PHILLIPINE PURSUIT

BY

Marv Mercer

This is a work of fiction. Names, characters, places and incidents either are a product of the author's imagination are used fictitiously. Any remembrances to actual persons, living or dead, business establishments, events, or locales are entirely coincidental,

Marv Mercer

THE PHILIPPINE ISLANDS

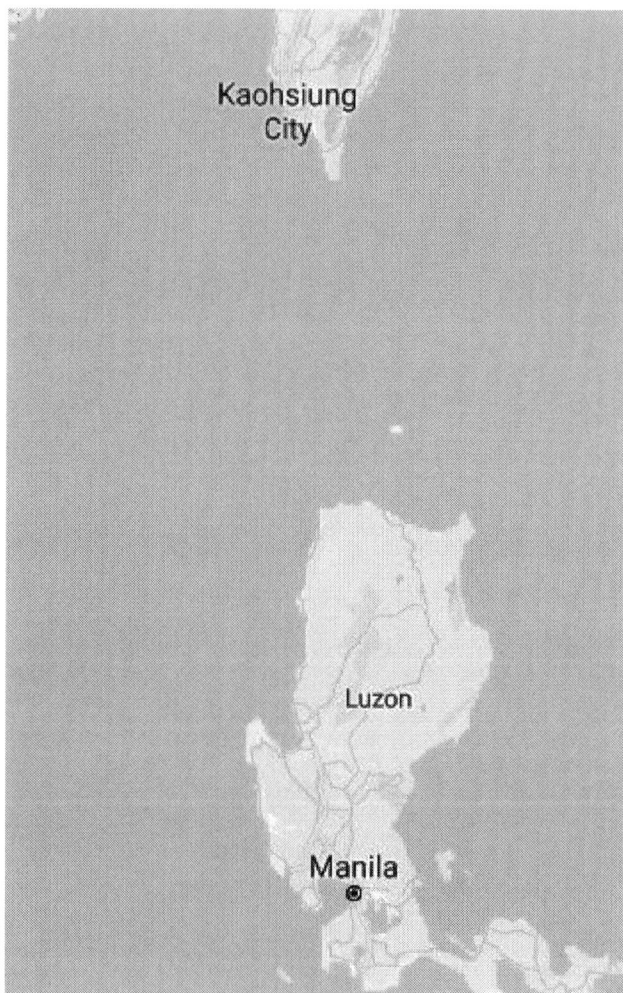

TAIWAN TO THE PHILIPPINES

Chapter 1

Sea

The Dragon Lady backed out of her slip at Taiwan's Kaohsiung shipyard after undergoing extensive repairs from damages incurred during a storm east of Taiwan. The cockpit was aft and the coach roof, that part of the cabin raised two feet above the deck, stretched forward almost to the bow. The mainmast was stepped to the top of the cabin rather than extending through it. A mizzenmast was just forward of the helm, a chart table located beneath it. The compass was mounted on the wheel's pedestal and clearly visible by the helmsman. The radar screen sat on a separate but lower pedestal next to it. Its radome was mounted on top of the mizzenmast under the wind generator turbine. The radar reflector was mounted high on the mainmast, below the masthead light.

The galley was forward of the main hatch. At the end of the sleeping area was another hatch which opened to the deck at the bow. As for the name Dragon Lady, no one could remember who came up with it after the comic strip character, but it seemed appropriate. After all, they were all a kind of reincarnation of Terry himself.

Once out of the confines of the harbor and into the Taiwan Straits, Al Cooperman gave the command to set the sails. Jeff Harris stood forward of the cockpit, used the hand winch to raise the mainsail. Earl Jamenson raised the jib and Mel Johnson, the mizzen.

Al set the course, a direction that would take the four southwest of Taiwan before turning southeast toward their next objective, Manila Bay in the Philippine Islands.

The sails set; the Dragon Lady was at her best as the ocean winds thrust her forward. Al was at the helm and Earl was in the cockpit with him. Mel and Jeff were forward; Jeff sitting on the cabin, his back against the mainmast. Mel was standing, supporting himself by grasping the mainmast's boom. Their eyes were on the Island that was slowly disappearing from view.

"How're you holding up?" a somber faced Jeff asked.

"What do you mean, holding up," Mel answered.

"I know that you and Shao-mei had something really special. It must hurt to leave her behind."

"Yeah, it is tough. However, I think that telephone call from you all telling me that the boat's repairs were made and ready for a sea trial put things in some perspective for Shao-mei and me. It was like an end to a fairytale. In our hearts we knew it, although we probably never really accepted it. But from that time on our relationship changed. We started putting some armor on our feelings to help mitigate the hurt that we knew was bound to come. I'm not all that sure it worked." Mel shook his head to dispel the sense of melancholy that was starting to encompass him."

"Well you still can keep in touch," Jeff remarked. "You never know what the future might hold."

"You're one-hundred percent correct," Mel answered. His disposition took an abrupt change. Gloom was replaced by cheerfulness, hopefulness. A grin appeared on his face. "Why am I being so morbid? Yes, we are going to stay in touch. She has the address of our Embassy in Manila and I told her I'd be writing her while on board and mail her a letter at our first port of call. But we've been talking about me. It seems you too left someone behind on Taiwan."

"You mean Kuo-ying. Yes, although I think we both considered our relationship temporary but more than just a one-night stand; if you know what I mean. Yes, I'll miss her. Funny, I don't even have her address."

"Well if you are ever in a mood to drop her a line, I'm sure that Shao-mei will be glad to forward your letter. I'm pretty sure she knows how to get in touch with her."

"I might do that; you can include it in your letter to Shao-mei."

As the two were talking they noticed that Taiwan had completely disappeared from view, but they knew it would never disappear from their hearts.

"Well, so much for reminiscing, let's go back and see if we can give Al and Earl a hand," suggested Mel.

"Good idea," Jeff said. He rose and turned toward the stern. "But who is the third person sitting with them?"

"It looks like Dave Hollingsworth, Al's CIA buddy; what is he doing on board?" a puzzled Mel asked.

"I don't know but let's find out."

Mel and Jeff made their way aft, holding on to the mainsail's boom for support.

"It is Dave Hollingsworth!" exclaimed Mel.

"What are you doing here?" Jeff asked Dave. "And how did you get aboard?"

"One question at a time," laughed Al. "C'mon sit down and I'll tell you all about it."

Mel and Jeff joined the others sitting on the bench seat that ran along the back and sides of the cockpit.

"When Dave found that our next port of call was Manila, he asked if he could join us. I didn't think you'd have any objections; especially after he helped us locate your girlfriend's cousin."

"No, I don't have any objections," Mel answered. "It just took me by surprise, that's all."

"When and how did you get on board?" asked Jeff.

"While everyone was saying their goodbyes at the shipyard I just slipped on board and made myself comfortable in the cabin. I didn't want to intrude on your personal moments, you know, like the proverbial third person on a date. I figured the best place for me was below, out of everybody's way. When it seemed that everything was shipshape, I felt it was okay for me to come up."

"Well then, welcome aboard," Jeff added. "We can always use an extra hand. How much do you know about sailing?"

"He's a great sailor, probably knows more about sailing than all of us put together," said Al, interjecting himself in the conversation.

"And the first thing Dave did was to fix our lunch," added Earl.

"Not much of a feast I'm afraid. Just some ham and cheese sandwiches," Dave added. "I figured it was the least I could do while everyone was scurrying around topside, raising sails and trimming the boat. As far as my nautical skills are concerned, I have done some sailing although I don't think I'm nearly as good as Al says, however, you'll probably find that my nautical skills are better than my culinary ones," laughed Dave.

"Hey, since you mentioned it, where are the sandwiches? I'm hungry," laughed Mel.

"I didn't know if you wanted to eat topside or in the galley," said Dave.

"Oh, I think up here would be great," Al said. "At least it is for me, I don't know about the rest."

Everyone enthusiastically agreed with Al.

"Okay topside it is. What would everyone like to drink?" asked Dave.

"We've got some Taiwan beer and soft drinks in the cooler under our seats. That should suit us all," answered Al.

"Okay, give me a minute and I'll be right back with the sandwiches."

Dave returned carrying a tray with enough sandwiches for each one to have two. The beer had already been retrieved from the insulated ice chest located under the rear bench seat.

"These are great!" exclaimed Jeff. "Welcome aboard once more."

While everyone was eating, Al made a small correction to the mainsail to more efficiently capture the wind. Then he tied loops around two spokes of the wheel that were located opposite each other, with the opposite ends of the loops tied to cleats on each side of the gunwale. That acted somewhat like an autopilot to keep the boat on course. Then he rotated his swivel chair so that he was facing the others and began eating his sandwich.

"Are you just going to Manila for the ride?" Mel asked Dave.

"Well yes and no," Dave answered. "Our embassy in Manila requested some help from me but there was no immediacy to the request so I thought this would be a nice alternate way of travel. I haven't had the opportunity to do much sailing in Taiwan, so this should be a pleasant diversion." Then he addressed Al. "You've got a great boat; I see it has Bermuda riggings. This is the first time I really had the chance to take a good look at her."

"I told you he knew his boats," remarked Al to the rest. "Yes, it does have Bermuda riggings. It's a fifty-one-foot ketch with an eight-foot beam. I found her in a shipyard in Long Beach.

"While we're all together this would be a good time to assign the watches," Al said to the group. "To be on the safe side, I was thinking of two of us to a six-hour watch. One can man the helm and the other will be the lookout. You can spell each other as you deem fit."

"A two-man watch is a good idea," chimed in Dave. "I don't want to put a damper on anything but these seas have been known to have pirates coming from Thailand and Indonesia."

"Pirates huh," Al said. "I doubt if we have anything to worry about but we best check our arms and ammo just to be on the safe side."

"I agree, six-hour watches are a good idea," Jeff said. "Have you made the assignments?"

"I figure you and Earl will have the first watch, then Mel and I will spell you at midnight." Then at six you and Dave can spell us. We'll let Earl fix breakfast. I'll make the duty roster so that we all will have a turn standing watch with each other and have a go at cooking meals."

It was around 8 PM, the crew had finished their evening meal. Jeff and Earl were topside manning their watch and Dave had joined them. Al and Mel had retired to their bunks to catch up on some sleep before they relieved the watch at midnight. Earl had the helm and Jeff was the lookout. All three were in the cockpit wearing all-weather jackets, coffee mugs in their hands and a thermos on the navigational table. The boat's wheel was tied off as before and the boat had no problem in maintaining its course.

There was a light northwesterly breeze and the current somewhat against the boat so that all sails were deployed to capture as much wind to keep the boat on its southwesterly course. Swells were approximately two feet high. There were patches of cirrus clouds in the sky illuminated by a three-quarter moon. The stars were out in all their glory!

"How did you all get together for this trip?" Dave was directing his question to both Jeff and Earl.

"We were stationed together at Udorn Air Base, Thailand during the Vietnam War," Jeff explained. "I was an Army lieutenant language specialist then. In fact, I learned to speak fluent Mandarin Chinese at the Army language school in Taichung."

"Yeah and did it come in useful when we found ourselves in Taiwan to make repairs on the Dragon Lady," Earl added. "I flew helicopters out of Udorn and on occasion ferried Al and Jeff on some of their clandestine visits to Laos and the Hmong tribes, but you know all about that. How long have you known Al?"

"Gosh, let me see," Dave paused. "It seems forever. We trained at the Farm together, and our paths crossed now and then, like in Taiwan. However, we were never stationed together. My forte was Asia; his was Europe except I guess for the one stent he spent in Thailand." Then Dave took a sip of his coffee. "What did you do after Vietnam?"

"Me, I went to work for my brother in his dive shop in Long Beach, California," Jeff answered. "That was where I ran into Al who was in Long Beach looking for a sailboat to fulfill a lifelong dream of his, sailing around the Pacific. When I learned of Al's plans I immediately asked to be included and suggested that perhaps Mel and Earl might also join us. I guess I was

13

looking for an escape from the boredom of civilian life and Al afforded me that opportunity. When Al agreed, I immediately called Mel and Earl."

"As for me," Earl added, "When my tour of duty ended, I returned to college where I received a law degree. I was working in the Boeing Corporation's legal department in Seattle; talk about boring. When I received the telephone call from Jeff, man I jumped at the chance."

"As far as Mel goes," Jeff explained, "at Udorn he was a first lieutenant Intelligence officer and the liaison between the CIA and the defense intelligence community. Someone in that community would come up with a requirement for some specific intelligence and Mel would pass the request to Al. After Mel's three-year tour with the Air Force ended, he joined an investment firm where, as I understand it, he excelled; accumulating a rather large savings and a long list of influential and successful clientele. However, according to him, the excitement of playing the market had gone, replaced by a sense of drudgery. He just burned out. He began to doubt his own judgment, afraid to give advice. As Mel put it, he needed a rest, an escape, a sabbatical. And when I called, that was all it took."

"Yeah, we like to think of ourselves as the four musketeers; you know, one for all and all for one," said Earl.

"I'm sure that was the case when you all rescued the Chinese defector in Kaohsiung," Dave remarked.

"A perfect example," said Jeff.

"If it hadn't been for Jeff's girlfriend, we'd never have known where he was," added Earl.

"And as I remember, you had a hand it that also," added Jeff to Dave.

"Well not much," replied Dave. "I just knew about the convention of the Taiwan Liberation Party and the fact that their leadership was to spring a surprise on everyone. Then it was just a matter of putting two and two together. However, I never fully understood all your involvement in that affair."

"I guess it started with Mel befriending the defector's cousin," Jeff explained. "She got him involved and then we all got involved; you know, as Earl said, one for all and all for one."

"And everybody lived happily ever after," remarked Dave.

"Yes, I guess you could say that," a somber Jeff replied.

"Well, I'm going to leave you to your watch and go below," said Dave. "Enjoy the evening, it seems perfect for sailing. Goodnight."

"Goodnight, thanks for the company," replied Jeff.

After Dave went below, Earl remarked to Jeff: "He doesn't know the half of it."

"No, and it is just as well. I think our whole Taiwan experience has left its toll on Mel," Jeff answered.

By the time Al and Mel relieved Earl and Jeff, the weather had changed. The cirrus had been replaced by low stratus clouds consisting of a horizontal layer of gray. Swells had increased to somewhere between three and four feet. The wind had increased from about five knots to ten, with gusts up to twenty-five knots. Both Al and Mel were wearing their heavy all-purpose jackets. Before Earl and Jeff went below, the mizzen sail was lowered; the Dragon Lady's position checked by the GPS and marked on the plastic sheet covering the navigational chart. Al adjusted the main and jib sheets. The white light atop the mainmast shone bright against the black sky and the starboard and port navigational lights gave off a distinct glow; red on the port and green on the starboard. Al maintained the helm and Mel as lookout, stationed himself on the bow but periodically he walked along the deck to stretch his legs and gain another vantage point.

"All's well," Mel remarked. He stepped down into the cockpit and filled his mug from the coffee thermos that was secured on the navigation table. "Want me to take the helm?"

"Sure," Al answered. "But no hurry; finish your coffee."

"With all the wave action, standing on deck is like riding a bucking bronco. Not much traffic, though. I noticed some tankers off on the starboard side. They're kinda hard to see, not like the cruise ship which passed us, probably on its way to Taiwan. It was all lit up like a Christmas tree."

"Yeah, I saw them on the scope. I imagine that the farther south we get the more the traffic. But it's a big ocean and lots of room for all."

"Right, I just hope all the big tankers take that same attitude," laughed Mel.

"Fortunately, they have radar too and should be able to spot us, and we them," Al said.

"Yeah, right, the operative word is 'should'," added Mel.

"Okay, I'll start my round, you've got the helm." Al picked up the binoculars that were on the navigation table and hung them around his neck and headed forward.

Mel kept his eyes on the compass' directional needle while resting his hands on the wheel, bringing it back to course when a wave caused the boat to stray a little. After half an hour at the bow, Al returned to join Mel in the cockpit. All's quiet on the western front, or I should say eastern front. I didn't see any lights at all," he reported.

Mel looked over to the radar scope. "Nary a blip on the scope either. We're all alone on this great big ocean."

"Kinda scary, huh?" Al commented.

"Not to me. Sometimes alone is good. When do you think we will see landfall?"

"You mean Manila? Obviously, it depends on our speed which depends on the wind. Once we make it into the Taiwan Straits we started moving at a pretty good clip. I figured we were running around 8 knots. Then we ran into a period of light wind and then it picked up again. I'd say we are probably back to somewhere between seven and eight knots. I checked our location when we began our watch and we were averaging about six knots, which isn't all that bad. Anyway, I figure that if we continue as we are, we'll probably reach Manila on our fifth day; probably see the northern island of Luzon after our third day."

"That's not too bad, four more days," commented Mel.

The watch changed at six in the morning. It was Dave Hollingsworth's turn at the helm and Jeff the official lookout. Earl fixed breakfast at five o'clock and Dave, Earl and Jeff had eaten before they relieved Al and Mel, who were now sitting around the galley table with Earl, enjoying eggs, sausages, hash brown potatoes, toast, and coffee.

"What's the weather look like for today?" asked Earl.

"Not bad," replied Al. "We have some early morning fog but the visibility is still over three miles. Once the fog burns off it should be smooth sailing. I checked the weather forecast along our route and they're predicting some squalls in the afternoon, but other than getting us a little wet, it shouldn't be bad."

"Great," said Earl. "Once I take care of the galley, I'll go up top and let you two get some shuteye."

"Roger that," replied Mel. "You did a good job with the breakfast; want a full-time job as chief galley mate?"

"You tried that once before but it didn't work then and guess what, it ain't going to work now," laughed Earl. "There is no way you're going to deprive me of the joy of your cooking."

"Well, you know that I can't compete with the likes of you when it comes to cooking," laughed Mel.

"Right, try your sweet talking on somebody else, maybe Dave, but I ain't biting," replied Earl. "Now if you two are finished eating I'll do the dishes and then go up top."

"We'll help with the dishes," offered Al.

"Just leave them," answered Earl. "It won't take me long."

"Okay, but don't say we didn't offer," laughed Mel.

"What mean we? It was Al who offered," laughed Earl. "I didn't hear a peep out of you."

"With that mean-spirited remark I'm going to hit the sack," replied Mel.

"Me too," said Al. "And by the way, I agree with Mel, it was a great breakfast, but unlike Mel, I wasn't surprised."

"Go to bed," said Earl.

Earl emerged from the cabin into an overcast sky and a stiff breeze that forced him to turn back and retrieve a heavier jacket. Having done that, he reemerged with a thermos of coffee to replace the one that was secured to the map table. As Al had predicted, the fog had burned off and visibility was unlimited. The main and jib sails were set, the mizzen raised, and the Dragon Lady was cutting a good swatch through the rolling swells.

Earl was tossed onto the side bench seat almost sitting on Dave's lap while struggling to keep the thermos level. Jeff was standing, his hands clutching the spokes of the wheel.

"Whoa!" exclaimed Earl. "I wasn't expecting that."

Dave freed the thermos from Earl's hand and leaning over, supporting himself on the edge of the deck, switched the old thermos with the new.

"As you can tell, the sea is getting rougher," Dave said. "Jeff and I were just discussing the need to run a jackline around the boat."

"Probably a good idea," replied Earl. "It's stowed under your seat."

Dave unlatched the door to the storage compartment and pulled out a coiled yellow web strap about one inch wide.

"Here Dave," Earl said. "Give one end to me and I'll tie it in the stern cleat and then you can go forward with the loose end."

"Right," answered Dave.

"While you two are rigging the jackline I'll try to hold her steady as she goes," announced Jeff.

"That would be greatly appreciated," said Dave.

Taking the one end of the jackline, Earl fastened it around the base of the stern cleat. While Earl was doing this, Dave donned his inflatable personal floatation device (PFD). He took the loose end of the jackline and slowly moved forward with one hand on the cabin railing. He wrapped the jackline around the starboard side and returning along the opposite side of the deck repeating the process. Once in the cockpit, he tied off the line to the opposite stern cleat.

"Okay," announced Dave, "we're all set. Anyone who has to go forward in this kind of weather should wear a PFD tethered to the jackline."

"You done good, thanks," said Jeff.

"Yeah, roger that," echoed Earl. "I thought I'd have to ride this bucking bronco all the way forward to secure the line."

"Well, it wasn't that tough, but it could get worse," answered Dave. "Best not take any chances."

"You got that right," agreed Earl.

"I'm going down below for a minute, want me to take the empty thermos?" asked Dave.

"Might as well," answered Earl. Then he turned to Jeff at the helm, "do you want a fresh cup?"

"That would be great, thanks." Jeff handed Earl his coffee mug which was sitting on the map table. It was a large ceramic one with a picture of an owl with large round orange eyes, embossed on it. Beneath it were etched the words '399th Intelligence Squadron, Udorn AB. Thailand; remnants of a bygone era. It was actually set in a beanbag holder to keep it stabilized during the unpredictable motion of the boat.

Earl filled Jeff's mug and replaced the thermos. Then he looked around, picked up binoculars laying on the map table. "I think I'll take a walk around the deck."

"Be sure you put on you PFD and connect it to the jackline," reminded Jeff.

"Roger that." Earl donned the PFD; a horseshoe shaped life preserver made of a buoyant material containing an inflatable chamber that provides buoyancy when inflated. He hooked it to the jackline. Then he stepped from the bench to the deck and started his walk, somewhat gingerly, balancing himself from the boat's pitches. At the bow he sat down on the cabin and eyed the surrounding sea.

"I don't see anything," he yelled to Jeff.

At that moment Dave came up from the cabin. "What's Earl's yelling about?"

"He doesn't see anything," answered Jeff.

Dave looked at the scope. "No blips, but it does look like we have some weather heading our way." Then he shouted to Earl, "I suggest you come aft, unless you want to get drenched. We've got some rain coming our way."

Earl ran his eyes across the horizon once more. "I think I see it coming from our starboard." Then he returned to the cockpit.

Earl, Jeff and Dave took slickers from one of the storage chests and donned them in preparation for the expectant foul weather. Jeff examined the sails. "Do you think we need to reef the sails?"

"No, I don't think so," replied Dave. "The wind is not that strong, gusts of about thirty knots."

"We were in stronger winds before and we didn't have a problem," commented Earl.

"Yeah, you're right. Nothing but a lost mainmast," an anxious Jeff replied.

"I'll tell you what, Earl and I will stand ready to reel in the mainsail if we find it necessary." Then turning to Earl, said: "Let's you and me put on our PFDs and connect to the jackline just in case."

"Right," replied Earl.

It wasn't long after Earl and Dave connected to the jackline that the rain did come. First in small pelts, then a downpour. The mainsail started flapping. Dave pulled in the mainsheet until the flapping ended. "All's well," he announced.

The rain stopped about as abruptly as it arrived. The sun came out, the wind subsided and the swells dissipated. It was smooth but slow sailing. Jeff, once again, secured the wheel. Allen and Mel, with sandwiches for all, joined the others on deck. Al, using the boat's GPS, determined their position and entered it on the boat's log and annotated the plastic cover over the map. Then using proportional dividers, calculated the distance since the last position was annotated.

"A little over 48 miles, not bad. About 8 knots," he reported."

"Yeah we were really moving," remarked Earl. "I'm surprised you could sleep with the way the boat was pitching and yawing."

"It was like my mother rocking me in my cradle," replied Al.

"Yeah, in those cotton fields back home," said Mel. "However, I was awakened by the rain."

"Well, it's Earl's and my watch," said Al to Jeff, "I'll take the helm and you and Dave are free to go below if you want."

"Who's got the next watch?" Jeff asked.

"According to the watch list, it's Dave and Mel; then you and I will have the graveyard shift."

"I guess it's my turn in the galley then," remarked Jeff.

"You got that right, and if you do a great job, we'll probably make you the chief galley mate," remarked Earl.

"Talk about a disincentive," laughed Jeff. "But, tell you what, I'll break out the rod and reel and see if I can snag a couple of fish for tonight's dinner."

"See," Earl turned to Al, "he is bucking for chief galley mate."

"Let's not get carried away," answered Al. "He hasn't caught anything yet."

"Speaking about catching something," Dave said. "It looks like we have company."

"What'd you mean, company?" queried Al.

"Over on the starboard, a school of dolphins or perhaps I should say a pod of dolphins, coming this way," answered Dave.

They all turned their attention to the right. Al focused his binoculars on the area in which Dave was pointing. "You've got good eyes there matey, dolphins they are."

"I can see them," echoed Jeff.

"Where?" questioned Earl, "I don't see anything."

"That's probably because they're coming towards us. Wait a minute, you'll see them." answered Jeff.

"I see them now," declared Earl. "How graceful they are."

There were about a dozen. The dolphins in unison sprang into the air and then dived into the water only to reappear and repeat the motion like a carefully choreographic water ballet.

"It looks like they're chasing a large school of fish," observed Al. "I can see the fish leaping out of the water trying to get away from the dolphins."

"How do you know they're dolphins and not porpoises?" asked Jeff.

"By their snout for lack of a better word," answered Al. "Here, you take the binoculars and have a look." Al handed his binoculars to Jeff, and then continued.

"Look at the snout, it's long and thin, the porpoises' snouts are blunter."

"Gotcha," answered Jeff. It looks like they're heading right for our boat."

"Those are flying fish that the dolphins are chasing towards us," exclaimed Dave. "It looks like they're gliding through the air."

"I've never seen flying fish before," remarked Earl. "How do they do it?"

"Don't ask me," answered Dave. "But they do it."

"Maybe we can net some," suggested Mel. "I'll get a net and if they get close to us maybe I can bring one in."

"Go for it," said Al. "They might be good eating fish."

"They are," interjected Dave. "They are commercially fished by the Japanese and Vietnamese."

"Come to think of it, I think the Tao people of Taiwan's Orchard Island eat them all the time."

"Well, here's your chance. They're coming right at us!" exclaimed Al.

And come they did. The dolphins were herding them right into the path of the boat. The fish hit the side of the boat. They hit the sails, where they bounced off and onto the deck before falling into the water. Some jumped into the cockpit, some hitting Al and Mel. Jeff and Earl picked up the ones that were in the cockpit and stuffed them in a burlap bag which Jeff had taken from one of the storage spaces under the bench seats. There were nine of them that figuratively speaking, fell into their laps. Jeff took one out of the bag and held the squirming torpedo shaped fish in his hands while the crew examined it. It was a little over twelve inches long. But what was so striking was a pair of pectoral fins just behind their head.

"They look like wings," observed Mel.

"Yeah angel wings or sails," added Earl.

"They look neat," observed Jeff.

"How do you cook them?" asked Earl.

"Just like any fish," answered Dave. "You cut off the head, scale and fillet em. Once you do that you've got about six or eight inches of meat for the frying pan. With all that jumped into the cockpit, I'd say we have enough for our dinner tonight. If you want, I'll do the honors, clean, fillet and cook 'em."

"How can anybody pass up a deal like that," said Al. "You do the cooking and I'll cleanup."

"And we can use the head and inners to chum with," added Jeff.

"Sounds good to me," replied Dave.

The evening meal was a feast. Dave breaded, seasoned and fried the fish fillets. Added to that was hash browned potatoes and stewed tomatoes; all washed down with Taiwan beer. As promised, Al took care of the cleaning chores and then he and Jeff retired into their bunks to rest for the graveyard watch. The night passed without incident. The wind and the swells were moderate and consequently not as much distance was covered compared to the previous night.

The day broke with a beautiful fiery red sky as the sun made its appearance. The weather forecast indicated a beautiful day for sailing, although as Al observed, "red at night, sailor's delight but red in the morning, sailor's warning."

The morning went fast. Jeff came up on deck to enjoy lunch with Dave, Earl and Mel. After that he took his rod and reel and went forward to try his luck at trolling. He dumped all the entrails of last night's fish feast into the water and let his fly float among then. It didn't take long! His line started to spin wildly from the reel. Jeff immediately pulled back on the reel and started adjusting the drag while keeping the line as taut as he could.

"I've got something big!" he yelled.

Jeff's announcement wasn't necessary. Those in the cockpit had heard the whizz of the line as it was being released from Jeff's reel. All attention was on the action in the water. Jeff started walking along the deck toward the stern as he kept playing his catch; his rod tucked against his body, the tip raised.

"Someone get the gaff," he yelled.

Mel grabbed it from where it lay and was ready to help Jeff bring in whatever was on the end of his line. They all saw it break water. Dave was the first to identify it.

"It's a Wahoo," he shouted. "I think he's tiring. Keep the line tight; don't let him throw the hook."

"Yeah, right," Jeff answered. He continued to play the Wahoo; tightening the drag a little more, so now he was reeling in more line than was being released. "I've got him." However, no sooner had Jeff uttered those words, the Wahoo started coming toward the boat rather than away from it. Excitement and pandemonium were in the cockpit as everyone yelled their encouragement. Jeff was backtracking toward the bow and reeling in the line as fast as he could. He knew exactly what his adversary was trying to do. By reversing his direction, the fish was trying to create slack in the line so that he could disgorge the hook that was embedded in his mouth. But Jeff was not about to let that happen. He could tell it was the last gasp of the fish that had put on a valiant fight but lost. Jeff reeled his catch alongside the boat and Mel was on the deck with the gaff to bring him on board.

As this was happening, Al joined the group. "Who can sleep with all the racket on deck?" he said.

"Man, talk about Johnny come lately" Earl replied. "You missed Jeff at his best."

At that point Mel and Jeff with the fish, climbed down into the cockpit. Mel laid the fish on the floor and all looked at the wiggling and squirming fish.

"It's a Wahoo alright," Dave announced. "Look at the silvery side and the pattern of irregular vertical blue bars. Watch out for those teeth, they're razor sharp."

The Wahoo looked to be over three feet long.

"Should we keep him or return him to the water?" Jeff asked.

"They're great eating," again Dave spoke. "We can fillet it or make steaks or both. We can eat some tonight and finished them tomorrow. Again, if you want, I'll do the honors."

"You do that, and you won't have to stand your watch," said Al.

"You got that right," remarked Jeff. "I'll stand your watch because I was supposed to be the cook tonight."

Everyone's eyes were on Dave as he placed a large cutting board on the deck just behind the cockpit. Standing inside the cockpit, he picked up the Wahoo and laid it on the cutting board. Jeff stood ready with a bucket of seawater. Dave cut behind the front gills and in front of the tail. Then he ran his knife along both sides just under the skin. Once that was done, he used his knife to lift up that part of the skin where he had cut behind the gill. Then using a rag and grabbing the part of the skin that was lifted, he pulled it away from the flesh all the way to the cut he had made by the tail. This he threw into the ocean. He turned the fish over and repeated the process on the other side. Then he cut the head away from the fish and threw it overboard; next the tail went into the water. Then, he trimmed the flesh. Lastly, he deboned the fish and cut it into steaks which he placed in a pan and carried it down into the galley, and placed them into the ship's refrigerator. Meanwhile, Jeff, using the pail of seawater flushed the board toward the ocean, carrying what was left of the Wahoo into the ocean. Then he scrubbed the board and made it ready for another catch.

All that done, Al checked the Dragon Ladies' position and marked it on the map. Then using a straightedge, he drew a line connecting the new position to the existing course line. He used the straightedge once more and drew a line from Manila to intersect with the latest position. Then using a protractor, he ascertained the compass heading to Manila.

"Okay guys, listen up," he announced. "Get ready to come about to a new heading of 273 degrees. Mel you take care of the Jib but watch out for the main boom. Jeff will handle the port mainsheet and Earl you handle the starboard."

"Aye, aye," replied Earl.

"Okay release the Jib sheets," Al commanded.

Earl and Jeff released the sheets and the Jib sail started to flutter in the breeze. Mel stood watch over the sail.

"Release the starboard sheet but keep hold of it," Al said to Earl, "and Jeff be prepared with the port sheet."

"Got it," replied Jeff.

"Okay, we're coming about," Al yelled as he turned the wheel to a southeastern direction.

Earl released the starboard sheet from its cleat creating slack on the line, while Jeff took up the slack from his side, causing the boom to come about. After the boat had come to the desired heading, Al commanded Earl and Jeff to secure the sheet. That done, the Jib sheet was tightened and secured. After that, an adjustment was made to the mizzen sail. The Dragon Lady was set on her new course to bring her into Manila Bay.

PARACEL ISLANDS

Chapter 2

Pirates

It was the fourth day. The sky was clear, although there were some puffy clouds off in the distance. The weather was hot but the breeze kept the temperature down. The Dragon Lady was clipping along somewhere between five and six knots. Everyone was on deck eating lunch. Jeff and Al were at the bow sitting on the deck with their backs to the cabin. Al was scanning with his binoculars. Earl was at the helm and Mel and Dave were looking at the radar display. Their eyes glued on the sweep, sandwiches in their hands, as it made its 360-degree scan of the ocean.

"What are those groups of islands to the southwest of us?" Mel asked Dave.

"Those are the Paracel Islands, Xisha to the Chinese," Dave explained. "It's an archipelago of some 130 coral islands and reefs. I think everyone and their brother claims them but in 1974 China established some military outpost on them ousting the South Vietnamese and I guess possession is nineteenths of the law, at least according to them."

"Why would anyone want them?" Mel asked.

"Two reasons," answered Dave. "One is fishing. Chinese commercial fleets out of Hainan Island use these waters. The second reason is plain old fashion money. Geologists believe there is a rich oil reserve to be found under these waters and China is laying claim to it. However, Vietnam and Taiwan also claim them. I guess the Philippines also want a piece of the action."

"Uh oh," uttered Dave. "It looks like we may have company."

"What'd you mean?" asked Mel.

"Look at those two blips," answered Dave. "They're coming in our direction at a pretty good clip. Best go forward and alert Al and Jeff."

"okay," Mel answered. Using the bench-seat as a step, he climbed onto the deck and made his way forward.

"Dave has spotted two boats moving fast in our direction," Mel informed Jeff and Al, when he reached them.

"From what direction?" Al asked.

"From our southwest, out of the Paracel Islands."

"The what islands?" Jeff asked.

"Yeah, right," answered Mel. "That's what I asked. It's a group of coral islands halfway between Vietnam and the Philippines occupied by the Chinese. Maybe you'll be able to use your Chinese again."

"Well let's join Dave and see what gives," said Al.

Once in the cockpit, Al said to Dave, "What's this about boats coming our way."

"Look at the scope," Dave answered, pointing to two moving blips on the screen coming toward them."

"What makes you think they're interested in us?" Al asked. "We're in international waters, aren't we?"

"As far as the charts indicate, we are," Dave replied. "But as I was explaining to Mel, the Chinese claim the waters around the Paracel Islands as their maritime boundary. I know that Philippines fishing boats have been fired upon by the Chinese and forced to leave the waters."

"Well hell, it's obvious that we're not a fishing boat, so I don't see what the problem is," remarked Al.

"I don't know if there is a problem," remarked Dave. "I don't even know if those boats are interested in us. However, there is another possibility which we need to be aware of, and that is the Chinese have also reported pirates out of Malaysia in these islands and they normally come in pairs. So, the bottom line is we need to be prepared."

"How do you know all this stuff?" asked Jeff. "I've never heard of any of this."

"You forget, I'm with the Embassy," replied Dave with a slight grin on his face.

"The U.S. doesn't have an Embassy in Taiwan," a skeptical Jeff answered.

"How soon we forget," laughed Dave. "No, we don't have an embassy on Taiwan, but we do have the American Institute on Taiwan. It's staffed with American diplomats on leave from the State Department to look after our interest."

"You're right, I forgot, so how come you know all this about China and pirates?"

"Like I said, I get paid to know," grinned Dave.

"I'm going to get a fix on our position," Al said. "Dave, you and Mel go below and bring our weapons topside. Jeff you go forward and keep your binoculars peeled to the southwest. As you said, Dave, we need to be prepared."

"Right you are," Dave acknowledged. "Let's go Mel."

"I'm right behind you," said Mel.

Both Dave and Mel made their way down into the cabin and retrieved four Beretta M9 holstered pistols, four extra clips, three boxes of cartridges, two M16A automatic rifles and four 30-round magazines. Dave already had his SIG 228 holstered around his waist.

Once topside, Al and Mel took the M16As from Dave and inserted one clip into each and laid them on the bench seat, then they did the same for each of the pistols; ready for whatever.

"Shall I continue on the same course," a nervous Earl asked.

"Absolutely," Al answered. "I've got our position nailed down, so if we find that those blips are hostiles we can radio for help."

Dave had his eyes fixed on the radar scope. "They're still heading our way. They may be Chinese just checking us out and, in that case, there shouldn't be a problem. Although we're in their so-called exclusion zone as it pertains to fishing, as you said Al, they can obviously see that we're not a fishing trawler and we're flying an American flag which should account for something."

"Yeah, but I'm not sure what," Earl laughed as he gave the wheel a little turn to the right to keep the Dragon Lady on her present heading. Mel released the starboard sheet to allow Al to tighten the port sheet, after which Mel secured the starboard sheet once again adjusting the mainsail to take full advantage of the wind.

"They should be coming over the western horizon any moment now," Dave shouted to Jeff up front.

"Okay, thanks," he answered and he started scanning the western horizon again.

"See anything?" asked Al.

"Nothing," replied Jeff, "Wait a minute, I do see something. Let me focus in on it."

"Where?" shouted Al, as he picked up a pair of binoculars.

"About 2 O'clock. I can make them out, two of them in what looks like inflatables, maybe Zodiacs."

"I've got 'em," yelled Al. "They're inflatables all right. I don't see any flags."

"Me neither," responded Jeff. "I count four persons on each boat."

"Right, total of eight, and they're not wearing any type of uniforms."

Mel and Dave were now looking in the same direction. They could barely make them out, specks churning up water.

"I don't like the looks of what I see," a concerned Al said to all those in the cockpit. "Earl be prepared to tie off the wheel if it looks like trouble." Al then turned to Mel. "Take one of the M16s up to Jeff and tell him to stand on the ladder in the forward hatch. That way he'll have some protection if it comes to any kind of a firefight. And let's strap on our sidearms, just in case."

Mel grabbed one of the M-16s and headed forward to Jeff. Jeff took the rifle from him and waved to Al acknowledging his instructions. Then while Mel was returning to the cockpit, Jeff opened the forward hatch, and climbed down to stand on a rung that allowed him to keep most of his body protected. The ladder was positioned at a forty-five-degree angle and thus he could lean against it to support his body. Then he rested his M-16 on the deck. He was ready!

Earl, Mel and Al strapped their Beretta M9 pistols around their waists. Dave already had his SIG 228 strapped on. The second M16 was laying on the back-bench seat. Earl had tied off the wheel. They too were prepared!

"I'm debating whether to have the three of you and Jeff hidden from view," remarked Al. "That way we can surprise them if they try to board us."

"On the other hand, perhaps showing our force and hardware might persuade them that we're not worth the effort," suggested Dave.

"I think you're right," agreed Al. "With Jeff forward and us low in the cockpit we will make a formidable foe."

"I wonder if we should lower our sails and go on motor," Earl said to anybody who was listening.

"That's probably a good idea too," replied Al. "That way we'll have more maneuverable in case we need it."

"Roger that," said Mel. "I'll lower the mainsail and Jeff can handle the jib. You and Dave can handle the sheets and the mizzen sail."

Mel walked forward and told Jeff the plan, and then he waved to Dave and Al to release the sheets and bring the boom parallel to the longitudinal axes of the boat. Once the boom was secured, Mel and Jeff lowered the sail and wrapped it around the main boom. Then Dave lowered the mizzen sail. There was a noticeable reduction in the forward movement of the boat until the engine came alive, and then the Dragon Lady resumed cutting a path through the waves. Jeff resumed his protective position down the forward hatch while Mel returned to the cockpit.

"Now it's a matter of just waiting," remarked Dave. "I've checked the radar and can't see any other vessels in the vicinity."

"They're getting closer, "observed Al, binoculars focused on the approaching inflatables. "Uh oh, they're starting to separate, planning to come at us in two different directions. I can make out their faces. They're definitely not Chinese military." After making these observations, Al checked the ship to shore VHF radio to ensure that it was on channel 16, the distress channel. Then picking up the mike and depressing the transmission button began speaking. "Mayday, Mayday, Mayday, this is the U.S. ketch Dragon Lady. I repeat, Dragon Lady, Dragon Lady, position North 16 degrees, 21minutes, 51 seconds; East 111 degrees, 57 minutes, 45 seconds, again, North 16 degrees, 21minutes, 51 seconds; East 111 degrees, 57 minutes, 45 seconds, facing imminent threat from a pirate attack, need help to repel. Repeat this is the ketch Dragon Lady at North 16 degrees, 21minutes, 51 seconds; East 111 degrees, 57 minutes, 45 seconds, need assistance to repel pirate attack. Over." Then Al released the transmission button and picked up   the M16 from the back bench.

There was no need for binoculars now. The men in the two inflatables were clearly visible. They were brown skinned and wore red and yellow bandanas around their heads; their expression intense, menacing; their eyes fixed on the crew of the Dragon Lady. The helmsmen were steering 50 horsepower outboard motors. One of the boats crossed in front of the Dragon Lady while the other crossed behind.

The Dragon Lady's radio was receiving a message but it appeared to be in Chinese. Al turned to Mel, "go take Jeff's place and tell him to get his butt down here on the double. We need to know what we're receiving."

"Right," Mel answered. He entered the cabin and made his way forward through the passageway and changed places with Jeff who in turn made the reverse trip to the cockpit.

While this was going on the inflatables were still circling in opposite directions like wolves stocking their prey; coming closer with each revolution. Earl swore that he could see a gold tooth in one of the pirates' mouth.

As soon as Jeff made his appearance from inside the cabin Al told him what was needed and Jeff responded. Taking the mike and depressing the transmit button he spoke in Chinese into it. "This is the ketch Dragon Lady please repeat your last transmission; over." Then he released the transmission button and waited. Nothing. He again depressed the transmission button and repeated his message. After which he released the transmission button. Nothing. He was about to repeat the process again when a voice came through the radio's speaker. Jeff listened and then answered in Chinese. Then a couple more transfers of information and Jeff placed the mike in its cradle on the radio.

"It was the Chinese military on Woody Island in the Paracels. They received our distress message and relayed it to the Peoples Liberation Army Air Force on Hainan Island. They have scrambled two Jian-7 fighters to come to our assistance. The ETA is 30 minutes."

"That's good news," remarked Dave.

"Yeah if we can hold 'em off for thirty minutes."

"Hey man, there ain't no way they're going to get my boat, not over my dead body!" exclaimed Al.

"Let's hope it doesn't come to that," Earl said.

The pirates were encircling closer and closer, faster and faster as if they were trying to get Al and the crew distracted. Then the encircling stopped and each inflatable came to idle off each side of the Dragon Lady. Then the pirates started discharging rapid bursts into the air from automatic rifles.

"Damn, have they been watching our Western movies," Dave remarked. "It's just like Indians encircling the wagon train before preparing for the main attack."

"Yeah, I wonder if that volley of fire is the same as shooting across our bow wanting us to stop".

"My guess is that they are assessing the situation and planning their next move," Al said. "I see one guy with a walkie-talkie to his ear."

All this time Earl was at the wheel maintaining their present course. "When they start to make their move Earl, you need to keep low. Don't give them a target but keep the boat on course," instructed Al. "Dave you take the starboard flank and I've got the port. Jeff's got the stern."

"It looks like they have plenty of fire power and won't be afraid to use it," Jeff observed.

No sooner had Jeff made his observation, the inflatable on the Dragon Lady's port side started approaching closer and turned so that it was parallel to the Dragon Lady and traveling at the same speed while the inflatable on the Lady's starboard maintained its distance, also going parallel to the Dragon Lady and with its weapons displayed. The pirate in the inflatable on the port side used a bullhorn and speaking in broken English, ordered the Dragon Lady to stop.

"And if we don't?" yelled Al as he removed the clip from his M16 and reinserted it once again; the message obvious.

"You not fight us," the pirate replied. "You no win."

"Maybe, maybe not, but you'll be the first to go down," Al answered.

The pirate holding the bullhorn turned to one of his companions as if to ask 'what did he say?'

Then Al shouted to Mel at the forward hatch. "Mel, show him what we can do."

Then Mel released a shot that whizzed just over the head of the pirate causing his helmsman to immediately pull away from the Dragon Lady and out of range of any future shots. Then there was more conversation between the inflatables via the walkie-talkies. Then a burst from the opposite side and then a crisping sound as shells hit the water forming a line of ripples that ran from the Dragon Lady's bow to its stern.

"Damn!" exclaimed Al.

"What was that?" echoed Jeff.

All turned to the starboard and saw the immediate threat. The inflatable on that side had mounted a swivel gun on its bow and raked the water along the side of the boat.

"I don't think we are a match for that," a concerned Dave remarked.

"Yeah, he can sit there out of our range and make Swiss cheese out of our hull," remarked Jeff.

"Want me to kill the engine?" asked Earl.

"No, just reduce speed enough to allow us maneuverability, but show them that they've made their point," answered Al. "That will give us some time to think about alternatives."

"Well we best think fast," Jeff said. "We're being approached from the portside again."

The inflatable on the portside approached within thirty yards of the Dragon Lady. Then the bullhorn once again: "As you see you not win a fight. Put down your weapons. We will board. No harm come to you."

"How do we know that?" yelled Al. "What do you want?"

"Put down weapons. We board," was the reply.

"It seems that they have a limited vocabulary," observed Earl.

"Give us a few minutes," shouted Al.

The pirate on the bullhorn turned to a member of his gang as if looking for a translation or advice. Then a reply, "five minutes, no more."

"What now?" asked Earl.

"I don't know," answered Al. "If they want our boat then it'll do them no good to sink it. In that case we can make a standoff. Jeff, get on the radio again and see where those Chinese fighters are."

Jeff immediately depressed the transmitter button and began transmitting. "Woody Station this is the Dragon Lady, where are your fighters?

We are about to be boarded. I say again, Woody Station this is the Dragon Lady, where are your fighters?' Then Jeff released the transmission button and listened for a reply.

The reply came in the sound of a sonic boom as two delta winged jets swept down from the western skies and made one pass over the Dragon Lady and her two adversaries. Everyone's eyes were upon them; the crew of the Dragon Lady and those in the two inflatables. Their reactions were different. From the Dragon Lady there were cheers and 'high-fives; from the inflatables expressions of surprise and disbeliefs.

The two Jian 7s gained altitude only to make another pass, this time lower. Red spewed from their wing guns as they sprayed the water in front of the inflatables; one Jian 7 to each inflatable. Gestures of rage and contempt erupted from those in the inflatables. Then one parting shot in defiance from the swivel gun was being made ready when it was interrupted by a shot from the Dragon Lady's bow. Mel's aim was true! The swivel gun's gunner fell. There was no time for another attempt; the two Jian 7s were making another pass. Both inflatables began a rapid retreat from the area.

"A great shot!" Al yelled to Mel. "I didn't know he was in your range."

Mel arose from the forward hatch and holding his M-16 in his hand, walked aft to join his mates in the cockpit.

"'I' didn't know about the range either," said Mel. "I guess the boat just drifted a little closer or I was just lucky."

"Whatever the reason, you saved our butts," said Jeff. "We were sitting ducks with our eyes on the jets."

"I know, that's why I had my sights on the gunner and when I saw him inject a magazine into his gun, I thought a shot might at least distract him."

"That it did," laughed Al.

As they all watched the pirates depart, Al turned to Jeff and said: "Jeff, get on the radio and thank those pilots for us. They might have just saved our lives."

Jeff picked up the mike once again, depressed the transmission button and began taking in Chinese. Woody Station this is the Dragon Lady, I repeat, Woody Station do you read me, over." Then Jeff released the transmission button and waited. Then he repeated his call once again and waited. Then the acknowledgment was received and a short conversation ensued after which Jeff replaced the mike. Then he turned to the rest of the crew, "Woody Station will relay our thanks to the pilots. I was also told that a Chinese patrol boat is now on course to intercept the pirates and bring them to justice."

"That's great news," remarked Al.

"Well, that explains why the jets didn't take out the pirates," observed Earl.

"Well, all's well that ends well," Al said. "Let's hoist the sails and get underway."

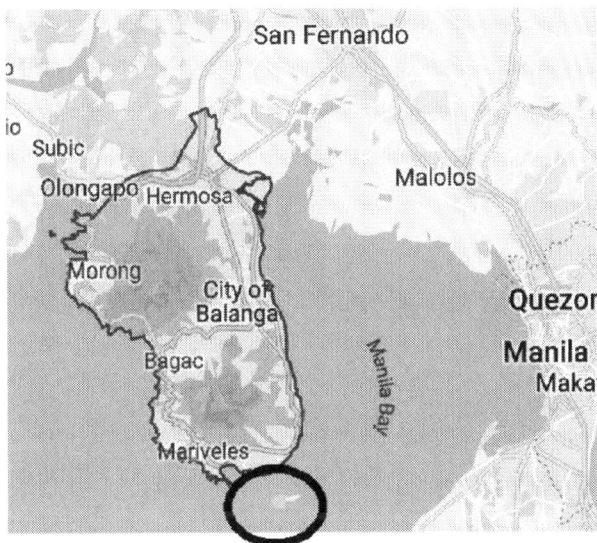

Bataan Peninsula with Corregidor encircled

Chapter 3

Bataan

The Dragon Lady was fully dressed once again; her sails raised and proceeded on a course to Manila Bay. The excitement was over, the weapons stowed and the crew was returning to some semblance of normalcy. The rugged mountains of the Bataan Peninsula were coming into view.

"Steer for the highest peak," Al instructed Jeff who was at the helm. "That's the 4,000 feet high Mount Natib."

"Does that mark the entrance to Manila Bay?" asked Jeff.

"Well yes and no," answered Al. "The mountain marks the entrance to Manila Bay on its east, opposite the South China Sea. However, we're going to put in at Subic Bay which is northwest of the mountain and opens to the sea."

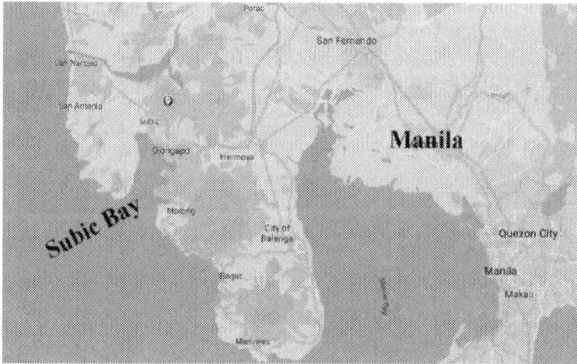

SUBIC BAY

"Why the change in plans?" Jeff asked.

"We've got Dave to thank for that," Al explained. "He's been in contact with the embassy which has been in contact with the powers to be at the Subic Bay Navy Base. It's a large ship repair and supply facility. Now what has that to do with us you ask?"

"Ok, I'll bite," answered Jeff. "What has that got to do with us?"

"They have a marina that supports a lot of privately-owned boats of the station's personnel. It's secure and thus we shouldn't have a problem leaving the Dragon Lady berthed there while we take in the sites of Manila and the Luzon Peninsula. We can also replenish our supplies and fuel."

"Sounds like an ideal situation," remarked Jeff, "remind me to thank Dave."

"Okay, why don't you thank Dave," Al said, grinning.

"Did I hear somebody mention my name?" Dave said as he was climbing out of the hatch, followed by Earl and Mel.

Jeff turned to face Dave. "I was just telling Al that I need to thank you for all the work you did in securing us a place to berth the Dragon Lady. So, thanks a lot. It will make us all feel more comfortable knowing that the Lady is secure in the hands of the US Navy. How did you swing it?"

"I knew that some of our embassy staff in Manila, including the Ambassador and Military Attaché keep their sailing boats there, so I called the Military Attaché before we left Taiwan to arrange for it. He in turn called the Admiral and since you, Mel and Earl are ex-servicemen, he was glad to extend you all the station's privileges."

"Let me say how lucky we are that you joined us in Kaohsiung," Earl said. "You probably saved our butt from the pirates and now found us a home base while we're in the Philippines."

"Gosh, I don't think I can take all the accolades that you are dumping on me," said Dave. "First, thank you for accepting me as one of your crew. You make me feel as I truly am one of you. Second, if anyone deserves credit for, to quote Earl—saving our butt—it is Jeff. It was his fluency in Chinese that got us air support from the Chinese. I couldn't have done that. However, that said, I'll be glad to accept all, and any praise you want to give me, deserved or not."

"Okay, enough!" Al interrupted. "I can't take any more of this. I think I'm going to throw up."

"I think Earl has a point," Mel decided to get into the act. "I'd like to add my thanks to Dave for just being part of the crew. I, for one consider him a crewmate."

"Hear, hear!" was echoed by all.

"Well, I guess we just gave Dave a great send off, although we'll not reach our destination for at least three more hours," announced Al.

"I think we need to give Dave a proper send off at the Subic Bay Officers' Club. I assume the navy does have one," Jeff added.

"I'm sure they must," inputted Dave, but if not, I'm sure we can find a club, bar or whatever outside the station."

"I haven't found a US base in the Far East that didn't have a gaggle of bars, restaurants, clubs, you name it, all equipped with booze, food and hostesses," laughed Earl.

"And Earl should know," laughed Jeff. "He must have sampled the offerings of every bar in Thailand, if not the Far East."

"Ah, guys you're embarrassing me," answered Earl.

"Yeah, I know," chimed in Al. "If it wasn't for the honor of it, you'd deny it."

Three hours later, around five in the afternoon the Dragon Lady approached Grande Island which guards the entrance to Subic Bay. The crew lowered all sails and Al allowed the boat to drift waiting for the navy launch that was to escort them into the bay. They didn't wait long. The expected navy gig came out to meet them. The coxswain turned the captain's gig 180

degrees and maneuvered it alongside the Dragon Lady.
Al and Dave were in the cockpit and Jeff, Earl and Mel
on deck placing bumpers along the Lady's port side.
The gig's coxswain brought his boat alongside the Lady
and Mel and Earl tossed two lines to two members of
the crew who tied them off forward and aft. Then Earl
and Mel secured their lines to the Lady's middle and aft
cleats.

The senior member of the gig's crew spoke to Al:
"permission to come aboard?"

"Permission granted," Al replied.

The sailor stepped over the gunnel, turned toward
stern and saluted the American flag atop the
mizzenmast. Then he faced Al and introduced himself.
"Boatswain mate 2nd Class Alexander, sir."

"Hi, I'm Allen Cooperman, welcome aboard."

"Thanks, is there a Mister Hollingsworth on board?"

"Yes, he's right behind me."

"I'm Dave Hollingsworth, what can I do for you?"

"Yes sir," the boatswain replied. "We have
instructions to check your passports and those of the rest
of the crew and, assuming everything is in order, to
escort you to pier 1 where you will be met by the Harbor
Master, a Filipino custom and immigration official and
the United States Defense Attaché."

"Very good," Dave replied. Then he handed the boatswain his red diplomatic passport. The rest of the Dragon Lady's crew handed the boatswain their green American passports. The boatswain briefly examined each of the passports comparing the photo on the passport to that of its recipient.

"If you don't mind, I'll keep these and hand them over to the custom and immigration official once we get to pier 1."

"Fine," Al answered. "Are we to follow your launch?"

"I'll have one of my men pilot your boat through the channel. The US Enterprise is currently on station and the harbor is pretty crowded."

"That will be fine," Al answered.

The boatswain turned to his gig. "Seaman Wolfisky, come aboard."

A young seaman came forward. "Permission to come aboard?"

"Permission granted," Al replied.

The seaman climbed over the gunnel, and like the boatswain, looked to the stern and saluted the American flag.

"Mister Cooperman, this is Seaman Wolfisky, he'll take the helm and pilot your boat through the channel to pier 1," introduced Boatswain Alexander.

"Welcome aboard Seaman Wolfisky, the helm is all yours," said Al.

"Thank you, sir," Wolfisky replied and stepped in front of the wheel.

"Well if you are ready, we'll cast off and escort you in," said Alexander.

"Fine," Al answered. "Once your boat is free, we'll start our engine and our boat will be in Seaman Wolfisky's hands."

"Very good sir," the Boatswain replied and then turned and returned to his gig.

Mel and Earl retrieved the lines from the Captain's gig and once the gig had pulled away from the Dragon Lady, removed the bumpers and stowed them.

"She's all yours," Al said to Seaman Wolfisky after Al started the engine.

"Aye, aye sir," Wolfisky said and pushed the throttle forward. The Dragon Lady was underway.

While the Dragon Lady was following its escort boat, Al remained with Seaman Wolfisky in the cockpit. The rest of the crew was on deck using the cabin as seats, following the movement of the escort.

When their boat left Grande Island behind and made the turn into the bay itself, everyone marveled at the sight they saw.

"It's the big E!" exclaimed Earl and he and everyone else gazed upon the 1,123-foot-long, super carrier, the US Enterprise with F-4 Tomcats aligning its flight deck.

"Man, what a sight," echoed Mel.

"I guess she's in for some maintenance, but what a treat," remarked Jeff.

"I flew by her once," mentioned Earl. "She was on Yankee Station and I was en-route from Saigon to Udorn. What a sight."

"I'm impressed the same as you guys, but what's the Yankee Station bit?" Dave asked.

"And Dave is our super-duper CIA agent. Anyone who's in the intelligence business knows about Yankee Station," joked Mel.

"Don't let them get to you Dave," Jeff interceded. "Yankee Station refers to a geographic position in the Tonkin Gulf where our carriers carried out air strikes against North Vietnam."

"Thanks Jeff," said Dave. "I figured it was something like that. I didn't think it was a baseball stadium although, I wouldn't have been surprised." Then Dave turned to Earl. "Hey Earl, did you ever land on a carrier?"

"What? Land on a carrier," Earl exclaimed. "My mother never raised any idiots. I like my landing fields to be on *terra firma*. Only navy pilots are crazy enough to try landing on a moving platform. That's just as crazy as bailing out of a perfectly good aircraft at 10,000 feet, huh Jeff?"

"Don't drag the army into your diatribe," replied Jeff.

"Diatribe, my what big words you use grandma," laughed Earl.

"The better to impress your peers, my son," Mel added to the banter.

"My, my, aren't we all in top form," laughed Jeff.

"Remind me to keep my mouth shut around these jokesters," added Dave to the merriment. "All I did was ask a simple question."

"Yes, but you asked it to a couple of simpletons," said Jeff.

As the bantering took place, the Dragon Lady continued on her course passing rows of destroyers, cruisers and one submarine berthed along a pier. Crossing another channel, they made a ninety degree turn and passed the wharf area containing warehouses and large cranes. At the end of the wharf was a smaller building with a sign indicating Pier 1 and the offices of the Harbor Master and Philippines Customs and Immigrations. The escort boat tied off to one of the pilings in front of the building while Seaman Wolfisky cut the Dagon Lady's engine and let her glide in a position behind. Two crewmembers of the escort boat were already standing by and tied off the Dagon Lady to cleats fixed along the edge of the wharf.

Boatswain Mate Alexander escorted the group into the Immigration and Customs Office, where he handed the passports he had collected to a Filipino sitting behind a desk. The agents examined the passports and called each member of the group by name, examined his passport, comparing the photo on the passport to the person he was addressing and then stamped it with an entry stamp. When he completed the entry formality, he welcomed them to the Republic of the Philippines and expressed his hopes that they will enjoy their stay.

That concluded, the boatswain escorted them next door to the Harbor Master's office. The office was small, equipped with only a desk, a swivel desk chair and two other straight back chairs. When they entered, they were greeted by a Navy Commander wearing service khaki, behind which was a Navy Captain wearing summer whites. The Commander first addressed the Boatswain Mate.

"Thank you, Boatswain Mate. If you'll wait outside, we won't be long and then you can escort these gentlemen to the marina where they can berth their boat."

"Aye, aye sir," the boatswain replied and then left the office.

"Welcome to the Philippines," the Navy Commander said to those remaining. "I'm Commander Scott

Gillespie, the Harbor Master and this is Captain Linville, the US Naval Attaché. I apologize for the lack of space. However, we won't keep you long. Since you are attached to the embassy, the Admiral has granted you special privileges. You'll be allowed to berth your boat in our marina at the standard rate. We have reserved space for you in the VOQ should you want it. It's not mandatory but probably a lot safer than the hotels in Olongapo City. However, there are a lot of acceptable hotels in Manila which is around sixty miles from the station, less than a two-hour bus ride."

Then Commander Gillespie took from atop of his desk some handouts which he distributed to everyone.

"First is the authorization for you to access the station and use our facilities. However, that does not include the Navy Exchange or the Commissary but, it does include the Officers' Mess and, as I mentioned before, the VOQ and marina. The other sheet of paper is our facility handout which we give to everyone visiting our station. It explains the do's and don'ts while aboard our station. It also includes a description of the currency used in the Philippines and, where you can exchange your American dollars for pesos; a list of the off limit areas which obviously doesn't pertain to you but, for your own safety you'd be well advised to avoid those areas; and a list of restaurants and available transportation. I trust you'll enjoy your stay. Any questions?"

"I have a couple," Jeff spoke up. "How do we get from the marina to the 'Q'. We'd like to have a kind of

farewell party at the club to say goodbye to Dave
Hollingsworth who will be leaving us."

"Boatswain Mate Alexander has arranged a carryall
to transport you and whatever luggage you have to the
VOQ. You can make whatever arrangements you want
with the Officers Mess which is in walking distance
from the VOQ. There is a station shuttle that makes
rounds around the station. You can catch it in front of
the VOQ. You can also use the jeepney service for
transportation around the station and into Olongapo
City. The cost is minimal and the details are included in
the handout I've just given you. There is also an auto
rental agency on station. They rent all sorts of vehicles
but the jeeps are the most popular and practical for
driving off station, again for a nominal fee."

"Very good, thanks," Jeff answered.

"Any other questions?" Commander Gillespie asked.

"Yes, I have one," Earl replied. "Mel and I have
friends stationed at Clark Air Base. How far is it from
here?"

"It's just a short distance," the Commander answered.
"No more than thirty-five miles. In fact, there is a daily
shuttle that runs from the station to the base. You can
catch it in front of the VOQ. In addition, each of your
quarters have a telephone with autovon connections, so
that you can call Clark from your quarters."

"Any more?" asked Commander Gillespie.

"No, none that we can think of now," Al answered. "Thanks for the briefing and the accommodations."

"My telephone number is attached to the authorization, should you have any questions just give me a call. As for the accommodations, you can thank Captain Linville, here."

"Let me add the Ambassador's welcome," Captain Linville addressed everyone. "And we are glad to have Dave Hollingsworth on board. We've been eagerly awaiting your arrival Dave. The Ambassador would like to meet with you tomorrow at 0900 hours. Assuming you will be staying at the 'Q' tonight, I'll arrange for a car to pick you up at 0700 hours tomorrow. I suggest you checkout of the 'Q' and bring all your luggage with you tomorrow morning. We'll find some accommodations for you in Manila. Just a word to the rest of you, you are a guest of the embassy so act accordingly. I'll give you my card with my office and home telephone numbers as well as the embassy's twenty-four-hour telephone number." Then Captain Linville reached into his top pocket, pulled out some cards and handed one to everyone.

"How do we get to the marina?" Al asked.

"That's easy," Commander Gillespie answered. "It's just across the channel from us. I'll walk outside with you and point it out. However, Boatswain Mate Alexander is standing by to escort you and your boat." The commander led the group out of the building to where the Dragon Lady was berthed. Then he pointed across the channel. "See the wooden building with the yardarm in front flying four pennants in its riggings? That's the yacht club where you'll register your boat. They are expecting you. By the way their grill serves great food, breakfast, lunch and dinner."

"That's good to know, thanks for all your help," Al said. Then the group shook Commander Gillespie's and Captain Linville's hands after which Al, Jeff and Dave boarded the Dragon Lady while Earl and Mel stood by to remove the lines from the cleats. Once the lines were removed, Mel and Earl boarded the Lady and Al followed the escort gig to the Subic Bay Yacht Club and Marina.

A boardwalk ran in front of the yacht club with five finger piers protruding from it. Each finger or pier accommodated twenty slips, ten on each side. After registering their boat, the group transferred their personal belongings to the Navy carryall that was parked in front of the Club. Earl and Jeff stayed with the carryall while Al and Mel motored the Lady to its assigned slip, number 79, farthest from the Yacht Club. Making one more inspection of their boat to ensure that everything was properly stowed; especially their weapons, Al locked the hatch and both he and Mel joined the others.

It was a brief ride to the five storied combination Bachelor Officers' Quarters (BOQ) and Visiting Officers' Quarters (VOQ). They registered at the desk on the first floor and all were assigned quarters on the second floor or second deck as the Navy referred to it.

Earl threw his B-4 bag on top of a queen size bed and looked around. A clock radio and table lamp were atop one of the two nightstands. A matching lamp and telephone were on the opposite night stand. The bedroom was separated from the sitting room by a three-foot wall protruding from each side and topped by an arch. A couch, end tables, table lamps and a coffee table completed the ensemble. A narrow hallway with a closet with mirrored sliding doors, led to the bathroom. The bathroom was shared by visitors assigned to the adjoining quarters. A small sign advised locking the door to the adjoining quarters when using the room and an admonishment to unlock the door when finished.

As Earl was surveying the room, Mel stuck his head out of the bathroom. "Sure beats the hooch's in Udorn."

"I'll say," replied Earl. "Too bad it's just you occupying the adjacent quarters."

"I know, you were hoping it was some gorgeous blond and you'd forget to lock the door to her room," laughed Mel.

"You'd have to admit, it's not a bad plan," said Earl.

"Can't argue," replied Mel. "Anyway, we're going to meet in the lobby at seven and walk to the Officers' Club. It's just a half a block away."

"Great! Knock on the door, we'll go down together."

"Will do," Mel said closing the bathroom door behind him.

Later that evening, Mel knocked on Earl's door and the two joined Jeff, Al and Dave in the VOQ lobby and then they all walked to the Officers' Club.

The entrance to the club was under a portico lined with palm trees, and through double doors. Upon entering, they passed the cashier's cage, cloakroom and manager's office before reaching the main dining room and bar. They headed for the bar area; a twelve-foot-long teak bar with stools and a brass-foot rail. Eight round tables, each surrounded by four swiveled barrel chairs were strategically placed within the area. There were not many patrons; four uniformed naval officers playing dice, and a trio of young women were seated at the bar. Only two of the tables were occupied.

Al picked the farthermost table and they borrowed a chair from the table next to them. Once seated, they were immediately approached by a Filipino barmaid.

"Good evening," she said, as she placed a bowl of peanuts and a cocktail napkin at each seat. "What can I get you?"

Each of the five ordered their favorite cocktail and the barmaid left with their orders.

"Since this is a kind of send off for Dave, I suggest that the bill be split four ways," said Jeff.

"You mean between you, Dave, Earl and Mel," laughed Al.

"Well, actually that's not what I had in mind," answered Jeff.

"How about just splitting in one way and giving the check to Al," quipped Earl.

"I agree with Jeff," Mel added. "This is a going away party to honor the newest member of our crew and it doesn't seem fitting that he should have to pay for his drinks."

"That's awful nice of you all but I can handle my own drinks," Dave said. "After all, it seemed we all agreed one for all and all for one, you know, like the three Musketeers."

"Dave has a point," Al added. "I think we should do it the old fashion way, let's roll for the honor."

"Great idea," Jeff responded.

"I'll buy that," Earl added.

"That's the general idea," laughed Mel.

"I'll get the dice and cup," Al offered. He rose from his seat and walked to the bar. The bartender was talking to three women. When Al approached, he turned from them to address Al.

"Can I help you?" he asked.

"Excuse me ladies," Al remarked to the ladies, ignoring the bartender. "I didn't mean to interrupt your conversation."

"That's quite alright," a strawberry blond with a pageboy hairstyle, said. "We were just inquiring about what there is to see in the area."

"Then you are new here," Al said.

"Well, I guess you could say that," another woman, with shoulder length blond hair, spoke. "We've been here a little over a week and haven't had a chance to leave the station."

"That's too bad," Al said. "Have you found out what's to see?"

The third member of the trio, tan complexion with black hair cropped close to the head, laughed "We've signed up for a Special Service tour of Bataan and Corregidor and were asking Juan if it was worthwhile."

"And what did Juan say?" Al asked.

"He recommended it very highly," the black-haired lady answered.

"That sounds like something perhaps my compatriots and I should do. How do we go about signing up?" Al asked.

"Call Special Services, I guess," giggled the lady with the pageboy hair. "There might be seats available. However, you'd have to do it first thing in the morning; the bus departs at 9:30 AM."

The conversation was interrupted by Earl. "Excuse me ladies, but we sent Al on a very important mission and it seems he got waylaid. I don't blame him for ignoring his partners, but our drinks have been served and we need to find out who buys, unless he wants to pick up the check himself."

"Leave it to Earl to mess up a good thing," laughed Al.

"A good thing?" the black-haired exclaimed. "What good thing?"

"Learning about the Special Service tour, of course," answered Al.

"Talk about quick on your feet," the pageboy lady quipped. "You're good."

"Well, if you ladies will excuse me, duty calls," Al replied. Then he turned to the bartender. "Juan isn't it? May I trouble you for a set of dice and cup?"

"Si, of course," grinned Juan, handing Al the dice cup filled with five dice.

"Thank you," Al said, taking the dice cup from Juan.

"Are you coming?" Al asked Earl.

"Naw, I think I'll stay here a little," Earl quipped.

"Hey, he's cute," the pageboy lady said.

"That may be," the black haired one, said, "but I'm hungry. Let's go to the dining room."

"What a party pooper," the pageboy lady laughed.

"Yes, leave it to mother Connie to look out for our best interest," the blond with the shoulder-length-hair laughed.

"You all can stay here, but I'm going to the dining room," the black-haired lady repeated.

"No, if you go, we all go," said the lady with the shoulder-length hair.

"Enjoy your dinner," Earl said to all the ladies. "I'm going to see if I can get someone to buy my drinks."

"Good luck," the lady with the pageboy hair style said.

"Thanks, I'll need it with the sharks I have to contend with."

The ladies left for the dining room and Earl joined his partners. "What's the game?" he asked.

"How about liar's dice," Al suggested.

"Naw, that takes too long," Mel commented.

"Where are we going that we have to be in such a rush?" Jeff said.

"Number one, I'm hungry and number two, I'm tired," Mel said. "Let's just roll one die and the highest number wins."

"You mean losses," Earl said. "I assume whoever has the highest number has to buy a round."

"That's correct, except in a tie of high numbers then there must be a roll-off of the high numbers to break the tie."

"Okay, I'll go first," Al said. He picked up the dice cup, removed four dice leaving the remaining die inside. He shook the cup and then turned the cup upside down letting the die fall on the table; a six.

Then Jeff rolled a four. "I like this game already," he commented, passing the cup to Dave who rolled a one. Next Earl rolled a five. Then Mel rolled a six, tying Al. Both Al and Mel rolled again to break the tie. This time, Al rolled a two. "Don't look good for you Mel," Al commented.

"Don't count your chickens before they hatch," Mel said, holding his hand on top of the cup, shaking it hard and then releasing the die on to the table; at the same time uttering "read it and weep."

The die rolled three times before coming to a halt; a five.

"I'm weeping tears of joy," Al said as he picked up his drink and toasted Mel. "Umm, a drink never tasted so good."

The game continued through three more rounds of drinks. As it turned out, Dave never had to buy a round. Then they all rose from the table and headed for the dining room. En route they passed the three ladies from the bar as they were leaving.

"Good night ladies," Al said. "Enjoy your evening."

"Thanks, you do the same," the black hair replied.

"Don't forget to sign up for tomorrow's tour," the lady with the page boy haircut said.

Once at the table Jeff asked, "what was that about a tour?"

Al explained about his conversation with the ladies while he was at the bar.

"That's not a bad idea," Mel remarked. "It will give us something to do tomorrow."

"Isn't it kind of late to sign up?" Earl remarked. "You said the tour was tomorrow."

"It might be," Al answered. "But my understanding is that it doesn't begin until nine-thirty. We could call Special Services first thing tomorrow and see if they have any seats left."

"Good idea," Jeff said. "I'll give them a call around seven-thirty and see what I can find out."

They finished their dinner, and found that Dave had prearranged to pay the check. When the rest objected, he just shrugged his shoulders and said he was on a regular salary and on per-diem as well and it was his way of thanking everyone for a great and exciting cruise. They all bid Dave farewell in the lobby of the VOQ, all agreeing that seven in the morning was just too early for everyone; everyone except Jeff, who had to set his alarm for seven-thirty to find out about the Bataan and Corregidor tour.

The next morning Jeff called Special Services and learned that the bus tour originated at Clark Air Base and included personnel from that base and Subic Bay Navy Station as well. The bus was a forty-passenger air-conditioned bus and there were still ten seats available. It was scheduled to arrive at the Special Services building around nine and depart at nine-thirty. Jeff made reservations for all with the understanding that the cost could be paid at the activity counter inside the Special Services building. A telephone call was made to the rest, awakening them, and plans made to meet in the lobby at eight and a quick breakfast in the club. Then Jeff called for a jeepney to pick them up at the Club and transport them to the Special Services building at nine o'clock.

Chapter 4

The letter

They held each other tight; Barbara curled under Allen's arm. The clock radio indicated one am. She raised her head and kissed Allen on the cheek.

"Gosh, I don't know what got into me," she whispered. "I'm not the sort just to go to bed with anyone."

Allen kissed her forehead. "I hope I'm not just anyone. You needed someone, I'm glad you chose me."

"Yes, you're right, I did need someone. But I don't do this with someone I've just met. I don't want you to get the impression I do this all the time or that I'm easy. In fact, it's been a long time since I've been to bed with anyone. It's, it's that you were so caring, so understanding; and looking at that cave and imagining what my father went through, just got to me."

"Hush, you don't have to explain. I'm glad I was here for you." Allen gently rolled over and softly kissed her eyes, then her nose and finally his lips fell on hers and then gently, ever so gently he kissed her and she reciprocated. Allen came alive again.

It was after two in the morning when Allen left Barbara's bed and returned to his room.

Eight-thirty the next morning Jeff finished his shower and opened the bathroom's adjoining door. He yelled to Al. "Al, I'm finished in the bathroom. It's all yours if you need it."

There was no answer. "Al, you awake?" he yelled again. Then he heard a faint but unintelligible remark coming from Al's bedroom. He peeped into the bedroom and saw Allen awaking in a somewhat stupor condition. "What time is it?" he asked, looking at Jeff.

"It's after eight-thirty and we're supposed to meet for breakfast at nine. The bathroom is all yours but, you need to get with it if you're going to join us for breakfast."

"Ugh," Al uttered as he threw off his covers and sat on the edge of his bed, his head in his hands.

"You okay?" Jeff asked. "You look like you're suffering from one horrendous hangover."

"No, just a lack of sleep," Al answered sheepishly.

"You went to bed the same time as we did," commented Jeff. "Is there something we don't know?"

"Just chalk it up to a restless night," Al answered. "I'll shower and meet you at the club. I shouldn't be too long."

"Okay, we'll save a chair for you, no problem." Jeff returned to his room, dressed and met Mel and Earl as he was walking down the corridor to the stairs.

"Well, good morning Jeff, where's Al?" Mel asked.

"He had a restless night and didn't get much sleep," Jeff answered. "In fact, I woke him up. He'll be joining us directly."

"Shall we take the stairs or the elevator?" asked Earl.

"You mean the ladder," laughed Mel. "You've got to get with it. We're in the Navy now. It's a passageway not a hallway; a ladder not a stair; a bulkhead not a wall and quarters not a room."

"What's with our boy wonder?" asked Jeff. "Has he been imbibing before breakfast?"

"No, I've been reading the evacuation instructions pinned to the bulkhead in my room," a grinning Mel replied. "In case of a fire, we're to take the passageway to the nearest ladder and climb down to the main deck."

"Man, what a wealth of information," laughed Earl.

"Back to the original question," commented Earl.

"Which is?" asked Jeff.

"Do we take the elevator or do we use the ladder?" answered Earl.

"By all means, let's take this passageway to the nearest ladder and climb down to the main deck," laughed Jeff. "I assume it will be near the elevator."

So, in the best Navy tradition, they walked down the passageway to the lit exit sign depicting a staircase and climbed down the ladder to the main deck. They arrived just as Peggy Jordon, Connie Munoz and Barbara Sinclair were exiting the elevator.

"Good morning ladies, did everyone sleep well last night?" greeted Mel.

"Good morning to you all," answered Peggy. "Aren't we missing one person?"

"How observant," Earl answered. "I wondered if anyone would notice if I wasn't present."

"Oh honey, I'd be the first one to send out the marines to look for you," answered Peggy.

"Is Allen going to join us?" a somber faced Barbara asked.

"He'll meet us at the club," answered Jeff. "I guess he didn't sleep too well last night and had a tough time waking up this morning."

"Are you all talking about me behind my back," Al said as he exited the second elevator.

"I told you he would be joining us," Jeff remarked.

"And good morning to you ladies," Al greeted.

"Good morning to you," Barbara replied to Al's greetings, her somber expression of just a minute ago turned bright; a complete transformation.

"We understand you didn't sleep well last night," Connie remarked. "Was it something you ate?"

"No, nothing like that," Al answered. "I think it had more to do with some pleasant thoughts and wonderful expectations."

"Well, I have some wonderful expectations of a good breakfast," said Jeff. "Shall we adjourn to the club?"

Lucky for Barbara no one was paying any attention to her or they'd see that her face had turned a crimson red.

They found two unoccupied tables which they pulled together. Peggy was flanked by Earl and Mel. Barbara sat between Mel and Al while Connie was between Al and Jeff. The breakfast was buffet style so after the waitress filled the coffee cups the group made their way to the buffet line. In addition to the normal breakfast items there was an omelet and waffle station. The men headed for the omelet station while the ladies stuck to the simpler fare; a small portion of scrambled eggs and a fruit plate for Barbara, Peggy selected eggs Benedict from the warmer and also added a fruit plate, while Connie selected a small carton of strawberry yogurt which she emptied in a bowl and topped it with crushed nuts.

"That's all you're going to eat?" Jeff asked as he set his 'all the works' omelet on the table and sat down beside her.

"That's all you're going to eat?" Connie answered.

"Touché," Jeff remarked. "Didn't mean to touch a nerve; it's just that doesn't seem worth the price of the buffet."

"It isn't, but this being Sunday, the buffet is the only thing on the menu, so what's a poor girl to do who is trying to watch her figure?" replied Connie.

"Well for one, you don't need to watch your figure," grinned Jeff. "In fact, I bet there are a lot of men, including me, who like nothing better than to watch your figure."

"And that's why I eat strawberry yogurt," laughed Connie.

"Watch out for Jeff," Al said, joining the conversation. "He's a smooth-tongued devil."

"Yeah, right," commented Jeff. "I already opened my mouth and put my foot into it when I questioned her meager selection of food. I'm sure Connie thought I was being obnoxious when all I was trying to do was sympathize with her for the price she had to pay for the little she is eating."

"Right," said Al, "you're only thinking of her."

"I am, I am," laughed Jeff.

"Right," Connie laughed skeptically.

Al then turned to Barbara sitting on his left, "and how is your bill of fare?"

"Well, now that you ask," Barbara answered looking into Al's eyes. "The eggs are okay, but the fresh fruit is delicious; pineapple, cantaloupe, watermelon, bananas and I think, guava."

"It does look delicious," observed Al. "I think I'll prepare a plate for myself. May I get you something while I'm up?"

"No thanks, I'm fine," Barbara answered, "but perhaps Connie would like some fruit."

"How 'bout it Connie, would you like some fruit?" Al asked.

"Yes, thanks for the offer but I'll get it myself," Connie answered.

While this conversation was going on Earl and Mel were talking to Peggy.

"You're from Miami, Florida," Earl commented.

"Yep, born and raised there," Peggy answered. "A native-born Floridian."

"Did you go to school there too?" asked Mel.

"What do you mean by school? Do you mean grade school, high school or college?"

"Yes," answered Earl.

"Yes, yes and no," laughed Peggy.

"Yes to grade school, yes to high school but no to college?" Earl replied.

"Hey, he broke the code," Mel laughed.

"Okay, where did you go to college?" Earl asked.

"FSU, Florida State University that is," Peggy answered. "Got my nursing degree and was offered a commission in the Navy and here I am, some ten years later."

"Why not the University of Miami," Mel asked.

"Ha, too close to home and too expensive," Peggy laughed. "How 'bout you all, where did you go to school?"

"You mean grade school, high school or college?" laughed Mel.

"Oh no, we're not going to play that game," Earl said. "I graduated from the University of Washington, did my flight training at Moore Air Base in Southern Texas, advance training at Big Springs, Texas and received my helicopter training at Fort Rucker, Alabama. Got out of the Air Force and got my law degree from the University of Washington, thanks to the GI Bill."

"Well, my career is not nearly as exciting as Earl's," Mel remarked. "I graduated from the University of Georgia, was commissioned via the Air Force's ROTC program. Became a Procurement Officer, as I said yesterday."

"Gosh, and you all got together to sail around the Pacific. I think that's great," commented Peggy.

"That we did," replied Earl.

"When are you all going to take us sailing?" Peggy asked.

"We need to ask our skipper," Mel replied. "How about it, Al. Peggy wants to know when we'll take the ladies sailing."

"As far as sailing, anytime the weather is favorable, but more importantly, when are the ladies available."

"Good question," Connie answered. "I start my class tomorrow, so I'll be tied up most of the week."

"Barbara and my schedules are pretty flexible," Peggy said. "So, all we need is a couple of days notice."

"I've got an idea," Al said. "Why don't we take the Lady out this afternoon? We can sail around the harbor. See how you like it. If everything goes well, maybe we can spend next weekend on the boat. I'll check out the weather and assuming it is favorable, I'll plot a course around the peninsula."

"I like that," Peggy agreed. "We girls can put together a picnic basket for this afternoon, right?" Peggy added, addressing Connie and Barbara.

"Absolutely" Barbara said.

"That's great, and we'll supply the wine," Mel volunteered.

"Then it is settled. What time and where shall we meet?" Connie asked.

"Right now, the time is a little after ten," Allen said, looking at his watch. "Let's meet at the Yacht Club, say at noon. We'll have the Lady berthed there."

"The Lady?" a puzzled Connie questioned.

"The Dagon Lady, you know, as in Terry and the Pirates," laughed Jeff. "It's the name of our boat. We named it after the character in the comics."

"Okay, if you say so," commented Connie. "I must confess I'm not familiar with Terry and the Pirates."

"Don't feel bad, Connie," Barbara added to the conversation, "I've never heard of Terry either, pirates or no pirates."

"I think it's a great name," added Peggy, "and I remember the comic strip, although it was a long time ago."

"A very long time ago," laughed Earl.

"Anyway, twelve o'clock at the Yacht Club," Barbara said.

At high noon the Dragon Lady was tied off at the wharf alongside the Yacht Club. The men were seated around one of the umbrella tables outside the club, when the ladies arrived carrying a couple of picnic baskets. The men rose to great them.

"Well what do you think of the Dragon Lady?" Al asked the ladies as they scrutinize the ketch.

"It is big!" exclaimed Connie.

"Well it's got to be to sail the Pacific," said Jeff.

"Just how big is it?" asked Barbara.

"It's 51 feet long," Jeff answered.

"Okay listen up ladies," Allen interrupted. "It's safety briefing time. As you've already noticed, the Dragon Lady is big. However, its seating capacity is somewhat limited. We can seat five, maybe six, comfortably in the cockpit but as you can see, we have plenty of room on the deck. The cabin has what is called a coach roof because it only extends two feet above the deck but it makes for a great seat. However, when on the deck you must wear a Mae West. We've checked out three of them from the Yacht Club and we'll give each of you one when you're aboard. Also, no one on the deck except the men when we're setting the mainsail. If we have to come about, we'll give you plenty of notice and two of us will be on deck to make sure that you're not hit by the main boom when it traverses the deck. Any questions?"

"If we can't be on deck until the sail is set, where can we be?" asked Connie.

"Good question," answered Al. "Also, let me modify what I said about being on deck. You can be on deck when we are under motor power, like when we motor from here to the main channel; it's just when we are rigging the boat for sail or preparing to get underway that you shouldn't be on deck. There will be plenty of room on the seats in the cockpit or you can sit in the cabin's galley, which is accessed from the cockpit. Any other questions?"

There being none, Al announced, "all aboard! Boarding is at the cockpit; be careful going from the pier onto the boat. Jeff and Earl will be standing by in the cockpit while Mel and I will assist you at the pier."

The ladies boarded without mishap, except for Peggy. Mel supported her as she stepped from the pier onto the boat's deck. Earl standing in the cockpit, reached up to assist her as she was climbing into the cockpit. However, she lost her balance and fell into his arms.

"My Sir Galahad," she whispered to Earl, her eyes locked on his startled face.

"Peggy doesn't miss a trick," Barbara laughingly commented to Connie.

"You don't mean she did that on purpose," a surprised Connie said.

"I wouldn't put it past her," Barbara replied. "She's had her eyes set on him from the very beginning."

All were aboard; the picnic baskets stowed in the boat's galley, each lady, adorned with a Mae West and seated in the cockpit. Earl was positioned up front, ready to receive the bowline from Mel. Al was at the helm, the motor idling.

"Cast off the lines," Al commanded. Mel and Jeff untied the bow and stern lines from the wharf's cleats; Earl retrieved Mel's line, while Jeff brought his with him when he boarded the boat. Soon he was joined by Mel. Al slowly pushed the motor's throttle forward and the Dragon Lady pulled away from her berth. Once away from the Yacht Club and into the main channel past the harbormaster's office, Al gave the okay for the passengers to go forward. Peggy was the first to accept Al's invitation, joining Earl at the bow. They sat next to each other enjoying the breeze that came off the bay.

Soon they were joined by Connie and Mel. Barbara and Jeff stayed in the cockpit with Al. The Dragon Lady made its way past the Station's maintenance yards, destroyers and finally the US Enterprise. They were in the eastern channel approaching the tree infested Grande Island.

"This appears as good a place as any to make ready the sails," Al announced. "Jeff go forward and ask the girls to join us in the cockpit. Ask Mel and Earl to stand ready to hoist the mainsail. Then you come back and help with the sheets."

"Will do," replied Jeff. "What about the jib?"

"Naw," answered, Al, "let's just use the mainsail for now. I think it should be sufficient."

Allen idled the motor while Jeff made his way forward to pass on Al's instructions, then returned and helped the ladies down from the deck into the cockpit. Once the ladies were seated, Al gave the command to hoist the mainsail. Mel and Earl unfastened the ties holding the sail to the boom and then Earl hoisted it. Once the mainsail was set, Mel unsecured the boom while Earl held it stationary. Mel then returned to the cockpit and removed the port sheet from its cleat while Jeff did the same with the starboard sheet.

"Okay Earl," Al yelled. "We'll take it from here."

Earl removed his hold on the boom and positioned himself forward of the mainmast so as to be clear of the boom's movement.

In the cockpit, Jeff and Mel allowed the boom and sail to swing to the wind. Then the sheets were secured. Allen killed the motor. The Dragon Lady was at sail.

"Okay, everyone you're free to move about," Al announced.

Once again, Peggy joined Earl at the bow. Jeff, Mel and Connie climbed onto the deck to enjoy the breeze and sights. They were passing the eastern side of an island with a white sandy beach.

"That's Grande Island," Earl announced. "It was the old Fort Went. It was supposed to be the first line of defense, guarding the entrance to Subic Bay but was never really maintained and not actually used in the defense of Subic and Manila Bay during the Second World War. All its guns have long gone and only their batteries remain. The Navy turned the old fort into a rest and recreation area for the military. They have cabins, ballparks, and a picnic area. That's where we'll have our picnic."

"How do you know about this place?" an impressed Peggy asked.

"Ah ha," Earl exclaimed. "The manager of the Yacht Club told us."

As Earl was describing Grande Island to those on deck, Al described it to Barbara and how they plan to use its picnic area for their repast.

"You think of everything, don't you," she commented.

"Well not everything," Al answered. "Actually, it was Jeff who asked the Yacht Club manager for the best place to put ashore to enjoy the feast we know you girls have prepared."

"Okay, you and Jeff think of everything," laughed Barbara.

Near the bow, Earl was continuing to impress everyone, but especially Peggy, with his knowledge. "That small tree infested rock is called Chiquita. Nothing is really on it but trees."

"How come you're so smart," a gleaming Peggy asked.

"Yeah, Earl how come you're so smart," laughed Jeff.

"I wonder if it is because he can read our navigational charts," Mel added.

"Now guys don't give away my secret. I'm trying to impress the ladies," Earl retorted.

"I'm impressed," Peggy said.

"So am I," added Connie.

"Eat your heart out guys," Earl retorted. "If you all could read then you might be able to make a hit with the ladies."

"Touché," answered Jeff.

"Okay, you score a point, but why don't you describe the land on our left?" asked Mel.

"What's to describe," responded Earl, "just lots of rocks and inlets."

"You all quit picking on Earl," laughed Peggy. "Don't pay them any mind Earl; they're just jealous of your superior knowledge."

"You got that right!" exclaimed Earl.

"You win. There is no way I can compete with you and Peggy," laughed Mel.

Once out of Subic Bay, Allen hugged the shoreline to alleviate any strong wave action as he passed the tip of the Bataan Peninsula and the town of Mariveles. Then he entered Manila Bay and sailed around Corregidor Island before turning about and returning to Subic Bay. Once in the bay the mainsail was lowered and fastened to its boom and the boom secured. Allen switched to motor power and headed for the Grande Island pier.

"All ashore that's going ashore," Al announced after Mel and Jeff climbed from the Dagon Lady to the pier and secured her. In the meantime, Mel retrieved the picnic baskets and some wine from the galley.

As they all disembarked, they could see cabins not too far from the beach. There was a picnic area just across from the pier which was their destination.

They had the area all to themselves although, they did see that some of the cabins were occupied. The picnic bill-of-fare consisted of fried chicken, potato salad and coleslaw. White wine was the beverage of choice although beer was also available. To the crew's credit, they did not over imbibe; they still had to navigate their return, albeit by motor power. It was dusk when the Dragon Lady tied off at the Yacht Club. The plan was to leave the Dragon Lady berthed along the wharf for the night and dock it in its assigned slot the next morning. Goodnights were said at the VOQ although both Allen and Earl would enjoy female companionship before the night was over.

The next morning was the beginning of a work day. Barbara and Peggy were on duty in the Navy hospital and Connie started her first day in class. The men ate breakfast at the yacht club. Afterwards they maneuvered the Dragon Lady to its assigned slot and discussed their future plans.

"We mentioned to the girls that we might take them for an overnighter this weekend if the weather cooperated," remarked Al. "What do you think?"

"We should be able to check out the weather forecast for the rest of the week," Jeff said. "The station has to have a meteorologist on board."

"Meteorologist on board? Jeff is really into this navy lingo," Earl remarked. "I swear he must have caught something from Mel."

"Hey when in Rome do as the Romans do," laughed Mel. "But I think an overnighter would be great with or without the girls."

"What do you mean, with or without the girls?" Al asked. "We don't need a weekend if we want to go someplace on our own. But we did kinda commit ourselves and I think a little female companionship would be great."

"I agree," answered Mel. "I was just thinking I'd like to take a trip inland, see some of the interior, maybe a trip to Clark Air Base. The Deputy Base Commander is an old Air Force buddy of mine. I'd like to look him up."

"That's no problem, we can do that, but obviously we're not going to sail to Clark," laughed Al. "But the question on the floor is shall we plan an outing for this weekend for us and the girls. I'm sure Barbara can find another friend so that the sides will be even; you know a girl for every boy."

"Hey, I said I was for it," Mel remarked somewhat defensively. "And I don't need anyone to fix me up either. It doesn't take a rocket scientist to see that you and Earl have latched on to Barbara and Peggy and I think that is great. But I'm okay with the way it is."

"Don't get me wrong," Al answered. "I'm not suggesting anything other than a weekend sail, not a weekend orgy. I just think it would be nice if we invited another lady to join us."

"I'm sorry," Mel apologized. "I didn't mean to imply anything by what I said. You're right, another girl would be nice."

"An orgy wouldn't be bad either," quipped Earl.

"Leave it Earl," Jeff laughed.

"Okay, it's settled then," Al remarked. "Jeff will check with the station's Meteorologist to see what the forecast is for this weekend."

"In fact, I'll take Earl along with me," Jeff answered. "Being a pilot, he can talk metrology. Now, assuming the weather is good, who'll notify the girls and someone should examine our choices of sailing destinations."

"I'll call Barbara and have her canvas the other girls to try to find a fourth," Al offered. "Mel and I will get with the Harbormaster and pick his brains as to what will make an easy sail and overnight port. After which Mel can check with his Air Force buddy at Clark and see what his calendar looks like. We can take the Clark-Subic shuttle to Clark or we can rent a jeep and do some sightseeing on our own, as well as visit your buddy. Dave Hollingsworth is planning to meet us at the club tonight. I'll give him a call to see if he can get any sightseeing suggesting from some of his collogues at the Embassy."

"Sounds like a plan," Jeff remarked. "Come on Earl; let's find a meteorologist or two."

"Ha, let's make it one," Earl laughed. "My experience is that when you ask two different weathermen. you'll get two different answers."

"So be it," laughed Jeff.

First stop for all was the Yacht Club, where discussions with its manager brought directions to the Station's meteorology department. Al used the club's phone to leave a message for Barbara. And then called and left a message for Dave Hollingsworth. Afterwards Mel called his buddy at Clark Air Base only to find that he was TDY to Hickam Air Force Base. Then Al, Mel and the manager studied maps of the western Luzon coastline looking for possible sailing routes and safe coves in which to lay anchor.

It was four-thirty and everyone was occupying a round table at the bar of the Officers' Open Mess.

"The weather forecast for the weekend is good; sunny with a light wind from the north-west, but no rain," reported Jeff.

"It looks like a go for this weekend," stated Al.

"How 'bout the girls, are they going to join us?" asked Earl.

"I haven't heard from Barbara," replied Al. "She's supposed to call me."

"How about Dave, what have you heard from him?" asked Mel.

"Haven't heard anything," answered Al. "I know he's planning to join us tonight. He was teaching when I called this morning so I left a message to let him know what we have in mind."

"Well it seems all that is left is to get a cup and dice and see who will be buying the drinks," Earl said.

"Right on!" exclaimed Mel. "I'll fetch the cup and dice." With that announcement, he rose from the table and walked to the bar returning with a leather cup containing five dice. "Since we're on a navy base it seems only fitting that we should play a little ship, captain and crew. What do you think?"

"If that's what you think then that's what it'll be," said Al. "You got the dice, go for it."

Mel shook the cup and let the dice roll onto the tabletop; a six, a five, two threes and an ace (a one).

"Would you look at that throw," said Al. "He's got his ship (a six), a captain (a five) and a crew of seven (2 threes and a one). No wonder our boy wonder wanted to play ship captain and crew."

The dice playing continued the round and each of the others had their turn. Al rolled ship (a six) but he never rolled a captain (five) so the rest of the dice didn't count. Jeff rolled and he never got a six (ship) so none of his dice counted either. Earl rolled two sixes, one five, a four and a three; a ship, captain, and a crew of thirteen (the extra six, the four and the three). Having the most crew, he was out. Al started the next round; he already had a ship so all he needed was a captain and then he could count a crew. He rolled and got his five and one four, one duce and two aces for a crew of eight. Jeff rolled a six, a five and a crew of ten; two fours and one two. Now it was up to Mel who already had a crew of seven. He rolled two deuces, and three aces which gave him a total crew of twelve. He was out. In the third round it was just Al with a crew of eight and Jeff who had a crew of ten. Al rolled; a pair of sixes, a four, a duce and an ace; a combined crew of twenty-seven.

"Damn!" Jeff exclaimed. He blew into the dice cup, shook it around for at least four times and let the dice flow onto the top of the table; five aces.

"Too bad we weren't playing poker dice, five aces would be pretty good," remarked Al.

"Yeah, right," answered Jeff. "I hope you all drown in your drinks."

"That's not very sportsman like," said Earl. "You ought to be pleased that you are buying your good buddies a drink."

"To you Jeff," Mel raised his glass in a mock toast. "For the giving person you are."

"Yeah, right," remarked Jeff. "Enjoy, and while you do, I'll start the throw to see who will be as fortunate as me and buy the second round of drinks."

Alas, it was Jeff again who had the honor to pay for everyone's drink. "Man, I'm not going to play with you shysters again. I don't know how you did it but I'm sure I was setup."

"Partner, how can you even think of a thing like that," Mel said. "If it was me that lost, I'd think I'd won."

"Run that by me again," remarked Jeff. "If you had lost, you'd think you had won."

"Well sure," Mel answered. "It would be my pleasure to buy you a drink, you know that."

"Well, do it then," laughed Jeff. "I don't want to deprive you of your chance for happiness."

"I would, but you wouldn't feel right if I rob you of your just deserts," laughed Mel.

"There Mel goes again," Earl chimed in. "He's only thinking of you, Jeff."

"Earl hit the nail on the proverbial head," laughed Mel. "I am only thinking of you Jeff, cheers." Mel raised his glass in a toast to Jeff.

"Hear, hear," everybody else said in unison.

"Gosh guys, I'm overwhelmed. Enjoy your drinks," Jeff responded.

"I see that Dave has just come in," Al announced, rising from the table and motioning to Dave who then joined them.

"Well Dave, do you have any words of wisdom to impart on possible excursions into the Philippines hinterlands?" asked Al.

"Yes, if fact I do," answered Dave, "Baguio."

"Okay, I'll bite," said Al. "What's Baguio?"

"Baguio is a mountain resort about 150 miles north of here," explained Dave. "It is sometimes referred to as Philippine's summer capital because of the cool climate at its 5,000-foot elevation. More importantly, it is the home of Camp John Hay, a DOD communication site, but more importantly an R&R site used by the military. It has great lodging facilities and a first-class golf course designed by no other than the golden bear himself, Jack Nicklaus. Our Embassy personnel also can use its facilities and since you are attached to our embassy, you too have access privileges."

"A golf course! Can we rent clubs?" asked Mel.

"I'm sure you can," Dave answered. "But I'm told the course is not for the faint of heart. I'm told there is one hole that you literally have to use a rope tow, because the fairway is so steep and the green is at the top. In fact, as I was told, there are places that have been leveled with 'ball-stops' to keep your ball from running down the mountainside."

"Whoa, that sounds awesome," Earl exclaimed. "How do we get there?"

"There are a couple of ways," continued Dave. "You can rent a car and drive. I understand it's not a bad drive, maybe six hours or so and through some beautiful country. Another way is to take a bus. There is public transportation from Manila to Baguio. I don't know, maybe even the Navy or the Air Force might have transportation since it is an R&R site."

"I like the idea of driving," interjected Jeff. "We can rent a jeep through Special Services. We all have International driver licenses and it should be a great way to see the country."

"Sounds like a plan," Al added. "We might even be able to squeeze in a few side trips."

"I bet Special Services can make lodging reservations for us, maybe even get us a t-time," added Earl.

"Hey, I almost forgot," Dave said. "I have a letter for Mel. It was sent in care of the American Embassy." He then reached inside his coat's pocket and pulled out the letter and gave it to Mel.

Mel looked at it, and the return address. "It's from Shao-Mei," he announced. He opened it and began to read. As he read, his expression became more solemn. Without saying anything he gave the letter to Jeff to read.

Jeff took it somewhat hesitantly, a premonition of what it might contain. His expression grave as he read it. "Damn!" he muttered. Then he re-read the letter. "That bastard, that damn bastard," he muttered, again his eyes fixed on the letter.

"What is it?" Al spoke, his concern obvious.

"Kuo-ying was in an accident and is in critical condition in a hospital in Kaohsiung," Mel answered for Jeff.

"What happened?" Earl asked.

"You remember Hung Li-chun?" Mel continued. "Kuo-ying was a passenger in a car he was driving. It seems he took a curve too fast. The car left the highway and hit a tree."

"That son of a bitch," uttered Earl. "We should have never saved his life; just let him rot in his overturned car."

"I've got to go back," Jeff said. "I want to be with her."

"What are you talking about? Who are you talking about?" Dave asked.

"I'm talking about Kuo-ying, a very special friend," Jeff said.

"You remember Han Yu-tai who defected from mainland China," Al interjected. "He was being held against his will by the Taiwan Liberation Party. You provided information on where their convention was being held which allowed us to free him."

"Yes," answered Dave. "I remember that part all right, and how you faked a fire causing the hotel in which he was a captive to evacuate allowing you to free the defector. But what about this Hung Li-chun?"

"Yes, well it gets kind of complicated," continued Al. "We befriended Kuo-ying, more specifically Jeff did, from Hung Li-chun. Apparently, they grew up together and he felt that she was his. Consequently, when we befriended her that made him jealous and he actually rammed the back of our car forcing us off the road onto the beach. However, he got the worst of the deal. His car veered off and actually rolled on its side. We pulled him out of the car and took him to the nearest hospital."

"Yeah, and the son of a bitch blamed us for the accident," added Earl.

"Kuo-ying recruited the defector, Han Yu-tai into the Taiwan Liberation Party," Jeff explained. "She was misled by the party, thinking that Han Yu-tai had volunteered to be the main speaker at the party's convention. When she learned the truth, she told me, and you know the rest of the story."

"Okay, I think I've got the picture," Dave said. "Now what's this about your going to see her?"

"As I said, she's a special friend," Jeff explained. "I want to be near her, to help her if I can. To let her know I care."

"There's no reason why we can't go back," Mel said.

"What do you mean we?" asked Al.

"If Jeff goes back, I'm going with him," answered Mel. "He shouldn't be by himself."

"I agree," said Al. "But there is a matter of visas. We never received any from Taiwan, only a letter of authorization which has expired."

"Hell Dave, you should be able to take care of that," Earl interjected. "Can't you?

Not only that, but my ole buddy probably can even expedite the process; right, Dave?"

"Yes, if that's what you want," answered Dave. "I still have connections on Taiwan. Visas shouldn't be a problem." Then turning to Mel and Jeff, said "Let me have your passports. I'll work on it first thing tomorrow morning. You just want visas for the two," looking at Al, "right?"

"Gosh, shades of Taiwan all over again, like when we were separated there," Al remarked. "I'm not sure that I like that, but if that's what they want then I'm for it." Then he turned to Jeff, "Would you like Earl and me to join you and Mel?"

"You can," answered Jeff. "But what would you and Earl do. "Mel, he has Shao-mei for company. You guys stay here and enjoy Barbara's and Peggy's company."

"Okay, but call us, keep us updated," Al said.

"Will do," answered Jeff. Then he turned to Dave, "Mel and I will go and get our passports for you and you can work on our visas while we check on airline reservations. "We'll want to leave as soon as we get the visas."

"I understand," Dave replied. "I'll have the Taiwan authorities' fax the visas. We should have them by late tomorrow or early the next day."

"You best call Shao-mei and let her know you're coming," Al mentioned to Mel.

"Once we nail down our air reservations, I'll give her a call," replied Mel. "We'll make reservations at the Kennedy Hotel."

"The Kennedy Hotel," Earl mused. "That brings some great memories. Maybe we ought to join them, Al."

"Yeah, right; I think we best stay right here. They don't need us."

"I wasn't thinking of them," grinned Earl.

"I know you weren't," laughed Al. Then he addressed Mel and Jeff. "Go get your passports while Dave is here."

"We're on our way, come on Jeff," Mel replied.

"I'm right behind you," said Jeff.

Jeff and Mel returned with their passports and gave them to Dave. "I'll get on these pronto. I'll call you as soon as I hear something."

The letter had taken its toll. Joviality was replaced by melancholy. Appetites were gone. Meals were left unfinished. Everyone returned to their quarters early and to a restless sleep. The following morning wasn't any better. The conversation around the breakfast table at the Officers' Club centered on Mel's and Jeff's upcoming trip.

"China Airlines has daily flights direct to Kaohsiung," Jeff announced. "It's about a two-hour flight."

"That's not bad," remarked Al. "I thought you might have to go through Taibei."

"Assuming Dave comes through with our visas this afternoon, will leave tomorrow," Mel added.

"What can we do?" Earl asked.

"Not much really," answered Jeff. "Mel and I did a lot of talking last night. We plan to stay at the Kennedy

Hotel. I don't know how far that is from the hospital. Obviously, we'll learn more when we check in to the hotel."

"How about money?" Al asked.

"We still have some NTDs (New Taiwan dollars-the currency of Taiwan) which will more than cover any taxi fare from the airport to the hotel and any immediate expenses once on the island. We have our traveler's checks so we're in good shape," Mel answered.

"You can have whatever NTDs Al and I have," Earl offered and then he looked at Al and said: "isn't that right, Al."

"You got that right," Al answered.

"Great," Jeff replied. "I'll buy them from you all at the going rate."

"Don't be ridiculous," Al said. "What's Earl and I going to do with the NTDs we have. We can't spend them here in the Philippines."

"That's right," Earl chimed in. "We're not planning to return to Taiwan unless, of course, you find that you need us. Then we'll be there in a heartbeat."

"Thanks," Mel said. "I can't foresee any reason why we should need you, but it's nice to know."

"Hey, that's what friends are for," echoed Earl.

The day dragged on; no one felt like doing anything. Jeff and Mel packed their clothes and toilet articles in their B-4 bags. They tried to busy themselves around the boat hoping to force their attention on anything except the pending trip so as to make the time pass faster. Conversation was forced. They played some games but the excitement and banter that usually accompanied these games were absent; they were just going through the motions. It was after four in the afternoon when they returned to their quarters in the VOQ agreeing to meet at six o'clock. Al received a call from Barbara who was told of the situation and they both agreed that tonight was probably not a good time for the ladies to join them. At six o'clock all the men met in the lobby of the VOQ.

"Hear anything from Dave?" Al asked Jeff.

"No, I was hoping you had heard something," answered Jeff.

"You can bet that if I had, you'd be the first to know," remarked Al. "If we don't hear anything soon, we'll give him a call. I'm sure he's been tied up all afternoon teaching his class."

"Yeah, I guess you're right, but this waiting is really getting to me," Jeff said.

"Well let's get something to eat, then, like I said, we'll give him a call."

They all went directly to the dining area, bypassing the bar. They had received their dinners and were in process of eating when Dave Hollingsworth, unnoticed, approached the table.

"You guys got room for one more?" he asked.

"Dave!" exclaimed Jeff. "We didn't see you come in. Do you have some news?"

"Do you mean do I have your visas?" Dave answered; a large grin on his face. "The answer is yes." With that news, he borrowed a chair from an adjacent table and sat down. Then he passed an envelope to each Jeff and Mel. "Inside you will find your passports with a visa stapled inside. In addition, I took the liberty of making reservations on China Airlines flight 1702 departing tomorrow at 2:30 PM. I've also arranged for an embassy van to pick you up at the 'Q' at one o'clock. I'd like to join you but I still have to teach, however I did arrange for someone from the American Institute to meet you in Kaohsiung and get you settled in at the Kennedy."

"Damn Dave, thanks a lot," said Jeff. "I don't know how to thank you."

"Man, I'll say," added Mel. "That's what I'd call beyond the call of duty."

"No problem," answered Dave. "I'm glad it worked out like it did. Our people in Taibei still have some good contacts within Taiwan's Department of Foreign Affairs in spite of our lack of official standing."

"Well Dave, you done good," remarked Al.

"I gotta say this, nothing but good has happened since you joined our crew," remarked Earl. "In fact, I'm going to buy the first round of drinks; part of our bon-voyage party for Jeff and Mel.

The mood of the group changed drastically. Gone was the melancholy of the past twenty-four hours. It was the old group who adjourned to the bar giving Mel and Jeff a proper sendoff. Later that evening Mel talked to Shao-mei and informed her of their plans and where they would be staying. He also learned that Kuo-ying was in the Kaohsiung Municipal Chung Ho Hospital, not too far from their hotel.

The embassy's van arrived at the VOQ right on time and picked up the group and transported them to Manila's International Airport. It was around 1:45 when the van dropped them off at the airport's international terminal. The Filipino driver told them that he had to deliver some papers for the embassy but he'd return around two and would be waiting for them in the arrival zone. Once in the terminal building, Al and Earl waited while Mel and Jeff queued in China Airline's passenger check-in-line. Jeff and Mel used their credit cards to pay for their fare and received their tickets and boarding passes. Al and Earl said their goodbyes with manly hugs and, watched as Mel and Earl cleared immigration and passed through the security checkpoint.

Al looked at his watch. "Two O'clock; that didn't take long. You wanta grab a sandwich or something?"

"Good idea," Earl answered. "I kinda like the idea of knowing they're in the air before we leave, just in case."

"My thoughts exactly," replied Al.

They found a snack bar where they purchased a couple of ham and cheese sandwiches and a couple of San Miguel beers and sat down at one of the tables.

"I'm missing them already," Earl said. "I sure hope everything turns out all right."

"Yeah, I guess we never knew how serious things were between Jeff and Kuo-ying, I mean I knew that Mel had fallen pretty hard for Shao-mei and I wouldn't have been too surprised if Mel had stayed in Taiwan but Jeff, I never suspected."

"Well I knew it was more than just a fling he had going with Kuo-ying but I assumed that once we were on the high seas, he'd get over it."

"Yeah, probably would have if it wasn't for that letter."

"Yeah, that son-of-a-bitch Hung Li-chun," Earl said as he took a swig of his San Miguel.

"Well we need to think of something to do while they're in Taiwan," said Al.

"We can always take the girls on the cruise we promised. Ask Dave to come along. That would even the sides."

"Good idea. I was also thinking you and I could play a round of golf. What was the name of the military golf course Dave was telling us about?"

"Baguio; high in the mountains. I'd like that, but I'd feel somewhat guilty going there without our two buddies."

"We need to do something. We just can't hang around the station. I say we go for it. We'll check it out and if it is as good as Dave says, we can always return with Mel and Jeff."

"Let's do it. Baguio and a cruise with the ladies. I like it."

Their conversation was interrupted by the announcement of the final boarding call for China Airlines flight 1702 for Kaohsiung. Al and Earl finished their sandwiches and beer and walked over to the observation window and watched as the Boeing 737 taxied to the end of the runway and lifted into the air. Then the two went down the stairs, walked through the baggage area and to the outside where they found the embassy's van waiting for them.

*   *   *   *   *

Jeff and Mel cleared Taiwan customs and immigrations and exited the arrival area carrying their B-4 bags, where they spied a Chinese man holding a sign which read 'Welcome passengers Mel Johnson and Jeff Harris'.

"That's us," observed Jeff.

"No, kidding," laughed Mel, "obviously, Dave's handiwork."

They walked up to their greeter and introduced themselves.

"Welcome to Taiwan Mister Harris and Mister Johnson," the greeter said, acknowledging their introduction. I am Mister Wang of the American Institute on Taiwan. Do you have any luggage to pickup?"

"No, we have just what we are carrying," replied Jeff.

"In that case, I'll bring the car around and meet you outside the baggage claim area," remarked Mister Wang.

"That's fine, or we can walk to the car," replied Mel.

"No, that is not necessary; I'm not parked far. I'll be driving a black Ford sedan. Just give me about ten minutes," Mister Wang said.

All three of them walked out of the baggage area to curbside where Mister Wang left them.

"Well we're here," Mel said. "It seems like it's been eons ago."

"Yeah, I know. What's it been, a little over a month?"

"Something like that" answered Mel.

It wasn't long before Mister Wang drove up to the curb. He opened the trunk from inside the car before getting out. He walked to the passenger side of the car and opened the rear door for Jeff and Mel. They sat in the rear passenger seats after placing their B-4 bags in the trunk and thanking Mister Wang for holding the door open for them. Mister Wang closed the rear door, walked around to the driver's side and got into the car. Then he turned to Jeff and Mel and said, "I understand that you want to go to the Kennedy Hotel, is that correct?"

"Yes," replied Jeff. "Do you know how far the Kaohsiung Hospital is from the hotel?"

"You mean the Kaohsiung Municipal Chung Ho Hospital?"

"Yes, I think so," answered Jeff. "It's the main hospital in Kaohsiung isn't it?"

"Yes. It is part of the Kaohsiung's Medical University. It's not too far, about a fifteen-minute taxi ride," Mister Wang answered.

Jeff and Mel checked into the Kennedy Hotel and then Mel called Shao-mei. At the conclusion of his conversation he turned to Jeff.

"Shao-mei said that the doctors have put Kuo-ying into a state of induced coma to help reduce the swelling in her brain. We'll not be able to visit until tomorrow. Shao-mei will meet us at the hospital tomorrow, around

10 AM. Although Kuo-ying will be unconscious, at least we'll be able to see her."

"Well I guess that will be some comfort," a grim Jeff answered.

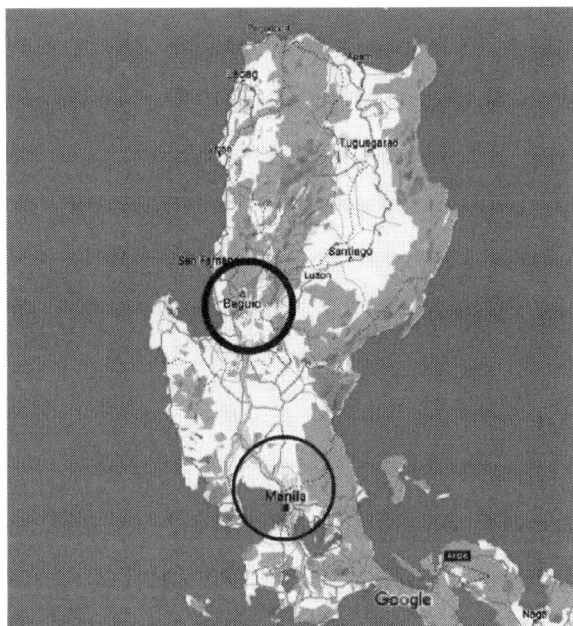

MANILA TO BAGUIO

Chapter 5

Baguio

115

That evening Al and Earl were joined by Dave, Connie, Barbara and Peggy for drinks and then dinner at the officers' club. Dave was introduced to the ladies. Upon the introduction to Connie he greeted her in Spanish to which she answered in the same language.

"You know Connie already?" Al asked.

"Connie is in the class I'm teaching," Dave answered. "She is one of my best students."

"I didn't know that you spoke Spanish," Earl commented.

"Yes, I'm fluent in Spanish," Dave replied. "That is one of the reasons I was transferred to the embassy in Manila. By the way, have you heard from your two missing partners?"

"Only that they arrived and were checked in at the Kennedy," replied Al. "I've got their room number and the Kennedy's telephone number."

"How about the condition of Jeff's friend?" Connie asked.

"The doctors have put her into an induced coma," answered Al. "Jeff's not sure what that means. They hope to get to the hospital tomorrow and learn more. One of them is to call and let us know how things are going."

"I sure hope everything turns out all right," Peggy said. "I hate to see a nice guy like Jeff, hurt."

"Agreed," said Earl. "At least he's got Mel with him."

"Well, when you hear from him make sure you tell him that all of us are thinking of him and he and his friend will be in our prayers."

"Will do," said Al. "I know he'll appreciate it."

"New subject," interjected Earl, "Baguio."

"What's Baguio?" asked Peggy.

"Baguio is a town up in the mountains about three hours north of here, with a first-class golf course," remarked Dave. "And, being the intelligent agent that I am, I bet that's the subject of your interest."

"Ah, you are so smart, or should I say intelligent," commented Al.

"Intelligent and smart will do," laughed Dave.

"Is that true, what do you think Connie?" asked Barbara.

"Oh no, don't get me into this," laughed Connie. "Remember, I'm still in class and he is my teacher."

"Yeah, I bet," commented Peggy. "I wonder what he's teaching you that is so hush, hush."

"Hey, don't pick on our buddy Dave," added Earl. "If Connie says he is teaching her, then he is teaching her, and probably doing a good job of it."

"No question," joked Peggy. "And I bet she is a quick learner."

"I'll drink to that," said Dave taking a swig from his drink.

"Okay, getting back to the subject of Baguio," Earl said. "Why don't we all go; make it a weekend trip."

"You really mean all of us?" Barbara asked.

"Sure, why not," answered Earl. "We could rent a van and drive through the county side; give us another chance to see the scenic side of the Philippines."

"Great idea!" exclaimed Al. "Why didn't I think of that?"

"Yes, Al, why didn't you think of that?" quipped Earl.

"Well ladies, and Dave, what do you think?" asked Al. "Are you all in."

"If we don't play golf, what will we do?" asked Barbara.

"I'm sure that there are other things we can play," laughed Peggy.

"Leave it to Peggy," laughed Connie.

"Baguio is a great place for shopping," interjected Dave. "I understand that the old market is a great place for bargains, and you can haggle."

"When did you have in mind?" Dave asked. "Both Connie and I will be tied up in class during the week."

"Why not the weekend? Memorial Day is a holiday isn't it?" asked Al.

"You're right, I plumb forgot. This weekend is a three-day weekend for most of the embassy staff, answered Dave.

"Okay, now we know that Dave and Connie will be free; how about it?" Al asked, addressing Barbara and Peggy.

"Hold on," interrupted Dave. "I just said that Connie and I didn't have class. I'm not speaking for her."

"Are you going?" Connie asked Dave.

"Well yes, I'd like to take some of Earl and Al's money on the golf course."

"Peggy, Barbara, are you two going?" asked Connie.

"It sounds great," answered Barbara. "I'm sure I can swing it. What about you Peg?"

"Where you go, I go," laughed Peggy.

"Well someone needs to chaperon you two, so count me in," said Connie.

"Yeah, right, I wonder who will be chaperoning whom," quipped Peggy.

"Okay, it's settled," Al announced. "Dave, see about getting us a tee time for Sunday morning, and see if there is lodging at, what was the name of the base?"

"Camp John Hay," answered Dave. "I'll check. I'm sure I can get us a tee time. The embassy normally has four times available for the Ambassador and his staff. Lodging maybe a little trickier, but I'm sure we can find accommodations in Baguio."

The evening ended with dinner and everyone excited about the prospect of the trip up the mountains.

The plans were completed: a rental van was reserved from the Navy's Special Services; Dave got a 10 AM tee time for Sunday, and Dave, to all's amazement, was able to snag the embassy's house it had in Baguio, which is used to host distinguished visitors. The Ambassador had planned to use it but at the last minute his plans changed and the house became vacant. The embassy's chargé d'affaires, a good friend of Dave's, alerted him to that fact and Dave was able to reserve it; a six-bedroom villa not too far from Camp Hay. Al called Mel and informed him of their plan. He got an update on Kuo-ying's condition; she was coming out of her induced coma and her prognosis was good.

At seven in the morning Earl and Al parked the
rented van in front of the VOQ where the ladies and
Dave Hollingsworth waited, their suitcases at their side.
The luggage was placed in the rear of the van and then
everyone boarded; Al in the driver's seat, Earl riding
shotgun. Barbara and Peggy sat on the seat behind them,
separated by a picnic basket. Dave and Connie occupied
the last seat.

"Okay navigator, what's our route?" Al asked Earl,
who had an opened map on his lap.

"First we have to get to MacArthur Highway,"
replied Earl.

"Okay," said Al. "How do we get to MacArthur
Highway?"

"Out the main gate and stay on the main drag, which
is Rizal Avenue, through Olongapo City," said Earl.
"According to the desk clerk at the 'Q', we should see
signs to MacArthur Highway. Once at the highway
intersection, we want to go north toward Tarloc."

"You got all that," yelled Dave from the back.

"Hey, I just keep driving until my navigator tells me
where to get off," laughed Al.

"I'm sure he'll tell you where to get off," laughed
Dave.

"Don't pick on Earl," admonished Peggy. "He
knows where we're going."

"I do? I mean I do," laughed Earl.

"Okay, then we're off," announced Al.

Al exited the Navy Station and proceeded past a whole slew of bars that they had passed on their tour to Bataan, joining the throng of people on mopeds, scooters, in jeepneys, sedans and buses, all vying for whatever space opened in front of them. The going was slow in Olongapo, but once through the city the traffic thinned and the competition for space was mainly with heavy-trucks, sedans and busses. The topography was flat but rising, with rice fields interspersed with palm and banana trees on both sides of the highway. Off in the distance, on the right, was the Mariveles Mountain Range, with its lush tropical vegetation. On the left, the foothills of the Cordilleras Mountains could be seen.

Thirty minutes had passed when the passengers' napping, gazing, or musing were interrupted by Earl's announcement. "MacArthur Highway's just ahead."

"Yeah, I see the sign," remarked Al. "What's the name of the town that we're supposed to be heading for?"

"Tarlac," answered Earl. "I was told that there are cafés and souvenirs shops along that stretch of the highway where we can take a break; look at souvenirs, local carvings and where the restrooms are clean."

"Great, I'm sure all of us would like a chance to get out and stretch our legs and use the facilities," remarked Al.

"Are we there yet?" asked Peggy, humorously.

"Just a few more miles, now; stay put like a good little girl," replied Earl.

Al turned onto the highway toward the town of Tarlac.

Earl saw it first and turned to Al, "see it up ahead, on the right, the Tarlac Café and Souvenir Store."

"Yeah, I see it. I particularly like the sign that says tourist welcome and clean restrooms."

Al parked in the store's parking lot, next to a large bus. Everyone disembarked and entered the store. They were greeted by rows and rows of souvenirs, clothing and Filipino handicrafts consisting of quilts, jewelry, palm fronds-woven handbags and baskets. There was even a small food section with locally grown products; jams and jellies. Off to the left was the café, and in the rear, everyone's main objective, the restrooms. The group used their respective restroom and returned to the large open bay to examine the wares before loading into the van and proceeding toward their destination.

"We're looking for Rosario," Earl instructed Al. "According to my calculation we should approach it in about an hour, depending on traffic."

"Traffic's not bad so far and it's moving nicely for the climbing we've been doing," remarked Al. "What's at Rosario?"

"Kennon Road, our gateway to Baguio," answered Earl. "According to the guy at the rental agency, there will be plenty of signs to alert us to the turn off."

They continued northwest along MacArthur Highway. The change in elevation was herald by the change in the terrain. The vast Sierra Madre was on their left. Its lush green vegetation was evidence of the rainforest and tropic pine that comprise this mountain chain; the eastern wall of Luzon Island.

As Earl had been told, they were alerted way in advance to the highway that would take them to Baguio. A gas stop was made in Rosario at a gas station and souvenir outlet where all took advantage of the restrooms and Earl purchased a guidebook of Baguio. Once these needs were met, they enjoyed their picnic lunch in the store's parking lot.

"Hey, listen to this," Earl announced. "I've been reading the history of this Kennon Road we're to take. It seems it's a result of a great engineering feat, or that's what the guidebook would like us to believe, but in fact it was the result of a great engineering screw-up."

"What do you mean?" Peggy asked.

"It seems that a United States Army Colonel named Kennon was in charge of the project and he decided to build the road starting at both its bases, here, and at its terminus in Baguio. The two ends were supposed to meet somewhere in the middle; operative word, 'supposed'."

"You mean like the meeting of the Union Pacific and the Central Pacific Railways at Promontory Summit in Utah in the 1870s?" asked Dave.

"Hey our resident spook knows his history," laughed Al.

"Takes one to know one," replied Dave. "But yes, I'm a railway buff. Actually, I think it was in 1869 that the transcontinental railway was completed and the famed golden spike joined the Union Pacific railway tracks with those of the Central Pacific."

"Well so far so good," Earl continued. "However, in this case Colonel Kennon and his engineers missed the spot that the two were to meet and a lot of adjustments to the roadbed had to be made and *voila,* we have San Francisco's Lombard Road only on a much larger scale. Here, look at the map."

Earl passed around the guidebook with a page depicting the zigzag nature of the road, for all to see.

"Maybe I should have brought some Dramamine," Barbara said.

"This looks like fun," Al commented, after seeing the map.

"Yeah, right, fun," Connie said. "I can see us now as we miss one of those turns and land at the bottom of a ravine."

"Not to worry," Dave quipped. "Our glorious leader will see us through."

"That's easy for you to say," quipped Earl, "but I'm riding shotgun; remember?"

The book was returned to Earl.

"Everybody ready?" Al called out.

Everyone gave their assent. Al turned the key in the ignition and pulled out of the parking lot. The access to Kennon Rod was across from the gas station and souvenir outlet. Al turned onto it after giving way to a couple of trucks and one touring bus. The first stage was an easy drive, climbing a little, but then the climb became steeper; the bus ahead of them passed the truck in front of it. Al, put the van's gear in low as he slowed behind the two trucks that were in front of him. He eased out from behind the truck directly in front of him to check the traffic. The roadway on the opposite side was clear, although Al had to accelerate fast because the first hairpin curve was not far ahead. Al shifted the gear in drive and stepped down on the gas pedal. The van accelerated. The speedometer indicated fifty miles an hour when Al pulled in front of the truck and braked, forcing the van to slow so that he was now sandwiched between the two trucks.

"You're cutting it kinda close aren't you partner?" Earl remarked.

"Yeah, I hear you," answered Al. "However, I need to get ahead of these damn trucks or we'll be sucking their fumes all the way to Baguio. Once I get past this first turn, I should be in a good position.

However, the truck in front made it easy for them. Its right turn signal was blinking as it pulled in front of a couple of shops that were located at the right of the bend of the turn. Behind the shops were a group of wooden houses.

"This must be one of the construction camps the travel book describes. They were built to house the workers who constructed Kennon Road. They're now occupied by the locals," Earl mentioned to Al.

"I wonder how many cars never made the turn and landed in the middle of someone's living room," remarked Al.

"Or at least in the middle of one of those shops located along the bend in the road," laughed Earl. "A little farther up, is camp 2, Twin Peaks." Then Earl announced to everyone: "Klondike Hot Springs Resort is located there, on the left, according to the guidebook."

"Look at that beautiful waterfall," Connie announced.

"Where?" Barbara and Peggy spoke almost simultaneously.

"On the right side, about nine o'clock," Connie answered.

"I see it!" exclaimed Barbara. "It's beautiful."

Al slowed a little so everyone could glance out the right and take in its spectacular view. "Everybody see it?" he asked.

Getting a positive response, he accelerated once more.

Without any trucks to slow Al's progress, they were making good time once again. Al caught up with the tour bus that passed the two trucks. He stayed a short distance behind it.

"I'm going to follow this bus all the way to Baguio," Al remarked to Earl. "Let it run interference for me, around all these curves."

"Good thinking," replied Earl. "Just stay far enough behind so that we don't join it if it fails to execute the turn."

"Amen to that," agreed Al.

"There it is, on our left, the Klondike Hot Springs Resort," Earl announced.

Al slowed, thus allowing everyone to view the hotel and its large swimming pool. Once past the resort Earl made another announcement.

"Okay everyone; keep your eyes peeled for Bridal Veil, on your left, and Colorado waterfalls farther up."

"I see it," yelled Barbara. "At least it's a waterfall. I assume it's Bridal Veil."

"Where?" Peggy asked.

"Straight ahead," Barbara answered.

Before anyone had a chance to see it, it became hidden from view by the roadway's hairpin curve onto a long bridge. Across the bridge a scenic turnoff was marked with a sign identifying Bridal Veil Falls. Al pulled into the turnoff and stopped the van. Everyone disembarked to view the narrow waterfall plunging down from atop a sheer wall of granite, creating a stream which continued under the bridge they had just crossed.

"It's beautiful," remarked Connie. "We don't have many waterfalls in Arizona."

"We don't have them in Texas either," Peggy commented.

"It is beautiful but it's nothing compared to the ones we have in Northern California," remarked Dave. "I'm thinking of Yosemite Falls in Yosemite National Park. That waterfall dwarfs this by comparison."

"Your right about the waterfalls in the northwest, especially in the Rockies," added Earl. Being an outdoor nut, I like waterfalls in all shapes, sizes and descriptions."

After some photographs, everyone returned to the van, and the trip up Kennon Road continued. Al's progress was slowed by a large truck in front of him. Oncoming traffic and a hairpin curve in front of them prevented Al from passing; however, that didn't stop a speeding black sedan coming up from behind him. It passed Al, and immediately pulled in front of him to avoid an oncoming truck, forcing Al to brake suddenly.

"Shades of Li-chun," Earl said.

"That guy's nuts," remarked Dave as he and the ladies grabbed the back of the seat in front of them, for support.

"He's going to kill himself, the maniac," remarked Peggy.

The car didn't stay there long. Once the opposite side was clear it accelerated and passed the truck. However, the screeching of his brakes was heard when he took the curve in front of the bus.

"And he's on his way again," remarked Dave, who was in a better position to see him take the curve.

"And good riddance," remarked Connie.

When the traffic permitted, Al, too, passed the bus and continued the climb. Another settlement marked by two lions' heads, was passed.

"This is camp 6," remarked Earl, reading from his travel guidebook. "It was one of the old construction camps but now it's a small housing area. After we take the next two turns, we'll see the Military Cut Off on the right, which is the road we want. It'll take us to Marcoville Street which is where our villa is located.

The house is near to both Session Road and to Camp John Hay's main gate."

Traffic began to slow as the group approached the outskirts of Baguio. "We should be approaching Military Cut Off soon," Earl said.

"Yeah, I think I see it right ahead, where the cars are turning," replied Al.

"Are we there yet?" Peggy asked.

"Gotta be soon," Dave said. "I can see the tall buildings of Baguio straight ahead."

"It won't be long," Earl announced. "We're going to take that turn-off just ahead, and from there, I'd estimate our ETA would be ten minutes."

"Oh, Earl I like it when you talk pilot talk," Peggy said.

"What pilot talk?" Connie asked.

"You know, ETA, estimated time of arrival," Peggy answered.

"Yeah, right," Barbara interjected. "You like it when Earl talks pilot; you like it when Earl talks, period."

"Hey, don't you be picking on Peggy," Earl said.

"If pilot talk is what turns Peggy on, then Earl will be entertaining us with ETAs, ETDs, A OKs ad nauseam," remarked Dave.

"Peggy, listen to them make fun of me; they're jealous of my superior knowledge," Earl quipped.

"I think I'm going to get sick," Al entered the fray.

"What superior knowledge?" asked Connie.

"The knowledge that enables Earl to recognize a mistake when he makes it, again," laughed Al.

"*Et tu, Brute*," Earl replied to Al. "I thought we were friends to the bitter end."

"Yeah, and the bitter end's a million miles away."

"A bitter end's a million miles away; where in the world did that come from?" asked Earl.

"From the musical, the *Unsinkable Molly Brown*," laughed Connie.

Then Barbara and Peggy blurted out with the chorus:

And he'll stay my friend,

Doesn't matter what the other people say.

He's my friend,

To the bitter end

Even though the bitter end's a million years away!

♪

"Gosh, what did we do to deserve all this?" Al asked.

"I didn't know we had members of the Subic Bay glee club with us," spoke up Dave, "but I'm not complaining mind you."

"Well I think we're in for a real good time, everyone seems to be in a party mood," laughed Earl.

"Hey, it's always party time, right girls?" remarked Peggy.

"Amen!" spoke Connie.

Al turned right on to the Military Cut Off. "What's the street we're looking for?" he asked Earl.

"Marcoville Street, it's on the left," replied Earl. "Judging from the map, it should be the third street."

Al slowed the van as both he and Earl looked for the streets intersecting from the left. "Okay, there's Leonard Woods Road, our road should be next," advised Earl.

The next road was Marcoville Street, and Al turned onto it. "What next Mister Navigator?" Al asked as he pulled over to the side of the road and stopped.

133

"We're looking for 510 Marcoville Street," replied Earl. "The house number on our right is 290, so I suspect our objective is in the third block on the right."

Al pulled away from the curb and drove slowly up the street.

Everyone was looking at the exquisite homes set back from beautifully manicured grounds, which fronted both sides of Marcoville Street.

"Gosh, talk about the high-rent district," observed Barbara. "All I see is money."

"You mean one of these is where we will be staying?" asked Connie.

"I like it already," remarked Peggy, "nothing but first class."

Al spotted what would be their home for the next three days. It was just as the others, set back from the street. He entered the circular driveway and parked in front of the double teak doors. They all alighted from the van and gazed upon the villa that was before them. The house itself, was of concrete-block covered by pastel-stucco. There was a grouping of palms placed in a floral bed at each front corner. A low hedge ran along the front, separated by the front entrance.

"Gosh, this had to cost you a bundle," remarked Barbara.

"Ha, Dave came through once again," replied Al. "This belongs to the embassy, right Dave?"

"Right you are," answered Dave.

"How come the embassy has a house in Baguio?" Connie asked.

"Baguio is sometimes referred to as the summer capital of the Philippines," explained Dave. "The Filipino president has a home here. So, when he or she is here, the Ambassador can be close by. In addition, Baguio is a nice place to host embassy guests; Congressmen for example. When it is not reserved, it is available to the embassy staff for a small fee. We were lucky, there was a last-minute cancellation and I was able to grab it. There should be a caretaker and his wife somewhere around here."

No sooner had Dave uttered these words, when a tall, middle aged man dressed in working clothes came from around the side of the villa. "*Buenos Dias,*" he greeted.

"You are the American guests? We have been expecting you."

"*Buenos Dias,*" answered Dave. "Yes, I am Dave Hollingsworth and you are Carlos, I presume."

"*Si Senor,* I am Carlos Garcia. My wife, Maria and I are the caretakers. We live in quarters behind the main house. Welcome to Baguio. May I help you with your luggage?"

"No, that is not necessary, but thank you for offering," Dave answered, "just show us where to put them."

"Of course," Carlos answered. "Maria will show you. As you probably know there are six bedrooms, three on each side of the house. Just inform Maria as to which bedroom is whose."

The luggage was unloaded and carried to the front door. At the same time a middle-aged-woman opened the door and held it open for the guests to enter.

"Welcome *Señors and Señoras.* I am Maria, the housekeeper. I will show you the bedrooms and you may make your selection. I will also show you the rest of the house."

"That is fine," Al said. "We'll just leave the luggage in the foyer, if that is alright. After we get the layout of the house, we'll decide who goes where."

"*Si Senior,* that will be fine. Just place the luggage there and I'll show you the rest of the house. First, let me show you the guest's powder room so that you may freshen up after your long trip."

Maria then directed them to the powder room off of the foyer. Those who needed, took advantage of the offer and afterwards they toured the villa. Opposite the powder room was a small sitting room with a small table just outside its entrance. On the table a guestbook for visitors to sign was placed, as well as information on what to do in Baguio. The foyer opened to a large living room equipped with all the amenities one would expect, including a large fireplace and a wet bar. A hallway between the foyer and living room led to the bedrooms; three on each side of the villa.

Off to the side, and separated from the living room, was a formal dining room with a table that could easily seat eight and which could extend to accommodate many more. Behind the formal dining room were the kitchen and an informal dining area, with a large oval table that was already extended to accommodate the six. From both the kitchen and the formal dining area, there was an access to a brick inlayed patio with a large propane grill, and a grouping of three wrought iron round tables and chairs. The patio was surrounded by flowerbeds and palms.

Each bedroom had its own bathroom and shower. In addition, one of the bedrooms on each side of the house was what one would call a suite containing a king-size bed, an extra-large bathroom with a two-sink vanity, an enclosed shower and a large walk-in closet. The others contained two twin- size beds.

"Well the arrangements are convenient," observed Earl, "the ladies on one side and the gents on the other."

"And neither the twain shall meet," laughed Al.

"Party pooper," laughed Peggy.

"Okay, who gets the master bedroom?" asked Al.

"I suggest we draw cards," Dave offered.

"I say it should be Dave, since he is responsible for these accommodations," said Earl.

"I agree," said Al. "It's all yours, Dave."

"Well, if you insist," responded Dave.

"Okay girls, I guess we need to make a decision, who gets the master's bedroom on our side?" asked Barbara.

"Did I hear correctly; did you say master's bedroom?" asked Peggy.

"Must have been a Freudian slip," suggested Connie.

"Very funny, you know what I mean, who gets the master bedroom?" remarked Barbara.

"Let super sleuth Connie have it," Peggy said.

"It's too big for me, one of you two can have it," Connie answered.

"Oh no, Peggy says it should be yours, and what Peggy wants, Peggy gets," laughed Barbara.

"Okay, if it makes you two happy, I'll take it," answered Connie.

"Boy that was quick. She didn't put up much of a fight, did she, Barbara?" Peggy quipped.

"No, she didn't, but the master bedroom is hers," laughed Barbara.

"Okay, now that we have that all settled, there's one thing I need to caution Connie about," explained Dave.

"Each of the master bedrooms has a red button right above the bed. It's an emergency button. You push it and an alarm is sounded in each of the other bedrooms as well as the Baguio police station. When the Ambassador is here, or some other distinguished guest, one, or both, of the twin bedrooms will be occupied by security."

"You hear that, Connie. You can't use it to signal your lover that the coast is clear because we'll all be in the know," said Peggy.

"Lover, look who's talking," laughed Connie.

"Okay now that we've taken care of the master bedroom, who gets the others?" ask Al.

"I'll take the middle room and Barbara can have the other, if that's alright with her," Peggy replied.

"It's okay with me," Barbara said.

"Fine," Al answered. "I'll take the middle room on our side, and Earl you can take the last one, okay?"

"Okay with me," Earl answered. "Now shall we distribute the luggage, and then make our plans for dinner?"

After the luggage was distributed, everyone gathered in the living room to discuss the plans for the rest of the day.

"Let's take a ride to Camp John Hay, kinda get the lay of the land," suggested Al. "I bet they have an officers' club, probably a commissary where we can get some breakfast goodies, maybe some steaks. We can take advantage of the grill outside and this beautiful weather."

"Sounds good to me," replied Earl. "What do you say, ladies?"

"Sounds like a plan," said Connie.

Everyone agreed, and with Earl as navigator and his map as a guide, they all headed for Camp John Hay.

They pulled up to the main gate and Barbara rolled down her window and presented her identification card to the Air Policeman at the gate. He examined it and then saluted. "Welcome to Camp John Hay," he said.

Barbara returned his salute. "Thank you," she replied. "Is there an officers' club on the station?'

"Yes ma'am. Just follow this road, past the Scott Hill baseball field and the Forest Lodge. It is on the left across from the Manor House. You can't miss it."

"How about a commissary?" asked Al.

"There is not a commissary as such, but there is a small shoppette with a limited amount of goods. There are also several restaurants, a base exchange and an embassy store. They are all in the same area."

"What's the embassy store?" asked Peggy.

"Ha, I know the answer to that one," spoke Dave. "It's the booze store which is run by the Embassy."

"Right you are, sir," remarked the Air Policeman, a grin on his face. "It's like our Class 6 store."

"How do we get to the golf course?" Dave asked.

"That's easy too; just keep on this road for about a mile. You'll pass the headquarters building, base housing and the barracks."

"Thanks a lot," Al remarked to the Air Policemen. "You've been very helpful."

"Yes sir, enjoy your visit," the Air Policeman replied, coming to attention, and once more rendering a salute.

It took less than five minutes to find the Officers' Club, but more importantly they found the Shoppette. It was part of a complex behind the Manor House and the Forest Lodge. Beside the shoppette were the Base Exchange, the Embassy Store, a movie theater and a restaurant. Al parked the van outside the shoppette and all disembarked. The shoppette had a good selection of meats, beverages and foodstuff. The group purchased six New York Strip steaks, some potatoes, a salad mix, salad dressing, milk, bananas and cereal.

"Do we have enough wine or do we need to visit the Embassy Store?" asked Dave.

"We're got enough for tonight, both white and red, but we probably should think of getting some tomorrow after our game of pasture pool," answered Earl.

Their shopping completed, the group returned to their villa where Earl and Dave took care of grilling the steaks, the ladies prepared the salad and the potatoes, while Earl kept their glasses charged with wine.

The night was ideal; a slight breeze rustled the palm trees' fronds, a quarter-moon shone down upon them and the night sky was punctuated by zillions of stars. Two of the outdoor tables were pulled together to accommodate all of them. At the conclusion of the meal, the ladies took care of the dishes, and then joined the men outside to breathe in the atmosphere. It was after nine o'clock when travel fatigue finally caught up with them and they made their way to their appointed rooms; all agreeing to meet at around eight-thirty for the men to plan their golf match and the women their shopping.

The next morning, they were all sitting around the table in the kitchen enjoying a light breakfast of coffee, and cereal topped off with slices of bananas.

"What time is our t-time?" asked Al to Dave.

"It's 10 A. M.," Dave answered. "I figure we'd get started around 9; that will get us there no later than 9:15, time to pick up some clubs, hit the driving range and do some putting."

"Sounds good to me," Al said. "You okay with that," he asked, addressing Earl.

"Absolutely," he answered. I'll definitely need time on the driving range. Hell, I haven't swung a club since I left the States."

"Uh-oh, sounds like somebody setting someone up for strokes," laughed Dave. "But swinging a club is like riding a bike, you never really forget how."

"Yeah, easy for you to say," added Al. "Actually, the first thing to go is the timing, and the golf swing is all about timing."

"So, what are you trying to say?" Dave asked.

"Listen to the men talk," Peggy chimed in. "It's like we're not even here."

"Sorry about that ladies," Dave remarked, "but we've got some serious negotiating to do."

"Well I think we'll have some serious negotiating to do this evening ourselves, especially if you have any special plans," quipped Peggy.

"Man, Peggy knows how to get to the heart of the matter," laughed Connie.

"Sorry ladies, we'll save our negotiation for the golf course," laughed Earl. "What are your plans for today?"

"I noticed Earl changed his tune real fast," laughed Barbara.

"Yeah, like he has plans for tonight," laughed Connie. "What about you Al?"

"What do you mean, what about me?" asked Al.

"What are we going to do?" Barbara asked Connie and Peggy, not giving Al a chance to answer.

"Listen to Barbara change the subject," Peggy laughed.

"Well she has a point," Connie said. "The boys have their day all planned, and obviously we're not included."

"You ladies can join us at the golf course if you want," Dave said. "We just assumed that golf wasn't your thing."

"Golf's not our thing, but shopping is," Barbara added to the conversation. "We'll ask Maria what she suggests."

"I'll leave you ladies my guidebook," offered Earl. "It lists where all the shopping is."

"I think Earl is trying to get into our good graces again," remarked Connie.

"Yeah, he's trying to get into Peg's good graces," added Barbara.

"Good graces, is that what it's called?" grinned Earl.

"I think it is time to change the subject," laughed Connie. "Earl, go get your guidebook."

"I'm going, I'm going," Earl laughed, as he rose from the table and went to his bedroom. He returned with the guidebook in hand. He gave it to Connie, opened to the section on where to shop.

"Listen up girls," Connie announced, as she read from Earl's guidebook.

'Baguio City is a bargain hunter's paradise. Prices in the flea markets and souvenir shops are not always fixed so your haggling skills will be put to good use. The whole length of Session Road is the city's premier shopping area. At its top is the SM City Baguio Mall on Luneta Hill. The Baguio City Market is at its base on Magsaysay Avenue, that runs perpendicular to Session. Specialty shops and restaurants are found in the city center where everybody goes for all their supplies.

A favorite place for tourists and visitors to shop is at the Baguio City Market where you can get anything and everything. Dry Goods, furniture, and antiques are on the upper floors of the Maharlika Livelihood Center, which are favored by bargain hunters.'

"Leave it to our Connie," remarked Peggy. "She'll find us something to do."

"Okay, next question, how do we get to Session Road?" asked Barbara.

"They've gotta have taxis here," remarked Dave. "I'm sure that Maria or Carlos can arrange for a pick up. I'll speak to Carlos and make sure you are taken care of before we leave for the golf course."

"Thanks Dave, thanks a lot," Connie said, all smiles.

Later that morning, as the men were getting ready to head to the golf course, Dave reported to the ladies that there would be a jeepney to pick them up at 10 AM. "To return you can hail a jeepney anywhere along Session Road. You'll also find them parked at the Baguio City Market. In addition, there're money exchanges up and down Session Road and at the city market. Now, lastly, here is a card for each of you. It has the address of our villa, so that all you need to do is present the card to the driver." Then he handed each of the ladies an address card.

"Dave, you think of everything," Connie said, taking her card from Dave.

The men had no trouble in accessing Camp John Hay, after Dave showed his State Department identification card to the Air Policeman at its main gate. They drove to the golf course, where each rented a set of clubs, checked in with the starter, hit balls at the driving range and practiced putting on the putting green. Five minutes before their scheduled t-time they reported once more to the starter at the number one tee, where each of them met their caddies; all young Filipino girls in their teens. Dave was first on the tee. His drive was down the center of the fairway.

"You can tell who's been playing golf alright," Earl observed as he approached the tee box and inserted a tee in the ground. He brought his driver back over his shoulder and let it rip only to see his ball slice out of bounds.

"Take a Mulligan," Dave said. "Obviously you were intimidated by my drive."

"Slow the swing down," Al advised Earl, as Al approached the tee box. His drive landed in the left rough, but was playable.

Earl took his Mulligan, slowed his swing and his drive joined that of Dave's in the center of the fairway. Using a three wood, the next shot found them all within fifty yards of an undulating green. Earl was the first to play and he chipped his ball onto the middle of the green. Then Dave was next and his chip shot landed in a sand trap guarding the green. Next Al's ball went left of the green but still puttable. Al's putt was short of the stick while Earl's lag putt was within two feet of the hole. He ended the hole with a bogey while Dave and Al ended up taking double bogeys.

"Man, talk about sandbagging," Dave remarked.

"I guess I forgot to tell you that Earl was on the University of Washington's golf team," Al admitted.

"Hey, that was a long, long time ago," Earl remarked. "I was just lucky."

147

"Yeah, lucky, right," a skeptic Dave remarked.

However, the game continued and after seven holes Dave was leading Earl by three strokes and Al was down five strokes. They were waiting for the foursome on the number eight green to complete their play, when a large thunder-like blast permeated the atmosphere.

"What was that?!" Dave exclaimed, looking toward the direction from which the sound came.

"Damn, Vietnam all over again," Earl remarked, searching the sky. A large bellowing cloud of smoke could be seen rising above the horizon.

"That was a bomb blast, no doubt about it," added Al.

Their three caddies were huddled together in an animated discussion, anxiety and fear displayed on their faces.

"I noticed that one of the golfers on the green is communicating with someone via his brick (portable cellular phone-a forerunner of today's cell phones)," observed Al, "maybe we can learn something from him." No sooner had Al made that statement than the course weather alarm sounded, indicating a suspension of play.

The threesome walked to where the golfers were still standing on the green. Dave introduced himself and showed one of the foursome   his id card.

"Excuse me sir, I'm Dave Hollingsworth with the State Department's Anti-Terrorist Department. Can you tell me what's going on?"

"The man who had finished talking on the brick, introduced himself. "I'm Colonel Jibrisky, Director of Operations at Clark Air Base. All I can tell you is that a bomb exploded on Session Road near the Philippine Military Academy. I've just called for a golf cart to transport us to the clubhouse. The course suspended play until they can learn more."

Dave turned to Al and Earl. "I don't like the sound of this; a bomb on Session Road. That's where the girls were planning to do their shopping."

"We need to get down there pronto," Earl said.

Al turned to one of the caddies. "Our game is over, what is the quickest way to the clubhouse?"

You can cross over to the number nine fairway and walk to the clubhouse from there," the caddie informed all.

"Okay, let's do it," Al said.

Chapter 6

Taiwan

Kaohsiung Municipal Chung Ho Hospital is one of three teaching hospitals that comprise Kaohsiung Medical University; a square U-shape construction, twenty-two stories in height, with the north and south wings being the outer two legs of the U and the central wing connecting the two. It is located at the corner of Tzyou 1st Road and Zi-You 1st Street and consists of 1626 beds and 12 departments.

The next morning the taxi dropped Mel and Jeff off under the large concrete marquee at the main entrance to the hospital. Mel had called Shao-mei from the Kennedy Hotel and she had given them specific instructions on how to get to the Neurosurgical ICU's waiting room on the seventh floor of the hospital. she would meet them there, and introduce them to Kuo-ying's parents. The information desk was at the center of the hospital lobby. Mel was directed to the north wing elevators on the left. Mel and Jeff joined a family of four entering the elevator. Mel pressed the 7th floor button and surprised the family by asking what floor they wanted. Hearing their answer, he depressed the button for their floor. Mel and Jeff were also benefactors of the children's practice of the English language by a chorus of "hellos" and "how are you."

The elevator opened to the seventh floor. A nurse's station was to their right from where Mel was given directions to the waiting room. It was large. Sofas and easy chairs were in groupings around the room. Shao-mei saw them enter the waiting room and rushed to greet them, embracing both Mel and Jeff. Also, there to greet them was Wang Yi-kwei, Shao-mei's cousin and defector from the mainland who Jeff and company rescued from the clutches of Taiwan's Liberation Party. Although Yi-kwei shook their hands, both Mel and Jeff felt a little tension in his greeting.

"Shao-mei then led Mel and Jeff to a grouping along the wall where she introduced them to Mr. and Mrs. Sung and their two children; Kuo-ying's younger brother and sister. Mrs. Sung, thin, short in stature with jet black hair favored her daughter. Mr. Sung was stocky, balding and medium height.

Shao-mei explained that Kuo-ying was in a state of induced coma. The doctors' attending her felt it was necessary to reduce the swelling in her brain.

"That doesn't sound too good," a somber Jeff commented.

"Actually, the doctors say that there is no danger and having Kuo-ying in an induced coma will relieve pressure on the brain and allow the brain to help itself in the healing process."

"How long will she be in this state?" asked Mel.

"According to the Neurosurgeon, that depends on the swelling. Once it goes down then he'll bring Kuo-ying out of the coma. He's optimistic about the outcome and believes Kou-ying will have no lingering effects. She may experience some loss of memory but that should be only temporary."

"Is it possible to see her?" Jeff asked.

"I'd say yes but I need to ask her parents," replied Shao-mei. Both Yi-Kwei and I have seen her. I'm sure they won't mind. I'll ask them now."

Shao-mei talked to the parents and they hesitantly agreed. Then she and Yi-kwei led Mel and Jeff to the nurses' station inside the ICU and explained to one of the nurses of their desire to visit Kuo-ying. The nurse escorted them to her room and then left them. Kuo-ying was in a deep sleep. Oxygen tubing called nasal cannula was inserted in her nose, a solution of some sort was being administered intravenously, and a medical display was monitoring all her vital functions.

They stood by her bedside and gazed at her.

"She looks so peaceful," Jeff remarked. "Just fast asleep."

"You're right," a voice from behind them said.

They turned and saw a tall, slender man in a white smock. His name tag bore the name 'Lin" in both Chinese and English characters.

"Oh, Doctor Lin," Shao-mei exclaimed. "Let me introduce two of kuo-ying's American friends."

"Mel and Jeff, this is Doctor Lin. He's the neurosurgeon that has been caring for Kuo-ying."

They both shook hands with Doctor Lin and then Jeff asked, "how is she doing?"

"She's doing as well as can be expected. She had a severe head injury and as one of you noted, she is asleep, a very deep sleep in fact. We have placed her in a coma. It reduced the metabolic rate of brain tissue as well as the cerebral blood flow. With these reductions, the blood vessels in the brain narrows, decreasing the amount of space occupied by the brain, and hence the intracranial pressure. With the swelling relieved, the pressure decreases and we are able to reduce or eliminate any damage to the brain."

"What's your prognosis?" asked Jeff.

"In Kuo-ying case, very good," answered Doctor Lin. "In fact, we're gradually bringing her to full consciousness."

"That's great, how long will it take?" Jeff asked.

"Perhaps by tomorrow if she progresses as I think she will."

"That's great news," exclaimed Jeff. "Will she be able to speak and receive visitors."

"Again, we will not know until she does regain consciousness and we perform tests, but I am very optimistic."

"Thank you, doctor, we really appreciate your informing us of her condition," Mel said. "Obviously she is in good hands."

"Thank you, now if you will excuse me, I'm going to examine my patient."

"Yes sir, thanks again," Mel said.

They left Kuo-ying's room and returned to the waiting room.

"Man, that was really good news!" once again, exclaimed a relieved Jeff.

"Where did Doctor Lin learn his English?" asked Mel to Shao-mei.

"He received his medical training in the United States, at Vanderbilt University in Tennessee," answered Shao-mei. "Now I'm going to speak to Kuo-ying's parents and make sure that they are aware of Kuo-ying's improved condition. I know that they will be relieved."

Shao-mei returned from her conversation with Kuo-ying's parents. "Doctor Lin had already informed them of his plans for Kuo-ying and obviously they are very happy."

"Well, I guess there is nothing more we can do here, what say we get a bite to eat," Mel said.

Everyone readily agreed; that is everyone except Yi-kwei who decided to keep Kuo-ying parents' company.

There was a small restaurant in walking distance of the hospital which Shao-mei and Yi-kwei had found earlier. Shao-mei, Mel and Jeff sat around a square table and ordered a large platter of pork fried noodles which they all shared. The conversation was stilted.

"Doctor Lin was pretty optimistic," commented Mel.

"Yes, he is regarded as the top neurosurgeon in Kaohsiung," remarked Shao-mei.

"I noticed that Yi-Kwei was kinda quiet," observed Jeff.

"Yes, he was really upset by the accident," responded Shao-mei. "He and Kuo-ying have been seeing each other after you all left."

"I noticed that he seemed to be very close to her parents," remarked Jeff.

"Yes, I think they reminded him of his parents on the mainland," Shao-mei said. "It's understandable. While we want Yi-kwei to consider us his family, and I'm sure he does, still, I think that Mr. and Mrs. Sung make him think of the mother, father and sister he left in Beijing, and which he'll probably never see again. We've never really talked about his family; my father's sister and brother-law. He must miss them very much, and I'm sure it hurts him to think about them."

"Yes, I'm sure you're right," Jeff said.

"Let me change the subject," Shao-mei said. "My father would like to thank you for what you did for me and Yi-kwei. Actually, I think he wants to show you off to his friends and business associates. He wants to host a dinner to honor you."

"You know that's not necessary," Mel replied.

"Yes, I know that, but he doesn't and it is a Chinese custom to honor your benefactors, and I'd like to honor you as well."

"Well, what can we say, Jeff?" asked Mel.

"If that's what the lady wants, then I say, let's go for it," smiled Jeff.

"Hen hao (very good)," replied Shao-mei. "We have no room at our home to entertain you properly so Father will rent rooms for you at the Tainan Hotel and that is where we'll host the dinner."

"Déjà vu all over again," remarked Jeff.

"Déjà vu? I don't understand," a puzzled Shao-mei remarked.

"How soon the lady forgets," laughed Jeff. "It was the dinner your uncle hosted for the four of us at the Hualien Hotel where we met you."

"It's nice to see you laugh," Shao-mei answered. "No, I didn't forget Hualien. How could I? It was an experience that changed my life," and with that last phrase she gazed upon Mel.

"And mine," Mel said, returning the gaze, clasping Shao-mei's hand.

Nothing more was said after that. They ate their meal, and afterwards returned to the hospital where they learned that Kuo-ying was semi-conscious and undergoing tests. However, Doctor Lin informed everyone that it would be tomorrow morning at the earliest, before he would know anything definite about her condition. Shao-mei used the opportunity while at the hospital to call her father to inform him of Mel and Jeff's consent to the dinner in their honor.

"I don't see any sense for me to remain here anymore today," Jeff said to Mel. Why don't I take a taxi to the hotel and you stay here and keep Shao-mei company?"

"No, let me talk to Shao-mei a little and then we'll both return to the hotel."

"Shao-mei is concerned that you might be upset on learning of Kuo-ying's and Yi-kwei's relationship," Mel mentioned to Jeff once they were in their hotel room. "She's questioning whether she should have informed me of the accident."

"Of course, she should have," answered Jeff. "I admit I was a little taken back, but it makes perfectly good sense that they should see each other. After all, she was responsible for Yi-kwei's association with the Taiwan Liberation Party. I know she felt responsible for what they did to him, and assisted us in his release."

157

"I've invited them to have dinner with us if that is okay with you."

"Of course, I'd like that. It will give me an opportunity to reassure her that she made the right decision. I would have come to see Kuo-ying regardless. I still have strong feelings for her whatever her relationship with Yi-kwei, and would have been disappointed if I were not told. What time do we plan to meet?"

"Shao-mei will call us around five from the hotel lobby. I figure we might as well eat here."

"Roger that. Now I'm going to lie down for a little while."

"Okay, while you do that, I'll call Al and Earl and bring them up to date and then I'll also rest a little. I'll set the alarm for four. That will give us a chance to shower and dress before Shao-mei calls."

Jeff was already up and had showered before the four o'clock alarm woke Mel. Mel showered and dressed. They were watching a Chinese game show on television when Shao-mei called. They met in the lobby. Shao-mei was alone; Yi-Kwei decided to eat at the hospital. They were escorted to a table for four in the hotel's dining room where they had a light dinner. Jeff thanked Shao-mei for writing Mel about the accident.

"I would have felt terrible if I had found out about the accident and not had the chance to see her; especially, God forbid, she died," Jeff assured her. "You were one hundred percent right to write Mel. I really thank you for that." Then he reached over and kissed her on the cheek.

After eating their meal, Jeff gave some flimsy excuse about having to return to the room.

"He wasn't too subtle, was he?" Mel asked.

"I think he was being the gentleman he is and I thank him for that."

"Shall I rent us a room?"

"Of course."

Around 9 A.M. the following day Jeff and Mel returned to the hospital. Shao-mei and Yi-kwei were already there. There was good news; Kuo-ying had recovered full consciousness. Her family was in the room with her at the present time. Doctor Lin had cautioned everyone that although Kuo-ying was conscious, she was still heavily sedated, and as a consequence she might seem somewhat incoherent, which was to be expected. He also emphasized that the visits should be brief at first. Perhaps longer visits tomorrow.

Mr. and Mrs. Sung and their two children entered the ICU waiting area and were greeted by Shao-mei and Yi-kwei. A brief discussion ensued.

"Kuo-ying recognized her family," Shao-mei related the results of her discussion. "She doesn't remember too much though, especially about the accident. But according to the Sungs she looked good and spoke well, although she was still drowsy. She was actually sitting up."

"Sitting up?" questioned Jeff.

"That's what Mrs. Sung said, but I'm sure she meant that her hospital bed was raised to support her."

"Never-the-less, that is great," commented Jeff.

"When can we see her?" asked Yi-kwei.

"Not for a while, I'm afraid. Mrs. Sung told her that friends we're waiting to see her, but Mrs. Sung was not so sure she really comprehended what she was told. The nurse is with her now giving her a sponge bath. My guess is it will be sometime this afternoon before the Doctor will allow visits, other than from her immediate family."

"Well, we'll just have to wait," Jeff said. He looked at Yi-kwei. Then walked over to him and speaking in fluent Chinese said: "Yi-kwei we need to talk."

"What about?" Yi-kwei answered with an unreceptive expression on his face.

"Let's move over to the corner so we'll have more privacy," Jeff answered.

They moved to the other side of the room, Yi-kwei still wearing the same indifferent expression.

"I know that you and Kuo-ying have been seeing each other," Jeff began. "I assume that it is more than just a causal relationship. I can understand that you might see me as appearing out of the blue, and possibly awakening some latent feelings in Kuo-ying that might affect your relationship with her. I just want you to know that I'm here out of a sincere friendship for her, nothing more. I have no intention of coming between you and her. I feel relieved that her recovery is progressing as well as it appears, and that's what I intend to tell her when I see her. I'll also let her know that I'll be returning to Manila and joining the rest of the crew."

"That's fine for you to say," Yi-kwei responded. "But what about Kuo-ying? Do you think that you can just enter her life again, say hello, and leave without it affecting her? Yes, I have some strong feelings for her. I believe she has those same feelings for me. I know she was hurt when you left. She thought that she would never see you again. I think that I helped ease the pain of your separation. Now you appear, out of the blue, as you said. It's got to stir some old feelings. I don't want to see her hurt. This is my concern."

"I appreciate your feelings, but when we separated it was as sincere friends. I don't think Kuo-ying thought of me as nothing more than as a good friend who helped her when she needed it most. And that need, by the way, was to rescue you. Her feelings had to be for you. That's why she was so upset when she saw how you were betrayed by the Taiwan Liberation Party. She knew how strongly you wanted a platform to denounce the regime on the mainland, and how she was responsible for introducing you to the leaders of the

Party. Consequently, she felt responsible for your betrayal."

"I never thought of it that way, I felt that I was getting Kuo-ying on the rebound."

"Nothing could be further from the truth. When I have an opportunity to talk to her alone, I'll mention how glad I am that you two are seeing each other."

"You'd do that for me?"

"Not for you, but for Kuo-ying and myself. Now shall we go back to the others? Maybe go out to lunch and hopefully we will be able to see her when we return."

"I'd like that." Yi-kwei's whole mien changed. Cheerfulness replaced gloom; relief replaced forebodingness.

"What was that all about?" Mel asked Jeff upon his joining them.

"I did some real soul-searching last night while you were with Shao-mei," Jeff answered. "Although I have real feeling for Kuo-ying, maybe even love, I had to admit to myself it was going nowhere. Basically, I told Yi-kwei he had nothing to fear from me as far as Kuo-ying is concerned. Kuo-ying and I separated as good friends then and, that's how it will be when I return to Manila. You know, I feel kinda relieved after admitting that to myself."

"Did we make a mistake in coming here?"

"No! Definitely not! As I said, I do have real feelings for her. I want to remain a good friend and to be available if ever she should need me. And, it afforded you an opportunity to see Shao-mei, which you would not otherwise have done."

"You're right there! I never realized how much I missed her until I saw her again."

"That's great. Now, I'm looking forward to Tainan and the soiree in our honor."

"Amen to that," replied Mel.

As suggested, the group returned to the same restaurant where they ate the day before. It was at this time that Shao-mei informed Mel and Jeff about the plans for the, as Jeff described it, soiree in their honor.

"My father reserved the banquet room at the Tainan Hotel for the day after tomorrow," Shao-mei explained. "There's to be about fifty of his friends and business associates, and some of my close friends. However, as he put it, the dinner is to show off his American friends. He also has reserved two rooms for you at the Tainan Hotel."

The subtlety of the individual rooms did not go unnoticed by either Jeff or Mel.

"He'll arrange transportation for you from Kaohsiung to Tainan. He's really looking forward to the event to repay you for what you did for me and Yi-kwei. He's very excited and wanted me to say that he wants to give you 'the cook's tour' of his new reprocessing plant. I asked him what he meant by the 'cook's tour.' I was not familiar with that expression. He told me to never mind, that you would understand. I think he wanted to impress you with his knowledge of English."

"I'm impressed," Mel laughed. "A cook's tour is an American expression that means a complete tour. It has its origin in the 19th Century English explorer Thomas Cook and, not a culinary cook."

"Yeah," added Jeff. "It means he wants to show us the 'whole nine yards'".

"The whole nine yards, now I am confused," Shao-mei added.

"Ha, I don't know why," said Jeff. "I don't know where it came from but I've heard it since I was a kid. Simply put, it too, means everything."

"Well my father wants to give you the cook's tour and the whole nine yards," laughed Shao-mei.

After lunch they returned to the hospital and were pleased to find that Kuo-ying was up to receiving visitors. Yi-Kwei was first. He stayed with her for about twenty minutes, in which time he informed her of Jeff and Mel visit. Jeff was next. Kuo-ying had fixed her hair and had taken the oxygen tubing from her nose. The front of her bed was raised to the sitting position. She looked tired.

"*Ni hao,*" she greeted, her face aglow. "I couldn't believe it when Yi-kwei told me that you and Mel were here."

Jeff sat down on the chair next to her bedside. "Once I learned of the accident, there was no way I couldn't come; and Mel too."

"How did you hear of the accident?"

"Shao-mei wrote Mel and he told the rest of us. Al and Earl wanted to come but, someone had to stay and hold the fort. I keep them informed of your progress, which obviously is great. You look fabulous."

"Hold the fort; you and your crazy American Expressions, and looking fabulous? You've got to be kidding."

"Not at all. Mel and Shao-mei are outside. I didn't know that you knew Shao-mei."

"I met her through Yi-kwei. We've been seeing each other."

Jeff took note of the somber expression that came over her face. "That's great, and I'm not surprised. That's the way it should be. He's a great guy." Saying that, he gave her hand a gentle squeeze.

"Thanks." Her eyes started to moisten.

"You need to rest. I'll call Mel and Shao-mei in, just to say hello and then we're going to skedaddle."

"There you go again with your crazy American expressions," smiled Kuo-ying. "There is no way I can pronounce it, and I bet it can't be translated into Chinese."

"The closest I can get to Chinese is, we're going to leave and let you get some rest." Jeff laughed and rose from his chair, gave Kuo-ying a kiss on her forehead and left, only to return with Shao-mei and Mel. Both gave Kuo-ying a kiss and told her how well she looked; that she was in their prayers and that they would return tomorrow. Then, they left Kuo-ying so that she could get some much-needed rest after all the excitement of their visit.

The following day, Mel and Jeff returned to the hospital where they once again visited Kuo-ying. They were pleased to learn that her condition was upgraded and Doctor Lin had informed her family that if her health continued to improve, she would be discharged soon. She'd still have to undergo therapy but that could be done in her hometown.

That afternoon, Shao-mei's father arranged for a taxicab to transport Mel and Jeff to Tainan, where they checked into their rooms at the Tainan Hotel. Their evening was spent at the Chiang's home where they enjoyed a family dinner prepared by Shao-mei which Mister Chiang was quick to mention. The following day Mister Chiang personally gave Jeff and Mel a cook's tour of his recycling plant. It began with the outside area where scrap material was stacked in piles. They watched as the scrap material was transferred to a long conveyer belt that moved the scrap into the processing facility. Next, they were escorted into the processing facility where Mister Chiang gave them hardhats to wear. They watched the scrap metal be shredded in small pieces by repeated blows from a steel drum on which small hammers were mounted.

"That's called a hammer mill," Mister Chiang explained. "As you can see, the shredded pieces fall through the openings in that grate located below the hammer mill, and onto another conveyer belt. Then, a magnetic drum separates the ferrous material from the nonferrous material. After that, we use a Cyclone air separator system that works like a giant vacuum cleaner, and sucks the non-ferrous material up into a hopper while the ferrous material continues along the conveyer belt."

As they walked through the plant following the process, Mister Chiang pointed to several employees who were stationed at points along the conveyer belt. "Their job is to remove any questionable material from the ferrous material before we ship it to steel mills in Kaohsiung to be used again," Mister Chiang explained.

"What about the non-ferrous material that's sucked up into the hopper?" Mel asked.

"It goes through the non-ferrous processing line where Eddy Current Separators, separates non-ferrous material, like aluminum, and farther down the line an Induction Sorting System pulls out additional non-ferrous material, like stainless steel. These we send to foundries, again in Kaohsiung," Mister Chiang continued his explanation.

At the conclusion of the tour they entered into Mister Chiang's office where they sat around a coffee table. An employee brought in tea and soft drinks, and set them on the table.

"I use to reprocess plastics, but I find that there is a greater demand for reprocessed scrap metals," Mister Chiang explained. "The problem I have, is getting a sufficient amount of metal to make the system pay for itself. I'm thinking of establishing an office in the United States, perhaps with Shao-mei, to locate sources of scrap, and arrange for its shipment to us." Then he turned to Mel, "I understand that you have a business background, and connections with companies in the United States."

"I was a stockbroker in the States," remarked Mel. "Most of my dealings were with individual investors, and not companies."

"Nevertheless, I'm sure you could be of great assistance in helping Shao-mei find sources, if I should decide to go that route," Mister Chiang replied.

"Well, of course, I'd give Shao-mei any assistance I could," smiled Mel.

"Mister Chiang, where did you learn your English?" asked Jeff. "You speak like a native."

"Ha, you are too kind," answered Mister Chiang. "I'm afraid my English is not nearly as good as your Chinese. However, to answer your question, I went to the logistic school at your Wright-Patterson Air Force

Base in Ohio. Then I did, how do you say it, a stint with our Combine Services Forces, where I was a liaison with your Military Assistant Advisory Group. So, I've had many opportunities to use English."

"When we put into Kaohsiung to repair our boat, Colonel Lu of your Combine Services Forces provided us a lot of help," remarked Jeff.

"Lu is a common Chinese name, like your Smith," laughed Mister Chiang. "I'm afraid that the Combine Services have a lot of Lu's."

"Yes, of course," laughed Jeff. "You're right, but this Colonel Lu is with your Foreign Affairs Police, and he provided us with some temporary visas, so we could travel around Taiwan."

"You probably mean Colonel Lu Chi-tien, who works for a colleague of mine, General Chin. In fact, General Chin replaced me when I retired," smiled Mister Chiang. "I'm glad that he was able to help you. I must remember to call General Chin, and advise him of Colonel Lu's assistance."

"That would be nice," interjected Mel. "If it wasn't for Colonel Lu, we would never have met Shao-mei."

"And never have come to her and Yi-kwei's aid, for which we all are in your debt, and for which I am delighted that tonight we can honor you for that. It is too bad that your other companions aren't here."

"Yes, I know they will be disappointed when we tell them of your generosity," Mel said.

169

"Not generosity but gratitude," smiled Mister Chiang. "Now, I'll have one of my people drive you back to your hotel so that you will have an opportunity to rest before this evening's dinner."

"If I'm not mistaken, I think that Mister Chiang was trying to recruit you?" Jeff mentioned to Mel, when they were back at their hotel.

"It sure sounded like that. He's got quite an operation. I bet I could help him."

"Yes, and Shao-mei," laughed Jeff.

"Yes, and Shao-mei."

Chapter 7

The bombing

Al, Earl and Dave made it across the ninth fairway to the course's parking lot. They immediately found their van and proceeded to drive off the base but were stopped by the Air Policeman at the main gate.

"Be advised that Upper Session Road is closed to all traffic north of the Ben Palispis Highway due to a bombing in the old district," he advised the group.

"I'm with the Embassy," Dave informed the sentry. "Will that make a difference?"

"I don't know, I'm just to advise those leaving the base about the road closure," he answered.

"Thanks," Dave answered, and then Al drove the van up Loakan Road and turned on to Session Road. Once, he had to pull to the side of the road to allow an emergency vehicle to pass, and then he continued until he encountered members of the Baguio Police Department at a temporary barricade blocking traffic from proceeding farther. Dave showed the policeman his State Department Identification Card.

"I'm the Embassy's point man on terrorism," he informed the policeman. "I'd like to meet with the authorities."

"Yes sir," the guard replied, examining his ID card. "However, you can't enter at this point. We have to keep this road clear for emergency vehicles."

"What do you suggest?" Dave asked. "In addition, we have friends who might be injured."

"Yes sir, I understand. We have a lot of people looking for their friends or relatives. However, Sessions Road is closed to all but emergency vehicles. However, the city is using Burnham Park as a staging area and a first aid station. You might try there."

"And how do we get there?" Dave asked.

"Turn left and go about half of a mile to Kisad Road. It borders on the west side of Burnham, and from there you can access the park."

"Very good, thanks a lot."

"Yes sir, good luck."

Al turned left and then turned right on to Kisad Road. They traveled for about a mile, and spotted a large expanse of green dotted with pine trees and a sign identifying the area as Burnham Park. They entered the park via Absad Santos Drive where they encountered another roadblock. Once again Dave showed his ID card.

"I'm the Embassy's point man for terrorism. I need to talk to whomever is in charge," he informed the policeman.

"Yes sir, that would be Inspector Abrigo. You can park in the baseball field's parking lot over to your right, and walk to Central Control. It's just past the artificial lake. It's the communication van with the extended awning. You should find him there."

Dave thanked him, after which Al parked the van. Then they began their walk across the manicured grass. A lot of activity could be seen on the green between the lake and Sessions Road; parked emergency vehicles, an ambulance with its red lights flashing exiting the park, two ambulances parked by a pavilion with emergency aid people administering to the injured under the pavilion's cover. Al spotted the communication van; a large camper-like vehicle with antennae protruding from its top. Uniformed policemen and army soldiers were standing under a green awning that extended from its side.

"You go ahead to the communication van while Earl and I check out the pavilion," Al said to Dave. "Maybe we can find out about the girls."

"Good idea," Dave answered.

Dave continued toward the van while Earl and Al headed toward the pavilion.

"Do you see what I see?" Earl asked Al.

"Yes, I think I do. It's Barbara," a relieved Al answered. "And why aren't we surprised; after all that's her calling. And, I assume, where there's Barbara there is also Peggy and Connie."

They walked over to where Barbara was just finishing dressing a wound on a small boy while a woman, presumably his mother or sister, watched anxiously.

"Well Florence Nightingale, what a pretty picture you make," Al remarked.

Barbara turned and recognizing Al and Earl, released the boy to his guardian, and then immediately went to Al and embraced him in her arms. "Oh Al, it's awful, so many hurt. Who would do a terrible thing like this?" tears welled in her eyes.

"I don't know honey. But thank God you're safe."

She withdrew from Al and turned to Earl, "Peggy and Connie are somewhere around here. We've trained Connie to be quite a nurse. There are so many hurt, and for no damn reason; it's insane," her tears turning into anger.

"I guess you never finished your golf game." A voice from behind them said. They turned around and saw Peggy and Connie.

"Where's Dave?" Connie asked. "We assumed you were all right."

"Yes, we heard the explosion on the golf course, and then learned that a bomb had been detonated in the market area. We were worried about you all, and got here as fast as we could," answered Earl. "Dave is talking to the authorities now. He should join us soon."

"Where were you when the bomb exploded?" Al asked.

"We weren't that far away, actually," Connie answered. "We were having lunch down one of the side streets."

"We could feel the ground shake, and the noise was deafening," Peggy added.

"The Philippine National Bank building was hit," said Barbara. "We were told it blew off the whole front side. I don't know how many were trapped inside. We saw some policemen and told them we are trained nurses from Subic and asked if there was anything we could do. One of them directed us over here. A doctor Rodriguez is in charge and he put us to work immediately."

"Yes, and although I'm not a nurse, I can speak Spanish so they had me help in the processing of the injured," Connie explained. "Those who didn't have any life- threatening injuries were treated here. All the seriously injured are immediately transferred to the Baguio General Hospital."

"Is there anything we can do?" asked Earl.

"I think we have done all we can do," Barbara answered. "They haven't brought anyone in for a while."

"Let me check with Doctor Rodriguez," Peggy answered. "He's the one with the white smock talking with two of the paramedics near the ambulance." Peggy ambled over where Doctor Rodriguez was standing. He turned and smiled.

"Excuse me, Doctor Rodriguez," she said. "Our friends have joined us and they were wondering if there is anything they can do to help."

Doctor Rodriguez looked over where the group was standing. "How kind of them." Then he turned to the two paramedics and held a short conversation with them in Spanish. After which he addressed Peggy. "I think most of the recovery work is finished and it looks like most of our effort here is also finished. Let me walk over with you and personally thank all of you for your kind and compassionate help." Then he and Peggy walked over to the group.

"*Hola,* Doctor Rodriguez greeted Al and Earl. "Thank you so much for offering your services, but as I told *Senorita* Jordon all the recovery work is finished." Then he turned to Connie and Barbara, "And *mucho gracias* for all your help. It has been indispensable. I will see that your superiors at the Subic Bay Naval Hospital are informed of your generosity in volunteering your services. You have been true to your calling. As I mentioned earlier, we can wrap up what little is left here. Go and enjoy the company of your companions."

"Thank you, Doctor Rodriguez," Barbara said. "I'm so glad that we could be of help."

"Yes, thank you Doctor Rodriguez," added Connie.

"Yes, and I hope that they get the bastards that did this cowardly thing," added Peggy.

"Yes, it was a cowardly thing to do," replied Doctor Rodriguez. "Unfortunately, we have a lot of political unrest in the Philippines, but it has been mainly in the south, in Mindanao."

"You think this was a terrorist attack?" Al asked.

"I don't know, but the authorities I have talked to seem to think so. Well, don't let me detain you. Thanks again for all your help." Doctor Rodriguez turned and left.

"Well ladies, you did yourself proud," remarked Earl.

"It was so useless, all the injured," Peggy exclaimed. "I don't know how many were killed. The serious injured, and I guess the dead were taken to the Baguio General Hospital."

"People like to make news at the expense of the innocent," remarked Al. "Problem is that news sensationalism feed these attacks. I know it's news, and I guess it has to be reported, but at the same time it just promotes more attacks like this one. I guess we might as well head back."

The group met Dave as they were returning to their van.

"I thought I saw you all while I was waiting to speak with Inspector Abrigo," Dave explained. "Then I confirmed it, by using one of the policemen's binoculars. You don't know how relieved I was, as I'm sure Al and Earl were," Dave said, addressing the ladies.

"What did you find out from the Inspector?" Earl asked Dave.

"Not much, too early to tell. Nobody's claiming responsibility, but Inspector Abrigo told me the bombing has all the footprints of the MNLF."

"What's the MNLF?" asked Al.

"Moro National Liberation Front," answered Dave. "They want complete independence for the Moro people. Inspector Abrigo told me that this was the first attack of this kind this far north, although there had been a scattering of small bombings around Manila."

There wasn't much conversation on the ride back to their Villa. Dave reported what he knew about the bombing to the Embassy. Al tried to call Jeff and Mel, only to find that they had checked out of their room at the Kennedy Hotel, but had reservations for the day after tomorrow.

"I left a message telling them that all of us are okay, and that we'd be returning to Subic tomorrow, just in case they hear of the bombing," Al reported.

The dinner that night was a somber affair consisting of some wine and snacks after which they retired as couples; Al with Barbara, Peggy with Earl, Dave with Connie. They needed the safety and consolation of each other's arms. The next morning, they departed Baguio arriving at the Subic Bay Navy Station shortly after noon.

*   *   *   *   *

The television was turned on in Jeff's room, as he dressed for the evening affair. His attention was drawn to the screen by the view of a skeleton of a building surrounded by rubble, and people being interviewed by a newscaster. As he watched he learned of the disaster that had struck Baguio earlier that afternoon. He picked up the telephone and called Mel informing him of what he had learned from the TV's newscast.

"You know that Al, Earl, Dave and the girls are in Baguio. They were to play golf while the girls did some sightseeing," Jeff said. "I sure hope that they are all right."

"From what you said, the bombing was on Baguio's business street," remarked Mel. "Even if they were in Baguio, I assume that they would be on the golf course."

"Yeah, right, but how about the girls?" Jeff asked. "Who knows where they might be. I'm sure they're alright but I just have an uneasy feeling."

"Can we call them?" asked Mel.

"I guess we could," answered Jeff. "But do you know where they're staying?"

"That's a good question. When I talked to Al, all he said was that it was a house that the Embassy had in Baguio. He didn't give me a telephone number, and dumb me, I didn't ask for one. And to complicate matters, he doesn't know that we're in Tainan."

"If he wanted to get in touch with us, he'd call the Kennedy Hotel. I'll call the Kennedy and see if anyone called and left a message."

"Good idea."

Jeff made the call and both he and Mel were relieved to learn that their compatriots were fine.

"They're returning to Subic tomorrow," Jeff advised Mel. "Perhaps we need to think of returning, or at least I should, now that Kuo-ying is recovering. You may want to stay and visit with Shao-mei a little longer."

"Let's see what tonight brings," Mel answered.

The dining room was located on the second floor of the Tainan Hotel. It was one of three, all the same size that were separated from each other by folding, floor to ceiling dividers. Round tables covered with white linen tablecloths were strategically located around the head table. It held a bouquet of cut flowers. Each table could seat eight. The customary lazy-Susan with cold appetizers was placed in the center of each table, along with place settings consisting of a red rimmed charger which held a china dinner plate; a pair of ivory chopsticks resting on a ceramic holder; a short ceramic soup spoon, and glasses of varying sizes for non-alcoholic beverages, wine and hard liquor.

Mr. Chiang, Mrs. Chiang and Shao-mei formed sort of a receiving line as they greeted about fifty of Mr. Chiang's business associates and their wives. Mr. Chiang was dressed in a dark blue business suit while his wife was elegantly dressed in a red satin, three-quarter length sleeve, two-piece skirt suite. Shao-mei looked stunning in a white, high-neck, sleeveless, body-hugging Mandarin gown adorned with a red floral pattern of plum blossoms. The dress having the customary slit up each side just above the knee allowed for easy movement. Mel and Jeff had the foresight to pack sport jackets but they had to purchase white shirts and ties from the hotel's gift shop to supplement their slacks and loafers.

Once everyone was seated, the flowers were removed from the head table and the food was served. First, a soup, then some stir-fry dishes, after which came a fish dish, followed by duck, lastly, the dessert consisting of an assortment of fruit.

Once the meal was finished, the dishes were replaced by bottles of wine and Kaoliang, a strong distilled liquor made from fermented sorghum. Mr. Chiang did the honors at his table by filling his wife's daughter's wine glasses and Mel and Jeff's liquor glasses. He then rose from his seat and welcomed his guests once more, and thanked them for honoring him with their presence. He introduced Mel and Jeff and described how they had met Shao-mei when she was visiting her uncle in Hualien.

No mention was made of how the four Americans thwarted the Taiwan Liberation Party's attempt to use Mister Chiang's nephew, Wang Yi-kwei, to further their political ends, or how Mel, Shao-mei and his nephew had actually walked across the mountains in an unsuccessful endeavor to evade capture. To do so, would open the door to too many questions about Wang Yi-kwei's background as a defector from Mainland China.

"Uh oh," Jeff quietly remarked to Mel, grinning. "Mister Chiang is really laying it on thick to his business associates."

"What do you mean?" Mel asked.

"He's been telling his associates how fortunate that you and Shao-mei were such good friends because you are a very successful financier in the United States, how you know all the right people, and how you would be a great asset to his company."

Before Mel could comment, Mr. Chiang raised his glass and proposed a toast to his American friends and to all his guests. That done then as if on cue, a person at each table rose and toasted Mr. Chiang, his wife, daughter and their American friends. And on it went, ending with the Chinese custom of *ganbe,* or bottoms up, where everyone drinking Kaoliang filled their glasses and consumed it in one swallow, turning the glass over to show it was empty.

When the evening was over Mel and Jeff returned to their respective hotel rooms.

The next morning over breakfast, Mel confided to Jeff: "When I saw her standing in the receiving line wearing that Mandarin gown, she was so beautiful, I knew right then and there I wanted her for my bride."

"My my, why am I not surprised," Jeff commented, a slight grin on his face. "Hells bells, what took you so long? I knew it as soon as you jumped at the chance to return to Taiwan."

"I don't know, I guess subconsciously I always did. It was just seeing her last night that I really realized that I wanted to spend the rest of my life with her."

"And how does that gorgeous hunk of womanhood feel about you?"

"Last night when we were together in my room, we knew we wanted to be together for the rest of our lives. We did a lot of talking, especially about the difference in our religions; she being a Buddhist and me a Christian."

"Is that going to be a problem?"

"Not to me. Actually, as Shao-mei explained, Buddhism is more of a philosophy than a religion. They don't believe in labels like 'Christian', 'Moslem', 'Hindu' or 'Buddhist'; that is why there has never been any wars fought in the name of Buddhism. They do not preach or try to convert. They will explain Buddhism if an explanation is sought. That's what she did to me, explained about her belief. Hey, we even talked about her father's idea of setting her up in business in the United States."

"You mean with that American financier who knows all the right people," laughed Jeff.

"Yeah, I guess that's it," laughed Mel.

"Okay, so what's next?"

"I have to formally ask her father for his permission to marry his daughter. I plan to do that this afternoon."

"Well you shouldn't have any problems in that respect; especially after the big build-up he gave you last night. I thought you were already part of the family."

"I sure hope you're right. I have to admit, I am a little nervous. Shao-mei is supposed to set the stage for me. I guess I'm also a little apprehensive; you know, about Chinese customs and all that."

"Hey, no sweat. It's just like in the States. She'll make all the decisions and you'll just say, yes dear."

"Yeah, right."

"Now, on a more personal note, does this mean you'll not be returning with me?"

"No, we discussed that also. I told Shao-mei I had to return to the Philippines to see Al and Earl. She understands, but I won't be making the rest of the voyage with you all."

"You'll be missed, and I can honestly say that Shao-mei's company has to be a hell of a lot better than the likes of Al, Earl and even me," laughed Jeff

"Hey, I can't argue that point," Mel joined Jeff in laughter.

"Okay, you go seek the permission of your future father-in-law. We can meet later this evening and finalize our return plans to Manila. By the way, how're you going to get to you father-in-law's home."

"Shao-mei will pick me up. We're going to take Mr. and Mrs. Chiang out for lunch and that's when I'll pop the question."

"Yeah, and I bet it will be no surprise to anyone," laughed Jeff. "Also, Shao-mei will drive us to Kaohsiung. She wants to see Kuo-ying and give her and Yi-kwei the good news."

"Yes, and we can make our farewells to Kuo-ying too. Should I see about booking our return flight to Manila for day after tomorrow, and also call Al and Earl to let them know of our return plans."

"Yes, but don't let the cat out of the bag about Shao-mei and me. I want to tell them myself."

"Right on."

Later that afternoon, Jeff made reservations for two on a 4 P.M. flight from Kaohsiung to Manila. Then, he actually found Al in his quarters in the V.O.Q. and gave him the details of their return flight. Afterwards he packed his B-4 bag while waiting for Mel to return. As Jeff surmised, Mister Chiang was not surprised when Mel asked his future father-in-law for permission to marry his daughter, and who readily gave his consent, welcoming him to the Chiang family.

It was after three when Shao-mei and Mel arrived at the Tainan Hotel. Jeff greeted her with a great big hug. "You know how I feel, for that matter, you know how all of us feel. We couldn't be happier."

"Thank you," she answered. "We have a lot of planning to do. Mel is going to call his parents tonight. Then we need to set a date."

"I'm going to my room now, throw everything in my B-4 and meet you down here," Mel said to Jeff. "You can check-out for both of us, and then we'll be on our way to Kaohsiung. We can say our goodbyes to Kuo-ying tomorrow and head out to the airport in the afternoon."

"Fine, sounds like a plan," Jeff answered. "What about you, Shao-mei; what's your plan?"

"I'll drop you off at your hotel then go to the hospital and see Kuo-ying and return to Tainan tonight."

"Will you be all right driving by yourself at night?" Jeff asked.

"Yi-kwei will be with me," Shao-mei answered. "Kuo-ying is doing well, and he needs to get back to work. He'll still see her though, but unless things take a turn for the worse, it will be on the weekends."

At the Kennedy Hotel Shao-mei made her goodbyes. She embraced both Mel and Jeff, holding Mel a little longer.

"I love you. It won't be long." Mel whispered as he gently pressed his lips against hers. Then they separated. Mel held the car door open for her, and Shao-mei entered, not looking at Mel so he would not notice the tears t welled in her eyes. Mel stood and watched as she drove away; he too feeling the pain of separation albeit a short one.

Shao-mei drove to the hospital where she informed both Kuo-ying and Yi-Kwei of her engagement. Needless to say, both were pleased. She visited for about half-an-hour and then she and Yi-kwei returned to Tainan.

After a western breakfast the next morning, Mel and Jeff checked out of the hotel and took a taxicab to the hospital. Kuo-ying was sitting in a recliner when Mel and Jeff entered her room. The color had returned to her cheeks. Both Mel and Jeff noticed the change.

"You look great," Jeff greeted, and then kissed her lightly on the cheek.

"*Xièxie,* (Thank you)," Kuo-ying replied, a big smile on her face, her eyes aglow. "You always know how to say the right thing."

"That he does," Mel remarked, but in this case, he is one hundred percent right. You do look great, like your old self again." And he too, kissed her on the cheek.

"Ha, you're no better than your partner," Kuo-ying replied. "I don't dare stand, or you'll see how thin I am. But enough about me, congratulation on your engagement. I know that you'll be very happy. Shao-mei is very fortunate."

"Thank you," Mel answered. "I think I'm the fortunate one."

"When will you be released?" Jeff asked.

"Probably tomorrow or the next day. The doctors want to take some more tests, have me walking a little. My plans are to return to Taidung, stay with my parents, and undergo therapy at the clinic there. If things go well, I'll return to the National Chengkung University, and start teaching at the beginning of the next semester."

"That's great," remarked Jeff. "And I know that Yi-kwei will be there in your corner helping you along."

"What corner?" Kuo-ying laughed. "You Americans have the funniest expressions. But, yes, Yi-kwei and I have become very close since you abandoned me to play sailor boy with your playmates."

"Ouch, that really hurts," laughed Jeff. "But seriously, I am happy for you. I know that Yi-kwei has very strong feelings for you."

"Thanks," Kuo-ying expression took on a more somber note. "And I was only kidding when I said you abandoned me. I will always have a special place in my heart for the American who came to the rescue of a stranded lady in distress."

"Hey, don't forget me," Mel spoke up.

"Never! I'll never forget the four Americans who came to my aid when I was betrayed by the Taiwan Liberation Party. I was beside myself, didn't know what to do, had no one to turn to, and all of you became my knights in shining armor. No, I'll never forget any of you."

Mel bent down and kissed Kuo-ying on her cheek once again. "And you will always be a part of us. And a part of my wedding plans."

"I'd like that," Kuo-ying remarked, her face aglow.

"I can only echo what Mel said," Jeff added. "You know you'll always have a special place in my heart too. But I'm going to have to abandon you again. Mel and I have to leave; we have a plane to catch."

"I understand," Kuo-ying said. "You don't know how much your being here has help me. Now hurry up and go before I start to cry."

Jeff reached over and holding her two hands, kissed her gently on her lips and mouthed goodbye. The lump in his throat prevented the words to come out. He turned and he and Mel left.

189

Chapter 8

The Mission

Mel, Jeff, Al, Earl and Dave, along with Barbara,
Connie and Peggy were at the Navy Officers' Club
sitting around two tables that had been joined. Drinks
had been served, and a celebration was well underway.
Two days had passed since Mel and Jeff were met at
Manila's Ninoy Aquino International Airport by Al and
Earl. Mel broke the news of his engagement on the
drive back to Subic Bay, and that he would not be
sailing with them when their cruse commenced. Al
arranged for the celebration, calling it a good news bad
news event.

Al using his and Barbara's half empty glasses struck
them together emitting a sharp ping which got
everyone's attention. "Okay, listen up. It's toast time."
Then Al rose and turned toward Mel. "Pard, you've
been a part of us from our days in Thailand. You've
been our shipmate for the last umpteen days. We've had

great times and a few hair-raising experiences. We're brothers. And your leaving will create a void that will always go unfilled. We love you." Then Al turned to the rest of the group. "Okay everyone, raise your glasses. To our comrade-in-arms and shipmate forever. We wish him nothing but the very best." Then turning toward Mel once again: "I think the Navy says it best, may yours and Shao-mei's future together consist of nothing but fair winds and following seas."

"Hear! hear!" was exclaimed in unison as Al sat down.

Earl rose and raised his glass. "As Al so eloquently put it, we're shipmates and in that vein: there are good ships and there are wooden ships but the best ships are friendships. To our great friend Mel. Bless you and Shao-mei."

Again, roaring cheers of hear, hear as Earl sat down.

Then Jeff rose. "Okay everyone, charge your glasses once more." Then to Mel, "here's to your sweetheart, a bottle and a friend. The first, beautiful Shao-mei, the second, may your bottle always be full, and the last, to everlasting friendships."

Once again, a chorus of hear hears as Jeff sat down.

Then Dave rose. "I'm a 'Johnny come lately', and can't really be called a shipmate, but I hope I can be called a friend. I echo what's been said. Not knowing Shao-mei, I know she is one lucky lady. Nothing but the best," and Dave sat down.

Hear hears were repeated.

"Okay Mel, your turn," Al announced.

Mel rose, his glass in his hand. "What can I say? I really never thought of us as parting." There was a slight tremble in his voice, a pause as he sought to compose himself. "We may not crew together in the future, but shipmates we'll always be. We may be separating, but parting, never. You all, and I include you Dave, will always be a part of me." His emotions took over and he had to sit down.

As soon as that happened, he was surrounded by Barbara, Connie and Peggy, each one waiting their turn to give him a big hug; all telling him how happy they were for him, and wishing him the very best.

"Hey, I never got that reaction," exclaimed Earl, but he joined the rest of the men and gave Mel a hug.

The following morning, after saying their goodbyes once again at the airport, the gang watched Mel's flight as it lifted from the tarmac on its way to Kaohsiung.

"Damn, I miss him already," Earl said, as the group was riding back to Subic Bay in their rental vehicle.

"It won't be the same alright," Jeff agreed.

"You're right there, but to change the subject, Dave wants to meet with us when we get back," Al announced. "He's lined up the Admiral's conference room."

"The conference room; what's up?" asked Earl.

"I really don't know. When he phoned me, all he said was that it is hush-hush, and he needed a secure area for the discussion," answered Al.

"Veeeeery interesting," Jeff said, imitating the character Wolfgang from the Rowan and Martin TV series: *Laugh In.*

"What time are we supposed to meet?" Earl asked.

"2 PM," answered Al. "We'll have a chance for lunch at the Yacht Club."

"Gosh, I don't think I can wait. The suspense is killing me," commented Jeff.

After finishing cheeseburgers and French fries washed down by San Miguel beer, the group arrived at the station's headquarters, a two-story, white-concrete building. In front was a large flagpole flying the United States flag, and directly behind the flag pole was a large anchor mounted on a forty-five-degree angled slab with the words, 'US NAVY STATION SUBIC BAY' in raised letters above the anchor's eye.

Dave was waiting for them in the lobby, and directed them to sign the visitors' log at the information desk

manned by a United States Marine. Once the signing
formality was over, the three were issued visitors'
badges. Then Dave escorted them down a long corridor
past the Admiral's office suite, to the Admiral's
conference room. It consisted of a long table with a
cushioned armchair at its head and eight armchairs on
each side. There were other straight back chairs
strategically placed along the side walls. To the left of
the head chair stood the Admiral's flag and mounted
along the walls were pictures of navy ships and aircrafts.
There was a door centered behind the head of the table,
presumably to the Admiral's office. A projection booth
was located at the end of the room. The office was
unoccupied at the time. Dave locked the door to the
corridor and asked the group to sit down.

"Gosh, this big room all to ourselves." observed Earl.

"All for us, thanks to the Admiral," answered Dave.

"So many choices, I don't know where to sit,"
remarked Jeff, a grin on his face.

"Well, why don't we take the chairs up front, two of
us on one side and two on the other side," Dave
suggested.

"Sounds good to me," Al commented and walked
around and took a chair opposite the door. He was
joined by Earl. Jeff and Dave sat opposite them.

"We've got pretty reliable evidence that the people
behind the Baguio bombing were members of the Moro
National Liberation Front or the MNLF for short," Dave

announced. "As background, the Embassy has been involved for some time in secret mediation between the MNLF and the Philippine Government. The Government is proposing that a truce be enacted and if it holds, to establish a Moro Autonomous Region in Mindanao."

"Where did this terrorist organization, I guess that's what you'd call it, get all their weapons?" Earl asked.

"Ha, I was hoping you'd not ask that question," Dave replied. "You know the old adage 'the enemy of my enemy is my friend'. Well when Russia was having a hell of a time in maintaining their control over Afghanistan, we supported the Mujahedeen in their attempt to expel the Russians. We airlifted Philippine volunteers to assist the Mujahedeen in their fight. Well what goes around comes around. It is these same Filipinos with the weapons we provided, who, when the Russians withdrew, returned to their homeland and took up the same fight, but this time against their government."

"Seems like I've read this story before," remarked Jeff.

"We've met the enemy and he is us," quipped Earl.

"I'm sure it was the thing to do at the time," remarked Al.

"So, where do we fit into this picture?" asked Jeff.

"As you know, I'm the Embassy's point man on terrorism," Dave began his explanation. "I'm also the

CIA's point man on terrorism. The real reason I was transferred to Manila was to act as the intermediary between the Philippine Government and the MNLF. I've been tasked to contact one of the leaders of the MNLF and try to broker a truce which, if successful, should end such terrorist attacks which we just witnessed in Baguio. To do this I need to slip into Mindanao clandestinely."

"Why clandestinely?" asked Earl.

"Because there are different factions within the MNLF; one faction seems willing to compromise on the subject of an independent Moro nation, and another faction that will not accept anything except the establishment of an independent Moro Nation, free from any Philippine interference. It's the first faction with which I'm to negotiate, obviously keeping such negotiations secret from the second faction."

"Uh oh, the plot thickens," commented Earl.

"I think I'm beginning to get the picture," added Jeff.

"I have to do some confessing," admitted Al. "After the Baguio bombing, Dave approached me with the idea of using our cruise for cover. We got a lot of good press, well the girls did, but so did we, in the unselfish manner in which we volunteered to assist the injured."

"Assisting the injured? When did we do that?" questioned Earl.

"We've got Dave to thank for that. The Embassy's Press Secretary made sure that our help was published in all the local and national newspapers; albeit embellished."

"Embellished? How about lied," Jeff added to Earl's bout of skepticism.

"Let me finish," Al interjected. "The articles played up our around the Pacific cruise, including our plans to sail to Mindanao and the Palawan Islands. So, it won't be any big deal if we are observed sailing around the coastline of Mindanao. All we have to do is sail around Mindanao; put in at Isabela, the capital of Basilan Province. That's where we and Dave will part company. The Agency will reimburse our expense, and indemnify us against any damage we might sustain."

"Uh oh, I don't like the word indemnify. Does that mean danger?" asked Earl.

"I can't see any danger," remarked Dave. You're just continuing your cruise. You might want to visit Isabela and other cities in the area. After all, that's what a cruise is all about."

"What Dave is implying," interjected Al, "is that he expects us to wait around while he does his thing and then return him safely to Manila."

"The operative word is safely," laughed Jeff.

"Well it's all voluntary," continued Al. "I didn't commit to anything, so what about it?"

"Hey, I'm in," readily agreed Jeff.

"You got my vote too," added Earl. "It's too bad Mel is not here; he'd jump at the chance to go along."

"Probably so," replied Al. "One of the reasons I waited until now is so he won't be tempted. Shao-mei would never forgive me."

"I agree with Al, although Mel would be a great asset," added Dave. "I really appreciate you guys helping me in this matter."

"That's what friends are for," replied Jeff.

The briefing for the group was held in the Admiral's conference room. The briefer was a Navy Captain on the Admiral's staff. With a large map of the Philippine Islands projected on a screen via a rearview projector in the projection booth, the Captain was describing the sea lanes to Mindanao.

"There are two sea lanes you can take," the Captain explained using a laser pointer to pinpoint the routes on the map. "One is via the South China Sea and the Mindoro Strait. This takes you west of Mindoro Island and east of the Calmian Group where you enter into the Sulu Sea. This time of year the winds should be in your favor as far as sailing goes; mostly from the northwest. The second route is via the Verde Island Passage and the Taiblas Straits, which separates Luzon and the Islands of Mindoro and Panay. This is perhaps one of the busiest sea lanes. This also dumps you into the Sulu Sea."

"Which one do you suggest?" asked Al.

"That depends. The intercoastal provides shelter from the monsoons coming out of Borneo, but this time of year that's probably not a problem."

"Famous last words," commented Earl.

"Obviously, you know how unpredictable weather is," laughed the Captain. "But the Philippine Atmospheric Geophysical and Astronomical Services Administration, I know that's a mouthful, PAGASA for short, provides real time updates. You'd do well to keep your radio tuned to their frequency. But back to my recommendation, the outside lanes provide strong winds which for those on sail are a plus. The inside lanes are good if you're under motor. With all the ships that use the intercoastal it might get dicey under sail. I know that the rules of the sea give sails the right of way over motor but. . ." And here, the Captain just shrugged his shoulders.

"How 'bout places to stop and replenish stores, get petro, things like that?" asked Jeff.

"Don't see a problem there, especially in the intercoastal but even on open waters, you'll be passing by the western coast of Mindoro Island, and although it doesn't have the cities you'd find on its eastern coast, there still are a few, such as Mamburao and San Jose that can provided good anchorage, and accommodate your needs," the Captain replied, using his laser pointer to locate the cities. "Farther south in the Sulu Sea there are Panay and Negros.

'Panay is roughly triangular in shape. Its largest city is Roxas, which is located on its northern coast. San Jose is the largest city on its western coast. Oton is another major city located on the tip of its southern coast. Other than these, the picking is pretty slim.

Then on the western coast of Negros Island you have Bacolod. It can satisfy whatever your needs. Next is the Island of Mindanao, and your final destination, Isabella."

"I'm not sure I like the term final," laughed Earl.

"Poor choice of words," laughed the Captain. "Any more questions?"

"I don't think so," Al replied after looking around at his colleagues, and saw them shake their heads. "Thanks for a very thorough briefing. Now we've got to huddle together and make some decisions."

"In that case I'll leave you to your own devices. Good luck." With those parting words, the Captain left the conference room.

"What do you think?" Al asked the group.

"I guess a lot depends on Dave's schedule," Earl commented.

"I agree with Earl," Jeff added. "What about it, Dave?"

"I really don't have a fixed time table," Dave answered. "My contact is a Catholic Priest in Isabella. What are our options?"

"Well as I see it, making a quick calculation, it'll take us about five days if we are on a twenty-four-hour sailing schedule. That's averaging six knots an hour," Earl commented. "If we limit our sailing to daytime, say, twelve hours, then we're talking eight days, assuming everything goes as planned; and of course, that's a big if."

"I don't feel good about an around the clock cruse unless it is imperative that we make Isabella as soon as possible," Al commented.

"Time is not critical, although it is important," spoke Dave. "What is critical is that we keep to our cover. We're supposed to be sightseeing. All night sailing would tend to blow that cover."

"Keeping our cover in mind, I think daylight sailing is the way to go," agreed Jeff. "We should find one or two interesting towns in which to spend some time doing the tourist thing."

"That sounds like a good plan," added Dave.

"Earl you're our navigator, how about you and Jeff get together with some navigational charts and plan our route. Dave, you use your Embassy sources and find a couple of tourist stops."

"Will do," Dave answered.

"Okay Jeff, lets hit the charts, and using an average speed of six knots let's get a fix on what overnight choices we have."

"We can do that, but a lot depends on what Dave comes up with for our tourist stops," replied Jeff.

"Granted," said Al. "So, Dave, the ball is in your court. However, that will not prevent the rest of us from doing some preplanning; for example, logistics."

"Roger, that," Earl said.

"I love it when you talk military," Jeff laughed.

"Okay, let's get something to eat, and afterwards we'll go to the Dragon Lady and start making plans."

"You all do that," stated Dave. "I'll return to the Embassy and get to work on my end."

The following day Dave returned, and they all huddled together to finalize their plans and review options.

"The Embassy has furnished me with a new passport," Dave explained. "They don't think advertising my association with the Embassy is a good idea, so I'm assuming Mel's identity since he's not on the cruise."

"So, you're going to be Mel Johnson from Atlanta, Georgia. How much do you know about Mel?" Jeff asked.

"Not much, I'm afraid. But I assume I won't need to know that much. Just from the three weeks I've been with you all, I think I already know enough about Mel to carry on any casual conversation. For example, I know he's from Atlanta, was a stockbroker and financial adviser and was a procurement officer in the air force. His last duty station was Robbins Air Force Base. He graduated from the University of Georgia. I should be able to wing anything else. After all, I don't foresee any lengthy interrogations from anyone. All the publicity we issued about the four Americans who unselfishly came to the aid of the injured in Baguio mentioned only names, no photos; only that they were sailing around the Pacific and the Philippines were one of their ports of call."

"That should work all right, but don't go giving any financial advice," laughed Earl.

The next few days were filled with planning; what provisions to take, what sea route to follow, what will the weather be like.

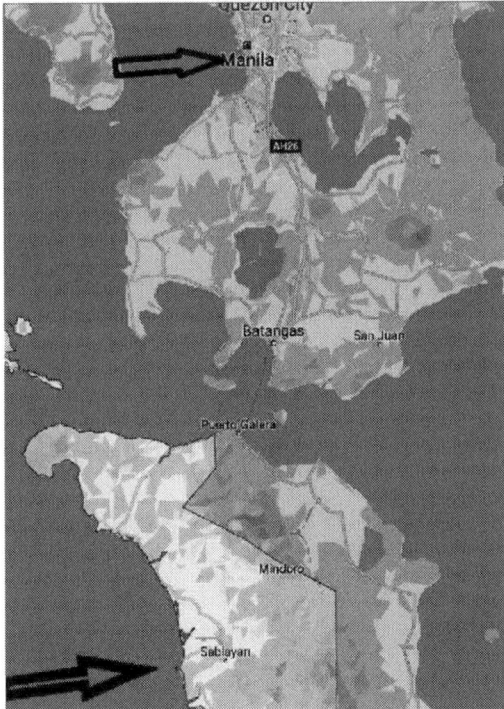

MANILA TO SABLAYAN

Chapter 9

Sea

Dawn was breaking. The sun had yet to make its appearance above the eastern mountains. There was a light mist off the water.

The group had spent the night on board, having made their goodbyes the evening before. Al was at the helm and Earl and Jeff were stationed at the bow, having released the bowline from the cleat that had held the 'Lady' fast to the pier. Dave had released the stern line and was in the cockpit with Al.

They made their way up the main channel, past the harbormaster's office, maintenance yards, destroyers and the US Enterprise, entering the eastern channel around Grande Island, on their way to the open waters of the South China Sea. Using their VHF radio, Dave received an update on the weather.

"It looks like we might be in for some rough weather," he reported.

"What'd you mean?" asked Al.

"In the South China Sea, four to six feet swells, wind out of the northeast at twenty knots, gusting to 30 and the forecast is for scattered showers," Dave answered.

"We won't have a problem with the swells, but we best lay a jackline and have our foul weather gear ready."

"Shall I call Jeff and Earl and let them know of the weather forecast?"

"Good idea; then they can lay the jackline while we're under motor."

Dave made his way forward to where Jeff and Earl were holding on to the mainmast and informed them of the possibility of rough weather, and Al's suggestion that the jackline should be laid. They returned to the cockpit, retrieved the jackline which was stowed under the bench seat, and wound it around the deck. Then Jeff retrieved two inflatable personal floatation devices (PFD) from the storage bin and placed them in easy reach of those in the cockpit.

"Well, we should be ready if, and when we do hit rough water," Jeff reported. "However, if the wind forecast is correct, we should be able to make good time to the intercoastal waterway."

"That's what I'm counting on," Al commented. "Once out of the bay we'll see the wind pick up and the swells get stronger. I'm going to set a forty-five-degree, southwest tack that will take us west of Manila, but not so far that we're out of sight of land, just in case. Then I'll switch to a southeastern course, and repeat the series until we make our first landfall."

"Sounds like a smart plan," commented Dave. "What's our first night's destination?"

"Lubang's Tilik Port," answered Jeff. "It's the entrance to the Verde Island Passage."

"What's there?" asked Dave.

"Not much, a Coast Guard Station and a navigational light. It's not one of your main tourist attractions, but it does afford a good anchorage and gives us an opportunity to stretch our legs on terra firma. My guess is that we could find some seafood restaurants there also."

"Sounds like a good place to RON," commented Dave.

"I like the way you picked up our lingo," laughed Jeff.

"You mean RON as in remain overnight. You guys in the military don't have a corner on acronyms you know. Hell, we've been using that in the Agency for I don't know how long."

"Yeah, well I bet you got it from us."

"S u r e we did," laughed Dave.

"Notwithstanding, I agree it appears to be a good place to RON," said Jeff. "What say Earl and I go forward and prepare to hoist the sails?"

"Good idea, but put on those PFDs," cautioned Al. "We don't know what we may encounter once we get out of the bay."

"Right you are," replied Jeff. "Here Earl, here's yours," Jeff said, handing Earl one of the PFDs. After the were donned, they went forward to await the set sail command.

The sails were set before leaving the protection of the bay and entering the South China Sea, and thus they didn't have to fight the winds and the roller coaster effect of high swells. When they entered the South China Sea, they were all pleased to find that the forecast of large swells and strong winds had not yet materialized.

As the Dragon Lady continued on her tack away from the mainland, the winds finally did increase, the swells became higher and the skies darker. Dave relieved Al at the helm, Jeff's eyes were glued to the radar returns and Earl was standing watch at the bow; his PFD donned and its lanyard connected to the jackline; a pair of binoculars hung around his neck. Al was plotting the boat's position on the plastic sheet covering the map on the navigational table.

"We've been making good time," Al announced. "I figure about 8 knots. I think it's time for us to come about and start our southeastern tack. But let's reef the mainsail first; I don't like the looks of the sky."

"Roger, I'll go forward with the boom crutch, and Earl and I will handle the mainsail," Jeff said.

Once Earl was advised of the plan, the boom was locked in place in the 'Y' shape top of the boom crutch. Then the main and jib sails were lowered. Jeff and Earl quickly secured the reefed portion of the sail to the boom. Once the reefing was completed, the boom clutch was removed, and the main and jib sails were raised again. Al tied off the mainsheet and Jeff and Earl returned to the cockpit and stowed the boom crutch. Al eased the tension on the mainsheet while Dave executed a 45-degree turn. When that was completed, Al trimmed the main and jib sails while Jeff trimmed the mizzen sail to achieve the maximum benefit from the wind. Once sails were set, and the Dragon Lady on its new tack, Earl prepared lunch for the crew; ham and cheese sandwiches, and potato chips washed down by San Miguel beer.

It was not long after that, that the skies opened up and the rain came; light pelts at first, but then the pelts turned into a regular bombardment. Visibility was nil. The running lights were illuminated. Everyone had put on their foul weather gear and Jeff, after being drenched from the swells that enveloped the bow, returned to the cockpit. Al was at the helm dissecting the swells, which had gotten to over four feet. Earl was watching the radar sweep rotate around the Plan Position Indicator's (PPI) display.

"No threats detected," he announced.

"By that, I hope you mean no ships in our path," Jeff commented.

"Roger that, good buddy," Earl answered.

Dave tuned the VHF to the PAGASA frequency. "No change in the weather forecast; gusty winds, high swells and scattered showers," he announced.

"Well we can give the Filipinos' weathermen an A, 'cause they sure are right about the weather!" exclaimed Jeff.

"How's the sails?" asked Dave.

"I trimmed the jib a little, and all sails are in fine shape," replied Jeff. "We've been in worst weather."

"Like off the coast of Taiwan," laughed Earl.

"Whoa! Dave yelled, as the Dragon Lady cantilevered above the sea, propelled upon the crest of a six-foot wave, and then came crashing down into its trough, sending a shock wave through the entire boat.

"That was a big one!" exclaimed Jeff.

"Yeah, I'll say," added Earl. "We don't need many of those."

"Roger that," mimicked Al. "I wonder if that is what's meant by a rogue wave."

"I guess it could have been," commented Jeff. "It sure wasn't like any of the others."

As Al was fighting the wave action, Dave was continually monitoring their position and annotating the chart. Jeff was checking the radar screen. Earl was handling the jib sheet, making small adjustments as Al maneuvered the boat to dissect the waves at a ninety-degree angle.

"The storm has been forcing us farther south than our projected course," Dave announced.

"I'm not surprised," Al commented. "Any indication on the radar when we'll come out of this mess?"

"Screen is solid dark green," answered Jeff. "I can't detect any clearing, and we're still alone out here."

"We'll correct once we get out of this weather," Al said. "We might want to revise our landfall."

Dave retrieved a large-scale map of the Philippines from the map drawer and entered the cabin to be out of the weather. After studying the chart for possible anchorage, he returned to the cockpit.

"On the western side of Mindoro Island, there are a couple of places which should offer suitable anchorage. One is Paluan Bay, and the small city of Paluan. It is just south of the Verde Island Passageway. We could RON there, and enter the intercoastal tomorrow. Or, a little farther south is a larger city named Mamburao located on Mamburao Bay. However, if we anchor there, we might be better off revising our original plan and use the Mindoro Straits as our connection to the Sulu Sea."

"Might be a plan; let's consider it as one of our options when we get out of this weather," answered Al.

Finally, the rain and wind started to subside. Visibility had increased. The sky was turning from black to grey. The swells had reduced in size. They had been in the storm for over five hours.

"I think I see light at the end of the tunnel, literally" Al said.

"I see patches of light green on the scope as well," Jeff agreed.

"I see sunlight peeking through the clouds due west," added Dave.

"Is it decision time?" asked Earl.

"What do you mean decision time?" asked Dave.

"Where shall we make landfall?" replied Earl.

"Dave, why don't you plot a couple of courses; one to our original destination of Lubang, one to, what did you say the name of the other two possibilities were?" instructed Al.

"You mean Paluan Bay and Mamburao?" answered Dave.

"Sounds like it, the one just south of the intercoastal," answered Al.

"Let me get a fix on our position and then I'll go below and plot some options."

Using the boats GPS system, Dave pinpointed the Dragon Lady's position on the map, and then taking the map, went below out of the weather. Using a straightedge, he lined a course from the boat's position to Lubang Island and then another line to Paluan, and then to Mamburao. Then using a pair of proportional dividers, he determined the distances to all three locations.

"I make we're about forty-two nautical miles from Lubang, thirty-five from Paluan, and a little less to Mamburao. We're southwest of all three. We could try for Paluan, and if it looks like it's getting too late we could put in to Mamburao Bay, and then decide what course to follow tomorrow. Or, there is another possibility. We could head southeast to Sablayan, on Pandan Bay. I figure it's the same distance south to Sablayan as it is to Mamburao Bay. The only difference, we'd be closer to Mindanao, but we'd be committed to the Mindoro Straits as our passageway, which means open water sailing as opposed to the intercoastal route. We also have an alternate port in Santa Cruz which is not that far from Sablayan, although it is a little north."

"That sounds like some good options. What do you all think?" Al asked the rest.

"I kinda like keeping south," remarked Jeff. "Heading back north, just adds more time to our trip."

"I agree also," said Earl. "Hell, open water sailing can't be any worse than what we had this morning, plus we'll have the advantage of stronger winds."

"Dave, you provided us with options, what's your opinion?" asked Al.

"I agree with Earl and Jeff," he answered. "I see no need in back tracking, nor do I see any advantage over the Verde Island Passageway, as opposed to the Mindoro Straits."

"Okay Dave, give me a heading and away we'll go," directed Al.

"Will do," answered Dave. "And, we will have Santa Cruz as a backup."

After receiving the new direction, Al set the boat on the new course, and the sails were trimmed accordingly. After a short while, Jeff relieved Al at the helm, and Dave went below and came back with a large thermos of coffee and four tin cups. The tack to Sablayan went smooth and uneventful; as Dave said: "the way it should go."

The first things that came into view, as they made the approach to their new destination were Mindoro's 8,163-foot Mount Banco and 7,756-foot Mount Iglit, part of the east-west mountain range. They entered the crescent shaped, Pandan Bay at dusk. Pandan Island was off to the

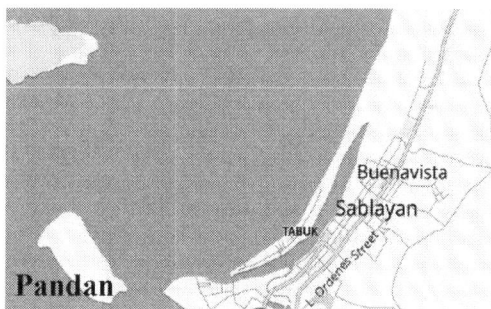

SABLAYAN

south, and another island, Sitio Tabuk, lay just off the mainland, and was separated from the mainland by a narrow waterway. Resting on the white sandy beach of the mainland were various colorful dugout canoes with outriggers and bamboo roofs, called Bancas. The Dragon Lady's sails were lowered, and Al motored up the narrow side of, and tied off at the pier on San Sebastian Street. A sign welcomed them to Buenavista, Sablayan. At the bottom was added, 'Foreign vessels must register with the Harbormaster inside the Municipal Building'.

The crew stepped off their boat to stretch their legs and look around. The pier was located on San Sebastian Street, on which were dive shops advertising half and full day trips to Pandan Island and Apo Reef. Farther down was a small restaurant and bar, and next to it was a hotel. The next street over was National Highway, which appeared to be the main drag, and on which the concrete municipal building was located. The crew headed for the restaurant and bar.

The Bamboo Shack Restaurant, was of wood with bamboo pleated, pull down curtains above the windows. The roof was of coconut frond thatch. The bar and six barstools were also of bamboo. There were ten unoccupied bamboo tables and chairs scattered in front of the bar.

"*Buenas Dia*s Señors," the bartender greeted, as the four sat down on the barstools. "What's your pleasure?"

"What kind of dinks do you have?" Earl asked for the group.

"We have San Miguel and Cerveza Negra beer, as well as cocktails."

"We want to try something that is uniquely Filipino," Al said.

"Well San Miguel and Cerveza Negra are Filipino beers, and we have rum drinks, but if you really want to try something unique then I'd recommend tuba. It is made from coconut milk and has a stinging sweet and bittersweet taste. We also have coconut wine, which is also made from the coconut, but you must not be fooled. It is a lot more potent than your American wines."

"I noticed that you use a lot of coconut products," observed Jeff.

"*Sí*, why not. We have a lot of coconut trees."

"Makes sense to me," Jeff replied.

"Okay decision time, what will it be, beer, or coconut cocktails?"4

"Well when in Rome do as the Roman's do," Dave spoke up. "Let's have coconut cocktails."

"Sí, the tuba or the lambanog?" the bartender asked.

"What do you recommend?" Jeff asked.

"Is your hotel close by?"

"We're not in a hotel but our boat is berthed at the pier, why?" Jeff asked.

"Well, I would recommend that you start with tuba, one shot, and if you don't have too far to walk enjoy a dinner with the wine," the bartender added, with a grin.

"What are you telling us?" Al asked.

"Lambanog is made from fermented coconut. It runs between 80 and 90 proof. We call it our poor man's vodka."

Al turned to the rest and asked, "what d'ya all say?"

After everyone eagerly consented, the bartender placed a shot glass in front of each and then filled the glasses with tuba. With a sense of trepidation, Al was the first one to try.

"Not bad," he reported.

"Hey, he likes it, Mikey likes it!" exclaimed Earl, mimicking the cereal TV commercial.

After the rest downed their glasses, Al asked the bartender "What's to do here?"

"You mean in the restaurant?" the bartender answered with a grin.

"No, I mean the town," laughed Al.

"Well there is the resort on Pandan Island, and there is Apo Reef," answered the bartender.

"We saw signs advertising boat trips to those places, what's there?" Jeff asked.

"Pandan Island is a privately-owned island with its own resort. You can visit there but they charge a small fee if you're not staying at the resort. They have a restaurant and bar, which if you eat there, they will deduct the fee from your check. Most people who stay at the resort do so for the beach."

"What about the reef?" Al asked.

"Apo Reef is the second largest contiguous coral reef in the world."

"That's quite a distinction," Dave commented. "What's the largest?"

"They tell me, it's Australia's Great Barrier Reef," answered the bartender. "Another?" the bartender asked seeing that everyone had consumed their tuba.

"Not for me, thanks," Jeff said. "I'll wait and sample your wine with dinner."

"Are you sending us a message?" asked Dave.

"Not too subtle there, Pard," commented Al.

"What's on the menu?" Earl asked the bartender.

In answer to the question, the bartender handed each a menu. The special of the day was flounder cooked in a lemon sauce served with rice or taro root. Other offerings included *Lapu-lapu* (grouper), mahi-mahi, chicken or pork adobo marinated in soy sauce, and breaded beefsteak, all served with the same vegetables.

Al and Earl selected the special; Jeff opted for the grouper and Dave for a combination of pork and chicken adobo. They all agreed to share a bottle of Lambanog wine.

"Bueno, would you like to eat at the bar or at one of the tables."

"We'll move to a table," replied Al.

The bartender placed the appropriate settings on one of the tables, after which the four moved to that table. Included in the place setting was a wine glass which the bartender filled with Lambanog. After they were all seated, Jeff picked up his glass of Lambanog and toasted: "to us."

"To us," was the instant response from all.

"Hey, this wine's not all that bad," Earl remarked.

"Yeah, I'd suggest you not get carried away," commented Jeff. "You know what the bartender said about its potency."

"You mean it's like sipping whisky?" Dave asked.

"Not like Wild Turkey or Crown Royal," Al commented.

"You got that right!" exclaimed Earl.

"Man, it does have a kick to it," Jeff observed after sipping a little from his glass.

"What say we take an excursion to the Apo reef," Al suggested. "It would be in keeping with our cover; you know, tourist taking in all the sights. Dave could use Mel's SCUBA gear. In fact, I was thinking we could sign up for one of those half-day tours; let them do the driving so to speak," Al explained.

"That's a great idea, a busman's holiday," Jeff exclaimed.

"Not only that, I bet we could finagle a trip to that private island, have dinner there before we embark on our next leg," Dave suggested.

"You mean free us from your cuisine of hamburger and beans," Earl laughed.

"Hey, you don't have to eat 'em you know," Dave quipped, feigning hurt.

"Aw, did I hurt your feelings," Earl replied. "Gee I'm sorry."

"Naw, you can't hurt my feelings, but just wait. . ." grinned Dave.

"Uh oh, I don't think I want to be in your shoes when Dave serves dinner," laughed Jeff.

"What's the big deal, I like Dave's hamburger and beans," responded Earl.

The group bantered back and forth while the bartender refilled their glasses. Their meals were finally served after the third refill. When the dinner was consumed and the bill paid, the group returned to their boat, albeit in a rather unsteady condition.

The group was awakened by loud knocking on the door from the cockpit leading down to the cabin. Al was the first to acknowledge it.

"What's that?" he uttered, still somewhat groggy.

"Sounds like someone's on board," Jeff said, rising from his berth.

Again, pounding on the hatchway.

"Who's there," Al shouted as he rose from his berth and slipped on his pants.

By this time everyone was awake. Jeff had reached for his Beretta M9 pistol.

"It is the police. Please present yourself and your credentials," a Spanish accented voice was heard from behind the hatch.

"Okay, wait a minute, we have to dress, we'll be right up," Al answered. Jeff stowed his revolver.

Al was the first one out of the cabin and into the cockpit, followed by the rest. A medium height, stout male in a brown uniform with a revolver hanging from a Sam Browne Belt, was waiting on the pier. The badge over his right pocket identified him as a policeman.

"*Buenos dias Señors*," the policeman greeted. "I see from the flag flying from the mizzen mast that your boat is registered in the United States."

"Yes, that's right, we're Americans," Al answered.

"Did you not see the sign requiring foreign vessels to register with the harbormaster inside the Municipal Building?" the policeman asked.

"Yes, but we arrived late and the Municipal Building appeared to be closed," Al answered.

"I see. Is this all of you?" the policeman asked, directing his gazed upon the rest.

"Yes, just the four of us," answered Al.

"Very well, please hand me your passports," the policeman directed.

"Wait, I'll get them, they are below," Jeff spoke.

"Good, I'll wait," the policeman answered.

Jeff climbed down the ladder into the passageway, got everyone's passports, and then surrendered them to the policeman still standing on the pier.

"Thank you. I'll take these to the Harbormaster, and you can get them from him once you register your boat and pay your berthage fee."

"We'll follow you to his office, if you don't mind," Dave spoke.

"Of course, you are free to do so. Are you ready now?" the policeman asked.

Dave looked around to the rest who readily acknowledge their assent. "Yes, lead the way," he answered.

After snapping closed the padlock on the hatchway, they all followed the policeman across the main street to the two-storied concrete building that was the Municipal Building, and into a small office marked Harbormaster.

The policeman handed the passports to a small, lean, middle- aged man sitting behind a gray metal desk, the desk plate identified him as the harbormaster. After speaking in Spanish to him, the policeman left.

The Harbormaster examined each of the passports, comparing the photo on the inside to each member of the party. Then he turned to the table behind him, on which was a log book in which he entered the details of each passport. Then he addressed the group.

"Welcome to Buenavista," he greeted. "What brings you here?"

"As you will note from the many stamps on our passports, we're sailing around the Pacific Ocean visiting as many countries as we can. While we were in Manila, we learned of the great Apo Reef and thought that would be a great place to visit."

"Oh yes, and let's see, you are Mister Johnson, is that correct?" the Harbormaster asked, after looking at the passports.

"Yes, that's correct," Dave answered.

"Well enjoy your stay. The Apo Reef is a beautiful sight with all sorts of sea life. Did you know it is one of the largest reefs in the world?"

"Yes, so we were told," Dave answered.

Then the Harbormaster handed each their passport based on the photograph inside. "How long do you plan to keep your boat berthed here?" he asked. "There is a daily berthage fee of twenty-five American dollars."

Al looked at Dave, "I'd say we're probably going to get underway tomorrow, weather permitting, wouldn't you?"

"Yes, I agree," answered Dave.

"Do you accept credit cards for payment?" Al asked the Harbormaster.

"But of course," he answered. Payment was made and the group departed the office.

"That was rather painless," Jeff remarked as they left the Municipal Building. "Let's check out the tours and have some breakfast."

"Roger that, Pard. Shall we go back to the Bamboo Shack?" Earl asked.

"Sure, why not, it's next to the slew of dive shops," answered Al.

"Just as long as we stay away from the tuba and the lambanog," cautioned Dave.

They stopped at the first dive shop advertising tours to the Apo Reefs and to Pandan Island, and learned that the shop offered combination tours of the reefs and the Island. Consequently, they booked a noon dive with a return stop at Pandan Island. Since the company runs regular scheduled shuttles to Pandan Island ending at 6

P. M., the group decided to take advantage of the little time available and see the island and have an early dinner.

"Man, it cost us a bundle," Jeff observed. "I think Americans and dollars are synonymous to these people."

"Well the Apo Reef is one of the most popular tourist spots in the Philippines so we shouldn't have been too surprised," said Dave.

"And don't forget who's footing the bill," laughed Earl.

At the Bamboo Shack the group partook of ham and cheese omelets with lots of coffee, and then returned to their boat to check their SCUBA equipment, and to fit Dave to Mel's buoyancy compensator (BC).

"How about the tanks, are they full?" asked Dave.

"I'll top them off," Jeff answered. "I'm not about to trust my life with these yo-yos," replied Jeff. "That's why we have our own air compressor on board."

After all the SCUBA equipment was inspected, they made preparations for an early morning departure the next day. At noon they all boarded a large Banca with a bamboo roof and outriggers on both sides, propelled by an outboard motor. Their dive bags were placed in the bow of the boat. Other than the so-called dive master and the operator of the outboard motor, they were the only ones on board.

Although their banca was larger than most, the group still had to sit in tandem to each other. Fortunately, the water was calm with light swells, ideal for the fifteen-mile trip to the reefs. The mangroves of Apo Island and the white lighthouse signaled the approach to the dive spot. Their banca anchored in the north lagoon. With the assistance of the two crewmen, Jeff donned his BC, after which his air tanks were strapped to the back of the BC. That done, Jeff sat on the side as the dive master fitted his fins to his feet. Then the dive master opened the valve on the tanks. Jeff, with his regulator in his mouth and his mask covering his face, took a deep breath, and gave the okay signal with his fingers. Then with one hand pressing his mask to his face, fell backwards into the water. Once under water he followed the anchor line to where it was embedded in the rocky bottom of the lagoon. This same procedure was followed by the rest of the group.

As agreed, they all gathered at the spot where the banca's anchor was positioned. Each of them inflated their BCs just enough so that they could maintain enough buoyancy to float just above the reef. They marveled at the reef and all the sea vegetation it contained, and at the variety of fish that called the reef their home. The water was clear offering complete visibility. At one point, Al signaled all to come to him so that he could show them a green moray eel that was observing him from its sanctuary in the rocks. As they proceeded along the bottom a stingray rose straight up and then propelled itself forward, like the US Marines' vertical takeoff and landing Osprey. Finally, they had had their fill; Dave's air supply was at the twenty percent mark so they all surfaced. Boarding the banca' was a lot harder than entering the water. One of the group held on to the side of the boat with his BC deflated, while the dive master removed his tank, then received his fins, one at a time and finally assisted the diver as he pulled himself over the side and fell into the boat. While this was taking place, the other three treaded water waiting their turn.

On the trip to Pandan Island, each of the group exchanged their diving attire for pull- over shirts, shorts and sandals which they had stowed in their dive bag. The dive boat pulled into the Pandan Island pier where the four disembarked with the admonition to return to the pier a little before six o'clock for the return trip to the dive shop. They really didn't need a reminder, since they had to retrieve their dive bags at the dive shop.

After a short walk across white soft sand, interspersed with palm trees, tourist lying on giant beach towels, or on white-strapped chaise lounges under large umbrellas, soaking up the sun, they arrived at the reception bungalow. It housed the office, bar, restaurant and dive shop. Nestled among the native trees and beyond the bungalow were the thatched roof guest lodges.

"You know, walking across the sandy beach makes me think of Mel," Jeff remarked.

"You mean like Hualien and Shao-mei?" commented Earl.

"What do you mean?" asked Dave.

"Ha, it is on Hualien's beach that we first met Shao-mei and her unscrupulous uncle," answered Al.

"I don't see any young things with which we could conjure up some conversation on this beach," observed Earl.

"It's just as well since we're not staying that long," Al laughed. "But I do see some of more senior folks, lawn bowling on the left side of the far hut."

"So, they are," observed Dave. "Who'd believe it?"

The first stop was the bar where they ordered San Miguel beer and engaged the bartender in some conversation.

"What's to do on the island besides lawn bowling?" asked Earl.

"Lawn bowling? What's that?" the bartender asked.

"You know, on that court just outside the lodges. Where they're bowling balls on the ground."

"Oh, you mean petanque. You call it lawn bowling?" replied the bartender. Petanque is a very popular sport in the Far East. Some people call it bocce ball. But to answer your question, there is snorkeling and SCUBA diving. There is the Apo Reef not too far from here."

"Yes, we know, we've been there, done that," said Jeff. "The problem is that we don't have much time."

"You can always hike to the Lagoon or to the Spanish Nose. It's a beautiful walk through our rain forest. If you're lucky you might see some of our Pawikans, large green sea turtles that are on the endangered list."

"Sounds interesting, how do we get there?" Dave asked.

"Just follow the trail to the right of the dive shop. There are signs that point the way."

"Good, thanks," Dave said.

"When do you serve dinner?" Earl asked.

"Leave it to Earl to ask about his stomach," laughed Al.

"Hey, I know we had a late breakfast, but all that diving has made me hungry."

"Actually, I'm with Earl," Jeff said. "I could stand to put something into my stomach."

"The restaurant opens at four. It's buffet style. You can eat all you want," the bartender answered.

"Okay, we'll pass on the Spanish Nose and sea turtles," said Dave.

"You don't need to on our account," said Earl. "You and Al can go, and Jeff and I will hold down the fort."

"You mean the bar," laughed Al. "But I have to admit I'd just as soon relax a little, drink some beer and wait for the buffet line to open."

"Maybe I'll take a quick walk to the, what's the name of that place, Spanish what?" Dave asked the bartender.

"Spanish nose; it's a rock formation on the southern side of the island that looks like a man's nose," explained the bartender.

"On the other side of the island; that doesn't sound like a short walk," said Dave.

"I guess that depends on how you define short," laughed the bartender.

"Yeah, you're right. I think I'll stay here and join my compadres in another San Miguel."

By the time the four finished another round of San Miguel beer, the buffet line opened and they pigged out on Filipino, Spanish and American dishes. Afterwards, they boarded the boat, returned to the mainland, collected their dive bags and were snug in their beds by nine.

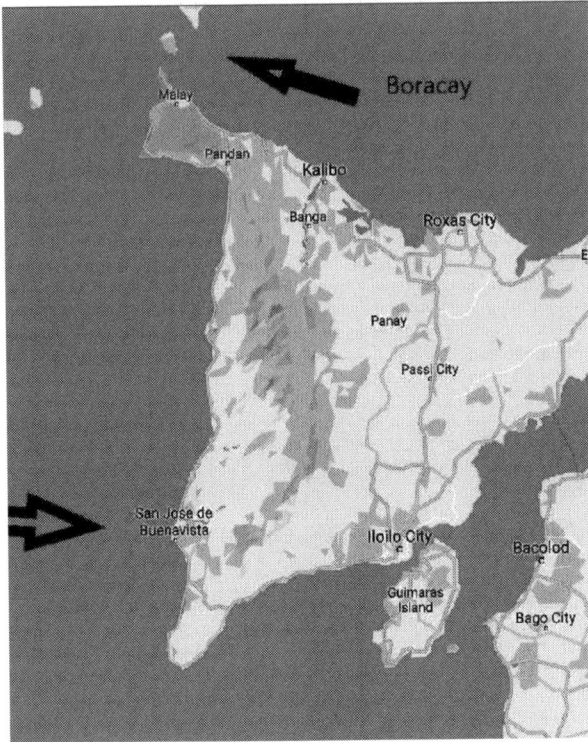

PANAY ISLAND

Chapter 10

At Sea continues

At dawn the next day, the Dragon Lady slipped out of its berth and made its way into Pandan Bay. A mist rose from the water and visibility was good in spite of a light morning fog.

"The fog should be lifting soon," Dave reported. "PAGASA reports good weather throughout the day; swells between three and four feet with twenty knot winds out of the northwest. Should be great for sailing."

They left the bay with sails set and trimmed. Pandan Island was on the left and the light from the Apo Island lighthouse was on the right as the Dragon Lady entered the Mindoro Strait.

"Ready for a little geography lesson?" asked Earl. "You notice that the Apo Light is on our right. Apo Island and the reefs actually split Mindoro Strait. We are in the East Apo Pass. We didn't realize it, but yesterday we crossed the pass on our trip to the Apo Reef. The Mindoro Strait is literally our highway to the Sulu Sea."

"Are you telling me we need to be especially alert until we get beyond the Apo Reef?" asked Al, who was at the helm.

"Roger that," answered Earl.

"Well Mister Navigator, I've already taken that into my calculations," commented Al. "We'll be doing some short tacks until we're beyond the reef, but it wouldn't hurt if you go forward and stand watch at the bow."

"Yes, and get into a PFD and connect to the jackline," said Jeff. "Although the swells are rather tame right now, that can change at any time."

"Actually, you're right; we're being sheltered somewhat by the islands. Once we cleared those, we're sure to see a pickup in the wave intensity. I'll play it safe and get connected," replied Earl.

"And I'll watch the radar," announced Dave. "By the way, what's tonight's destination, navigator?"

"We agreed on San Jose," Earl answered. It's a large city with good port facilities, and it's a good jumping off place for our next port on Panay Island. Assuming we have the weather you say we're going to have, we should make port before dark. Our alternate is Calintaan, a small-town north of San Jose."

The conversation over, Earl made his way forward amid the seesaw effects of the wave action. But as Earl predicted, once the Mindoro Strait's Apo East and West Passes merged beyond Apo Island, the wind became brisker and the swells higher. The boat pitched and yawed as it bisected the swells, as Earl so pointedly yelled from his position at the bow, "ride 'em cowboy!"

There was plenty of daylight left when the Dragon Lady motored into the San Jose Harbor, and took its place among the other boats moored alongside the 200-foot-long and 50-foot-wide wooden wharf that projected from shore. The second pier was 250-foot long, made of concrete, with a 100-foot-wide ramp. It provided berth to the larger cargo vessels. Al, et al, was picked up by a motorized tricycle, and transported to the end of the pier where the Caminawit Port Terminal was located. It housed a police substation and the harbormaster's office. It was in this building passports were checked, registered and harbor fees paid. In addition, there was a brief description of the derivation of the port's name: Caminawit. In the past, passengers from Manila, complaining of the long wait for the train that would take them to the town of Central, Mendoro, would remark: 'you come and wait'. That phrase was corrupted to 'Caminawit' and hence the name of the port.

The four, upon exiting the Harbormaster's office and exhausted by the all-day sail, decided to remain in the area rather than take a taxi to downtown. They quenched their thirst and appetite in the passenger terminal's café. The food wasn't gourmet by any stretch of the imagination, but when washed down with San Miguel, was eatable. After eating, they topped off their boat's supply of gasoline after which they 'hit the sack'.

The early morning departure was under cloudy skies and scattered rain showers, which as Jeff observed "put a damper on this leg of the trip; no pun intended." Their tack put the Dragon Lady on a southwestern course. However, due to the proximity of the Mindoro Strait to the ever-present reefs, the tacks were of about an hour and a half duration. When the Dragon Lady came about onto a southeastern tack, it found itself in the confluence of the Tablas Strait and the Mindoro Strait, separating Mindoro Island from Panay Island. The wind was sweeping down the strait and creating havoc with the weather pattern. The Dragon Lady tossed and turned, rose and fell on six-foot waves. The sails were reefed. Al fought to keep on course. It was so rough that there was no way the sails could be adjusted to allow the boat to come about on a new tack. Then as luck would have it, the boat came under the shelter of the coal mining island of Semirara. The cross-winds and the intensity of the waves subsided, thus allowing Earl and Dave to man the main and jib sails as Al brought the boat to a new southwestern tack.

"I think this was worse than the weather we ran into on our first leg out from Subic," remarked Jeff."

"You got that right," agreed Earl, who with Dave had just joined Jeff and Al in the cockpit.

"Earl, what was the resort island off the tip of Panay Island, you know, across from our alternate port?" Al asked.

"You mean Boracay," Earl answered.

"Yes, that's it. I was thinking we owe ourselves a break. Let's put in there, and lay over for a day, a kinda R&R. Maybe even book a room in one of their hotels and get a hot shower."

"You've got my vote!" Jeff exclaimed.

"Mine too," Dave echoed. "And we can add it to the State Department's tab."

"That's even better," Earl remarked. "I'll plot us a new course. It shouldn't take much of a change since Boracay is just a little north of our original destination, Sebaste."

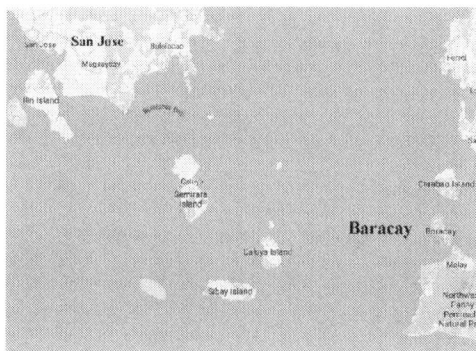

BARACAY

Al made one more course change, a southeastern tack that put them on a heading to Boracay. It was around four in the afternoon, when the Dragon Lady approached the bone shaped island with its white sandy beaches and coconut palm trees. The sails were lowered and Al, under motor, entered the small strait that separated Caticlan on Panay's mainland from Boracay. The Dragon Lady found berth at the Cagban Jetty Port; the main access point to Boracay.

White Beach, the main tourist beach located on the western side of the island is approximately two and a half miles long. A roadway traverses the center of the island, separating White Beach from Bulabog Beach on its eastern side. And a foot path separated White Beach from the businesses that cater to the tourist; small restaurants, dive shops, bars and massage parlors. Where the footpath ended, upscale hotels fronting the beach begin. Farther down, were the more modest priced hotels and native type bungalows with two, four and six-bedroom cabins. The group settled on one of the four-bedroom cabins: four separate bedrooms; one full bath and shower; a small living room, a kitchenette; an outdoor shower and a small charcoal grill.

"Not a bad location," Jeff observed. "The beachside bar is hopping."

"Yes, let's join the merry makers," suggested Earl. "I noticed that we're not too late for happy hour."

"To the bar then," Al agreed.

The four followed a gravel pathway to large pavilion, under which was a long bar surrounded by stools with about half of them occupied. A four-piece reggae band was playing at one end. The four selected stools at the opposite end, and was quickly greeted by the bartender who took their order; San Miguel Beer. Bowls of roasted peanuts were strategically placed before them. When the beer was delivered, Al started a conversation with the bartender.

"We only have one day to visit the island, what do you suggest?" Al asked.

"Only one day huh, well that depends on your interest," he answered. "We have all sorts of water activities; SCUBA diving, snorkeling, swimming. You name it?"

"Only one day, what a pity," came a female voice from a small party at the other end of the bar.

"Louisa, don't be so forward," laughed one of her companions; a petite blonde. Then she turned to the four," I apologize for my friend."

"For what?" Earl spoke up. "If the island is full of the likes of you all, then I'd say she's right; what a pity."

"Uh oh, Earl's on the loose," Jeff commented. "But I think he is right, it is a pity."

"Why don't you join us?" a male companion suggested.

Earl didn't hesitate; he grabbed his bottle of San Miguel and joined the party. Al looked at Jeff and Dave and questioned, "why not?" Nothing more needed to be said. The other three joined Earl. Introductions were made.

"You are Americans?" one of the group members questioned.

"Yep, Al replied."

"And what are you doing here," another asked.

"We're sailing around the Pacific and read about the beaches at Boracay," Dave answered. "We thought we'd give them a try."

"I know you all!" another exclaimed. "You're the Americans who came to the rescue of all our people injured in the bombing in Baguio a couple of weeks ago."

"Well, I don't know about the rescue bit," Dave said. "We were there and did what we could do to help out. Actually, our nurse friends from the Subic Bay Navy Station did most of the first aid work."

"Where are you all from?" Al asked.

"We're the fighting Marooms from UPB," another shouted.

"UPB?" Earl questioned.

"Yes, the fighting Marooms from the University of the Philippines, Baguio."

"Ah ha, that's how you knew about our help in the bombing," Dave remarked.

"Right you are, and thank you for that," was the reply.

"Yea, for the Americans," another student spoke up. "Let me buy your next round." Then he turned to the bartender, "Filipe, another round of drinks for our American friends."

"That's mighty nice of you but there is no need," Al said.

"No, no it is my pleasure, actually all our pleasure, right?" the student said, addressing the rest of the group. There was an immediate positive response.

"Very well, we accept with thanks," Jeff answered.

Then the celebrating began. Empty bottles were instantly replaced by full ones, as the students bombarded the group with questions: What states are you from, where did you go to school, how long have you been sailing. In turn the Americans learned that the students were doing graduate studies in computer sciences and mathematics, and were in Borocay on their mid-semester break.

Al could see where this was going. "Enough already, we haven't eaten yet and you're doing us in."

"We haven't eaten yet either, why don't we all go to Cocomangas Shooter Bar," a student suggested.

"Where?" Al asked.

"The Cocomangas Shooter Bar," was the answer. "Whoever is still standing after drinking fifteen shots of liquor gets a free tee shirt."

"That sounds just like something we really need," laughed Al.

"You mean something we can do without," added Earl.

"Earl, I can't believe you said that," laughed Jeff.

"Hey good buddy, I know when enough is enough."

"You all do your celebrating and get your tee shirts, I think we're going to eat here and then call it a night," Dave said.

Goodbyes were said, handshakes exchanged between the men and hugs between the ladies, after which the four staggered to the hotel's small diner and then to bed.

It was after nine in the morning when the four walked out of the hotel enclave and onto the white fine sand of the beach. The sun was at their back as it started its assent. They each carried a beach chair taken from a stack in front of the hotel's office, and placed them under one of the coconut palm trees that were scattered throughout the beach. That would be their command post as they surveyed the action at the beach. A mother was watching her children running to and fro from the gentle that encroached upon their space and just as quickly retreated into the surf. In another area children filled their pails with sand and emptied it in a pile; the start of their sand castle.

"I wonder where our bevy of quail are?" asked Earl.

"Snug like a bug in a rug, I expect," Jeff remarked.

"I don't understand why you didn't take one home last night?" laughed Dave.

"Ha, they knew what they were doing. You know, safety in numbers and all that," Earl commented. "Besides, I know my limitations. I couldn't do them justice."

"I think you underestimate your abilities," Al remarked.

"Maybe you couldn't do them justice, but I'm sure that they could do me justice," Jeff said.

"Listen to the man talk," Earl retorted. "I noticed he never made a move on them."

"As you said, safety in numbers. Anyway, what would those young maidens want with old codgers like us?"

"Experience," laughed Earl.

"Yeah, right, experience," said Dave.

"Well Dave, I can only speak for myself," quipped Earl.

"Okay, so much for boy talk, what's the agenda for today?" Al asked.

"You mean other than a relaxing day at the beach?" asked Jeff.

"I'd like to make a stop at the Bureau of Immigration's office," Dave said. "It's probably not necessary, but if anyone is tracking us, it will just reinforce our cover."

"That's fine, do you know where it is?" asked Jeff.

"According to the desk clerk, it's on the main drag not too far from the D'Mall. He gave me a brochure of things to see and do in Boracay. It includes a map of the area. We actually passed the mall on the way here," Dave answered. "We can catch a motorized trike in front of the hotel. You guys can stay here if you want, and just soak up the sun."

"If we are going to keep up our cover, I guess all of us should go. I mean, if you think we should check in with immigration, then all of us should be doing it," Al said.

"Perhaps you're right. We can explore the Mall and replenish some of our food stores," Dave said.

"When do you want to do it?" Earl asked. "If we're going downtown so to speak, we probable should also check our boat."

"Good idea," replied Dave. "We can do that and have lunch at one of the many cafés that's in that section."

At the Bureau of Immigration Office, the four presented their passports to the immigration official who examined them and then returned them with a parting statement to enjoy their visit. They walked to the D'Mall. Actually, a mall is a misnomer. It was a four-block area consisting of all sorts of shops and restaurants; a dental office, an optical shop, clothes stores, boutiques and souvenirs shops of all sorts and descriptions. The four had lunch at one of the myriads of small cafes and sandwich shops within the confines of the mall, and then ended up in the super market where they added to their store of foodstuff. Afterwards they hailed a motorized tricycle that took them to the docks where they stowed the items they had purchased, and made preparations for an early morning departure. Then it was a motorized tricycle ride back to the hotel where they spent more time under the coconut palms of the powder white beach. They ended the day enjoying happy hour at the beach bar, but to their disappointment most of the last night's jolly makers were not in attendance, and any thoughts of a night of debauchery had to be abandoned for a good night's sleep.

They woke early, had a hardy breakfast and made their way to the pier to begin another leg of their trip; this time to the port of Saint Jose Buenavista on the southern tip of Panay Island.

This leg of their journey was uneventful. The weather cooperated; following winds and mild swells. It was almost boring, but as Al exclaimed, "I'll take boring anytime!"

There was a single wharf at San Jose Buenavista. It ran parallel to the shore, before taking a forty-five degree turn into the Sulu Sea. This portion acted like a breakwater and formed a lagoon on its leeward side. It was on this side of the wharf that ships are moored. The parallel portion is connected to the shore by three access ways. The center one accessed a large warehouse and administrative building, while the other two accessed an area containing more warehouses.

Once moored, the four disembarked and looked at the wide expanse of concrete that was the wharf. Theirs was the only boat moored to the wharf. The ubiquitous motorized tricycle, this time with a metal covering, arrived and transported them to the administrative building where they showed their passports and paid the mooring fee. There was also a small information booth where they inquired about restaurants that were in the vicinity. They all opted for a steak house just a short taxi ride away, on Tobias Fornier Street. The taxi consisted of a motorcycle with a sidecar into which the four squeezed. The steak house was nothing fancy but there were a lot of

locals and as Earl observed, "that should speak for itself." The steaks were served with boiled potatoes, carrots and green beans. The four returned to the port, topped off the gas tank and spent the night on board the Dragon Lady.

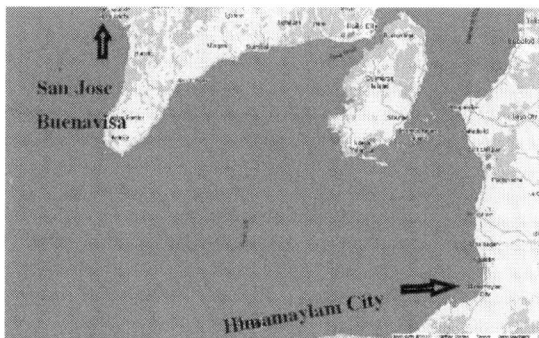

NEGROS OCCICDENTL ISLAND

Early the next morning the Dragon Lady motored out into the Sulu Sea, and set its sails for its next port, Himamaylan City on Negros Occidental, the western half of Negros Island. The Island is shaped like a boot. The tack that they were on took them southwest of the southern tip of Panay Island, before coming about on a southeast tack toward the ankle of the boot.

The sailing was smooth with following seas and favorable winds. The crew was beginning to get somewhat complacent. However, that mood was soon changed once they rounded the tip of Panay Island, and changed to the southeastern tack. That brought them into the Gulf of Panay, the large expanse of water separating Panay Island from Negros Island; their destination. In addition to swift east to west currents which brought with them high cross winds, and corresponding intensity in the wave action, it began to rain and the visibility dropped accordingly. The boat's foghorn was activated.

The crew donned their foul weather gear and huddled in the cockpit. The sails were reefed; Jeff's and Dave's eyes were glued to the radar screen. Al was at the helm with Earl standing next to him, binoculars hanging from around his neck. Water came spewing over the bow with each dip the boat took; the action of a bucking bronco.

"What's it look like on the screen," Al yelled to be heard over the roar of the wind.

"Not good," Dave shouted. "It looks like the weather is here to stay. There is nothing but dark green on the screen."

"Uh oh," remarked Jeff to Dave. "I think we have a problem."

"What do you mean, problem?" an anxious Dave asked.

"The screen just went blank," Jeff commented.

"Blank? let me see what I can do," Dave said.

Jeff gave way to Dave who started adjusting a couple of screws at the base of the radar but to no avail.

"We really need to be on our watch. The visibility stinks," observed Al

Jeff donned his PFD, connected it to the jackline and made his way toward the bow. Using his binoculars, he scanned the horizon in front and to the sides. Back in the cockpit, Dave maintained surveillance from the rear and sides.

At the helm, Earl asked Al, "You want me to spell you a little? You've got to be tired."

"Good idea," Al answered. "Just try and keep her on course. Obviously, that won't be easy, just keep making small corrections."

"Can do; Just like crabbing into the wind," Earl said, exchanging places with Al.

"I think I hear a horn or something but can't really tell over the noise of our horn," Dave reported.

Al turned off the boat's horn and listened. They all heard it, a sharp, piercing blast.

"We've got something coming toward us from our portside," Dave said. "Haven't been able to make it out yet."

Al scanned the portside. "I can't see anything," he remarked.

"I see it!" exclaimed Dave. "It's a ferry. Coming right at us!"

"We've got a ferry coming up from our portside. It looks like our paths may cross," a concerned Al mentioned to Earl. "Be ready to adjust course if need be." Al activated the boat's horn again.

"It's getting closer," Dave reported. "He probably can't hear the horn because of the rain and wind."

"I sure hope he can see us," Al said. He then turned toward the bow. Jeff was clinging to the mainmast, his eyes glued to the approaching threat.

The ferry was now clearly visible. "I don't see any change in his course," reported Dave. "I sure hope he knows the rule of the seas."

"You mean the one that motor vessels must give way to those under sail," questioned Al. "This is the Philippines. I wouldn't put too much faith in the rules of the sea here."

"With its bridge as high as it is, I doubt if he can see us," observed Jeff.

"What shall I do skipper?" a worried Earl asked, raising his voice to be heard above the piercing sound of their horn.

The ferry had not changed its course. It was taking direct aim on the sailboat.

"Give way, come about!" Al shouted to Earl. "It's almost on us!"

Earl turned the wheel hard to the right. Jeff held tight to the mainmast. The Lady's listed far to the right. The sails fluttered from the loss of the wind. Al released the port sheet causing the boom to swing lose. Before Dave's could adjust the opposite sheet, the ferry's wake pushed the Lady's stern aside causing her hull to rise out of the water bringing the boat precariously close to broaching. However, before that happened, Dave was able to secure the mainsail to the wind, giving their boat enough maneuverability to allow Earl to turn into the crest of the wave, albeit at a forty-five-degree angle but still listing. By the time the Dragon Lady was fully stabilized, and on a southwest tack, the ferry had disappeared in the rain. And much to everyone's relief, a picture was on the radar scope.

"The weather must have caused some sort of interference," suggested Dave.

"I guess," commented Al. He then turned off the foghorn. "We don't need that damn thing blaring in our ears. As far as the radar goes, I found that with all the jolting that was taking place, the connection to the antenna had come loose. It was just a matter of inserting the lead back into its hole and tightening the retaining nut."

Jeff returned to the cockpit. "Whew, that was close," he blurted out.

"I'll say," agreed Al.

"You did a great job in controlling the boat," Al commented to Earl. "For a minute there, I was afraid we were about to capsize."

"Yeah," Dave agreed. "That was a great bit of seamanship, riding that wave as you did. Not everyone could have the coolness to hold her into the wind amid all that was going on."

"Ah shucks guys," Earl grinned. "It just comes from all my training. After all, I was an Air Force pilot you know."

"Oh, here it comes," laughed Jeff. "I think I'm going to puke."

"Hey ole buddy, no need to do that, I just speak the truth," Earl remarked.

"Yeah, right," Jeff replied. "I too was impressed with the way you handled yourself and the boat, but I'll be damned if I'm going to add to yourself aggrandizing."

"Aggrandizing; you intelligence weenies always use such big words," razzed Earl.

"Oh, now you're hitting close to home," added Al to the bantering.

The joshing created a comic relief to what was a highly intense five minutes. However, the rain was still coming down, and the swells were still of their same amplitude. Al relieved Earl at the helm and adjusted the tack to the southwest. A more favorable sailing environment resulted. The boat was running with the wind, although the wave effect was still full of ups and downs. Still, the sailing became easier, no more fighting the current. Jeff and Earl went below and partook of coffee and sandwiches, then spelled Al and Dave.

All were topside when the boat was west enough to allow Al to come about and set a southeast tack for their destination, Himamaylan City. By this time, the rain had stopped and the winds subsided. The 8000-foot-high, Kamlaon Volcano with sugarcane fields on its lower slopes, was seen ahead of them. Himamaylan City was tucked into a natural cove with deep waters that made it a natural for boats of all sizes. Its concrete pier was parallel to the shore. The Dragon Lady tied off next to a fishing fleet consisting of five large bancas. The four disembarked and stretched their legs on the concrete. Dave walked up to two fishermen who were mending their nets next to their Banca and engaged them in conversation. Then he returned and relayed the result of his conversation.

"What did you learn," Al asked Dave.

"Himamaylan City is not all that big," answered Dave. "Just follow the road at the end of the pier and it will take you downtown. There you can find all sorts of restaurants, a large covered market and a public park."

"How do we get there?" Earl asked.

"By motorized trikes, what else," laughed Dave. "It's not a long walk to the main drag and there we can hail a cab, if that is what you call it."

"What about our boat? Do you think it will be safe?" asked Jeff

"As safe as any place we've been. These guys look like honest fishermen, but who knows?"

"Right, who knows," a skeptical Jeff asked.

"How about berthing fees?" Al asked.

"There's no fee. According to them, this is the municipal pier and anyone can tie up here."

"Well, what do you all think?" asked Al.

"I say let's lock the hatchways and go for it," Earl answered.

"I don't know if we have any other choice, unless we want to leave one of us to stand guard while the rest go in to town," Dave remarked.

"We haven't had any security problems so far," Earl said.

"Yeah, the operative words are 'so far'," Jeff replied.

"Hey we have the security alarm system which is connected to the horns. If anyone tries to force the hatchway everybody and his brother will hear," commented Al.

"Yeah, I guess you're right," admitted Jeff. "It's just at other ports there were so much going on and here, nothing," Jeff gestured with his arms.

"Well I'll tell you what," Dave said. "I'm exhausted from all the weather we've been fighting, and I'm sure everyone else is also. Why don't Al and I head in to town and get some takeaways and bring them back?"

"That's a good idea," Al said. "I know I'm not ready to hit the town. While were gone perhaps Earl can come up with something for our next destination. Some place where we might spend a day or two."

So that was the plan. Al and Dave walked to where the road from the pier intercepted the main roadway. With the help of the driver of a motorized trike and Dave's Spanish, they found a small café and brought back some *nasi,* (barbecue pork sandwiches), *Resh Lumpia,*(fresh spring rolls wrapped in a paper thin translucent crepe filled with fresh coconut tree heart, pork and shrimp and a garnish of scallion) and of course, San Miguel Beer.

"Man, I'll have to give you two a lot of credit, you've come back with a feast," Jeff remarked, after gorging himself with the *nasai* and *Resh Lumpia.*

"I echo that," Earl said. "A fitting end to what has been a really rough day on the sea."

After everyone had completed their sumptuous repast, Earl reported on what he found as an ideal spot for their next day's destination.

"Bugana Beach and Dive Resort on Campomanes Bay. It's not too expensive and I know that Dave and his CIA expense account can afford it. Here's how it is described in our tour guide: 'the bay has an existing port that caters to medium-sized sea craft'. That's us. To continue, 'the enclosed shape of the bay and islets in its opening provide calm waters even in harsh weather conditions. At the entrance to the bay is a wide expanse of coral garden with various species of

corals and fish.' And it is only about a four or five-hour sail from here."

"Okay, if everyone is on board with Earl's suggestion, I'll get on the radio to see if the resort has anything available. If they don't, I'm sure we can find other suitable accommodations close by in Sipalay City."

Everyone readily agreed and as luck would have it, accommodations were available and reservations were made.

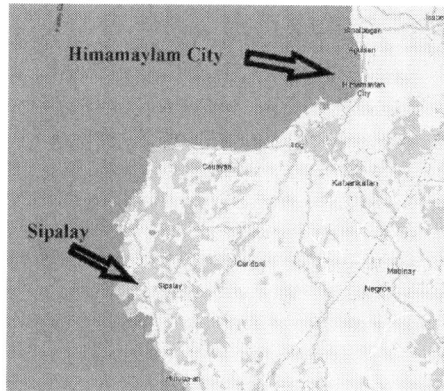

SIPALAY, NEGROS ISLAND

The next morning preparation was made for getting underway before the sun was up. Patches of blue sky were appearing over the Negros Central Mountain Range when the sails were raised. The Dragon Lady left the confines of the bay and entered Panay Gulf. The weather forecast was encouraging; four to five-foot swells with a ten-knot wind out of the northwest. A course was plotted that would take the boat west of the heel of Negros Island before coming about on a southeast tack aimed at Sipalay City's Campomanes Bay. Earl was at the bow, binoculars hung around his neck. The other three were in the cockpit; Jeff at the helm, Al at the radar and Dave relaxing on the bench seat.

"It looks like we've got everything going for us," Al commented. "Nothing on radar; no weather, no ships."

"Well let's not count our chickens before they hatch," Dave commented. "You know how fickle the weather is out here."

"Yeah, I know, but after yesterday we're due for a dose of good weather," Al replied.

"The sky looks pretty good right now," observed Jeff. "No dark skies on the horizon."

"That's now, but it can change," commented Dave.

"Dave, I never knew you to be such a pessimist," Al said.

"Not a pessimist, just a realist," Dave replied. "I hope you are right, but I remember that yesterday started good but ended bad. But I do agree with you, Al, we deserve some good weather."

The sun was in the ten o'clock position when Al decided it was time to change to a southeastern tack. Wispy cirrus clouds had formed high overhead. The temperature was in the high eighties.

"If it wasn't for the breeze, I'd say it was hot," observed Earl who had joined everyone in the cockpit.

"You got that right," commented Jeff, who just opened a bottle of beer, "hot and humid."

"What'd you expect?" laughed Al who was at the wheel. "After all, we are in the tropics, and it sure beats the pounding rain we contended with yesterday."

"Yeah, I know, you're right," Jeff agreed. "I'm heading below and changing into some shorts."

"Not a bad idea," added Earl. "I'll join you."

"Bring some sun block when you come up," Dave asked. "It won't take long to get a real burn, especially with the reflection from the ocean."

"Maybe it's time to rig the overhead canvas," suggested Al. "When Earl and Jeff come up, we'll do it."

"Great idea," replied Dave.

Jeff and Earl, dressed in shorts and tee shirts, returned to the cockpit. They took a wide piece of canvas from the storage locker under the bench seat. The canvas was attached at each end to aluminum poles and wrapped around two support poles. The canvas was unrolled and the two support poles were attached to special mounts on either side of the boat's transom. One of the canvas's attached pole was attached to the mizzen mast while the opposite pole was attached to the two supporting poles extending from the transom at forty-five-degree angles.

"That's more like it," Jeff declared. "What took us so long."

"The weather, dummy," replied Al. "The wind would have torn our cover to threads."

"I knew that," Jeff replied. "It was just a rhetorical question."

"There you go again, ole buddy, using those big words," Earl said.

"Just trying to increase your vocabulary. Pay attention, and maybe someday you'll be as smart as I am," quipped Jeff.

"Don't start comparing intelligence with Earl," interjected Al. "After all, he's a pilot."

"Oh, not you too. Has he got everybody bamboozled?" responded Jeff.

"Hey, what can you say, they call 'em as they see 'em," retorted Earl.

"I notice a small blip on the radar," announced Dave. "It's southwest of us, but not moving very fast."

"Hum, I'll go forward and see if I can spot anything," Earl said. With that declaration, and with binoculars around his neck, he climbed from the cockpit and balancing himself against the pitching movement of the boat, made his way forward. Using the mainmast for support, he scanned the western horizon. "I see something," he shouted.

"What is it?" Jeff yelled.

"Can't make it out," Earl answered. "Wait, now it's coming into focus. It looks like a sailboat without its sails."

"Whoa, what's that?" Jeff asked, as a brilliant red colored ball of light soared out of the western sky.

"It's a flare," reported Earl. "It came from the boat."

"What do you think?" Dave asked Jeff who now had his binoculars focused on the object.

"From what I can see it looks like a disabled boat. My guess is that the flare is a call for help," Jeff answered.

"We'll go and see if we can be of assistance," Al said, looking toward the southwest. "At the same time bring up some weapons. This could be some sort of ruse."

"Right you are," Dave agreed. "As we already know, there are pirates in these waters."

As Al was bringing the Dragon Lady about to a southwest course, Dave and Jeff went below, and inserted clips into four MI6A automatic rifles, strapped holstered M9 Beretta around their waist, and brought the rifles and two holstered pistols into the cockpit. The rifles were laid on the bench seat. Al strapped one of the pistols around his waist. Earl was recalled from the bow and he strapped a holstered Beretta around his waist. Taking one of the M16As, he went below and made his way to the forward hatch. Lifting it up, he braced both feet on two of the rungs of the ladder, and with his back leaning on the hatch opening, he laid his M16A on the hull. He was ready! They were ready!

Chapter 11

The Rescue

"Dave, get the coordinates of the boat and notify the Filipino coast guard that we are going to the assistances of a boat in distress," directed Al.

Dave moved the radar's cross hairs over the blip on the screen. "Latitude 9.54 degrees, longitude 121.28," Dave called out and Jeff wrote them down in a pocket size notebook. Then Dave radioed the Filipino Coast Guard and advised them of their position and that of the distressed boat. The coast guard acknowledged, and asked that they be advised once contact was made.

Al approached the distressed boat cautiously. They were close enough to view the entire boat with their binoculars.

"It's a dhow," Dave reported. "I wonder what it's doing in these waters. It looks like its sail is gone, only a stub where it should be. I can make out only one man, and he is waving some sort of cloth at us. However, I can't see if anyone might be hiding below the gunnel."

"Okay, let's bring in the sails and use our motor to approach him," Al directed.

Leaving the rifles where they lay, Jeff joined Earl at the mainmast and lowered the sails. Dave did the same with the Mizzen. Once the sails were lowered Earl and Jeff returned to their original position. Al motored to a position that allowed a complete binocular scan of the dhow. It revealed that only one person was on board, and he was at the rudder trying to keep his vessel's bow into the waves. Thus assured, bumpers were placed on the side of their boat and Al came alongside the dhow.

"*Alhamdulillah* (praise to Allah)," expressed a middle-aged man, bearded, wearing a skull cap. "I thought all was lost," the man said in English.

"Glad to be of help, what happened?" Dave asked.

"It was the storm; it took my sail and mast and water got into my gas tank."

"Where are you from, and where are you headed?" Dave asked.

"El Nido, on Palawan. I'm on my way to Mindanao."

"We're heading for Sipalay. We can tow you that far," Al said.

"*Baraka Allahu fika,* may Allah bless you. That would be most helpful."

Jeff got on the radio and notified the Philippine Coast Guard of the situation, then he turned to the man in the boat and said: "The Coast Guard wants to know your name, where you are from and where is your destination. I've already told them we were giving you a tow to Sipalaly."

"My name is Abdul Rahman ben Hasan. As I've already mentioned, I'm from El Nido, on Palawan. I'm on my way to Mindanao."

While Jeff relayed the information to the Coast Guard, Earl fastened one end of a line to the Dragon Lady's stern cleat and gave the other end to Abdul who fastened it around a cleat on his boat's bow. Once that was accomplished, Abdul took his position at the tiller of his boat and then Al slowly maneuvered the Dragon Lady away from the dhow allowing it to line up behind the Lady. Then he set a course for Sipalay.

Do you think we should risk the sails?" Dave asked.

"I don't see why not," Al answered. "Obviously we're not going to make as good time as we had planned but the sails will still be faster than the motor."

Once again, the sails were unfurled and after Al brought the Dragon Lady to its tack, he killed the motor. The Lady ploughed through the sea, the dhow bobbing some thirty to forty feet behind. Jeff was keeping it under observation. The line between the two alternated between slack and taut in tune with the rise and fall of the waves. As the dhow descended into the trough the line grew taut, grabbing the Dragon Lady only to release her when the dhow rose to the top of the wave. The going was slow.

They finally arrived at the Sipalay City dock where they made their farewell to a grateful Abdul, and then motored around the inlet that guarded the entrance to Compomanes Bay. They berthed their boat at the Compomanes pier and were picked up by the Bugana Bach Resort's jitney.

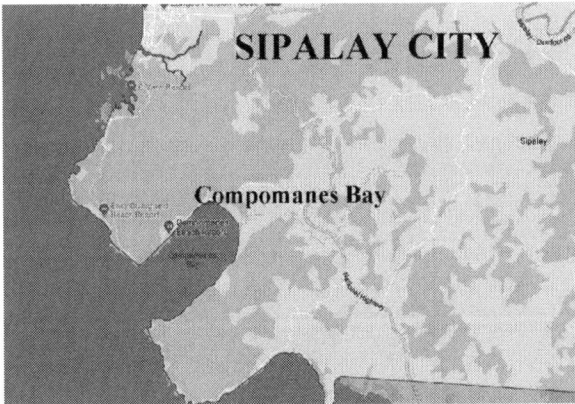

Campomanes Bay, NEGROS ISLAND

The resort fronted on the bay and its white sandy beach. In front of the several-storied main building was a gigantic boomerang shaped swimming pool with a hot tub that could seat ten. Off to one side was the poolside bar. Tiered on the side of a hill, were condo style villas, access to which was from a staircase that ascended the hill. Landings were at each level connecting a veranda shared by each of the units on that level. The resort's entire ground was covered with giant shade trees interspersed with coconut palms. From the beach, the pier was in walking distance to the hotel.

The group was given a second level, two-bedroom villa. On the veranda outside of each unit was a hexagon shaped wooden picnic table with attached seats and two deckchairs. The villa entered into a combination living room and kitchen. Off to one side was a hallway that connected to two twin bedrooms separated by a bathroom.

Once settled in, the four descended the stairs and walked to the dining room located on the first floor of the central building. About half of the twenty or so tables scattered around the room were occupied. A small dance floor was located at the far end with music from the 1950s provided by a three-piece Filipino band. Ceiling fans strategically placed moved the air. Lighting was subdued. Buffet tables lined the far wall.

A hostess met them and escorted them to a table for four, next to a party of eight seated at three tables pulled together. As Al and company were preparing to occupy their table they were interrupted by a voice.

"Welcome yanks."

The group turned and saw that the greeting came from one of the men sitting at the pushed together tables, who raised his drink as in a toast.

"Thanks, how can you tell?" asked Earl.

"Oh, you guys are easy to spot," replied another man from the same group. "Especially when we overheard the hostess speak to you in English."

"Yes, a dead giveaway," added one of the ladies at the table.

"And it's refreshing to hear a language that we can understand," added a third male member of the group.

"Well partially anyway," laughed the lady sitting next to him.

"Well it's obvious where you all are from," remarked Dave.

"Where's that, mate?" asked the first man.

"Down under, Aussies, if I ever heard one," answered Dave. "I'd say you fellows are a long way from home."

"Right you are but enjoying every minute of it," added another of the ladies.

"No sense in yelling at each other, why not add your table next to ours," suggested the original greeter.

"Won't that be crowding you a bit," commented Al.

"No problem we can all squeeze together nice and comfy like," was the reply.

And so, the tables were joined and introductions made: Richard Taylor, 6-foot-tall, trim, athletic, with a full crop of blond hair; his wife Alice, about 5'8"; slender, brunette with shoulder length hair; Richard's younger brother Robert, stocky, crew cut, also with blond hair. His 5'10", buxom, brunette wife was named Sarah. Then there was Milton Andrews, long hair, medium height, stout build. His redheaded wife, Ann, was pleasantly plump. Lastly, was Harold Young, also stout, over 6 feet tall, dark haired with a short mustache and goatee beard. His wife Andrea, was about 5' 8", lean, with close-cut blond hair.

"What's good on the buffet?" Earl asked.

"The *uga*'s good," answered Robert.

"*Uga,* what's that?" asked Earl.

"It's a local fish," replied Robert. "A bit salty, but not too much so, especially when washed down with Tapuy."

"Tapuy, what's that?" asked Earl.

"Tapuy, it's a rice wine, kind of sweet," answered Melton Andrews. "Not as good as our South Australian wines, but, hey, we're not in Australia."

"Amen to that mate," echoed Harold.

"But there are other choices, like spring rolls, barbeque pork and chicken, and the regular fare of vegetables. Not a bad assortment," added Richard Taylor.

"And you recommend the Tapuy wine?" asked Jeff.

"Yes, but there's always vodka," replied Richard. "They call it Lambanog, but it's their vodka, and of course Filipino beer."

"Well let's check out the buffet," suggested Al. And so, the four Americans partook of the buffet; accepting the Australian's suggestion of Tapuy wine.

"Where in Australia are you all from?" Jeff asked Melton Andrews, who he was seated next to.

"We all live in Adelaide, South Australia," replied Melton. "We're taking a little holiday from our digging."

"What do you mean, digging?" asked Jeff.

"We dig for opals. We have holes in Andamooka in South Australia. It's a little north of Adelaide."

"Gosh, that sounds interesting. How do you dig for opals?" asked Dave, overhearing the conversation.

"Well mate, it's like this," answered Robert Taylor, a grin on his face. "We find a little rabbit hole and start digging. Sometimes we're lucky and most of the time we're not."

"C'mon Robert, let 'em in on our secret," Richard said.

"I dunno. Can we trust these Yanks?" his brother answered.

"Oh, here it comes. I think we're about to be had," Earl commented, as all ears were now on the discussion of opal mining.

"No Yank, not at all," a sober faced Melton said. "It's just that we're sworn to secrecy on pain of death."

"Don't pay any attention to them," Richard's wife Alice said. "Digging for opals is a lot like digging for gold, only more dangerous. Opals are found in sandstone. The sandstone deposits north of Adelaide are ideal for opals. In fact, ninety-five percent of the world's opals come from Australia, and I dare say most of that comes from South Australia, or New South Wales."

"Yes, now you've gone and let the cat out of the bag," laughed Harold. "Now our Yank friends are liable to grab a pick and dig up all our opals."

"You mean they're not just lying around waiting for the plucking," Earl said. "If there's any work to it, you don't have to worry 'bout us. We ain't interested."

"Naw, there taint any work involved," replied Robert. "All you have to do is start with a pick and shovel, and dig a shaft some 20 meters or so. Climb down the shaft and start picking away at its side. It's nice to have a buddy like Richard here, on top to bring up all the dirt. Once you find a promising spot, then you really start picking, or if you really want to be adventurous, you can always blast away a seam with a little bit of dynamite."

"Yes, but it's advisable to get out of the shaft before igniting it," added Richard.

"Yeah, I can see the advisability of that," laughed Dave.

"Where have you all been in your tour of the Philippines?" asked Jeff.

"Let's see," answered Melton, "we spent four days in Manila, then did some SCUBA diving along the Apo Reefs. In fact, we just came from there."

"What did you think of it?" asked Earl

"It was nice but not like our Great Barrier Reef. Our Great Barrier Reef is over 2,000 kilometers long. You surely can't see it all in a day. Even a week doesn't do it justice."

"Your sure you guys aren't from Texas," asked Earl.

"What d'ya mean?" asked Melton.

"Well according to our buddy Al here, Texas has the biggest of everything," answered Earl.

"Hey, be careful 'bout what you say about the Lone Star State," interjected Al.

"Well, I don't know about your Texas, but we do know about our Island Continent, and we do have about everything a person could ask for and plenty more," Harold added to the discussion.

The banter continued, as did the wine. The conversation changed from opals to SCUBA diving, to sailing. The evening ended with a promise by Al to take their newly acquired friends on a sail around the bay the next morning, and with the four staggering Americans climbing the stairs to their unit.

"When did we agree to meet them for a sail around the bay?" asked Jeff.

"What do you mean we?" asked Earl. "As I remember the conversation, it was our skipper Al, that did all the offering."

"Why not, they seem like a likable group and they did buy the wine," answered Al.

"Yes, and back to the original question," interjected Jeff. "What time? With all the wine we consumed, I sure hope it's not early."

"Not too early," answered Al. "I told them we would meet them for breakfast around nine, and then plan the afternoon, depending on the weather. The bay's not all that big, but they say it has some great areas for diving and snorkeling."

"Nine! Damn, with all we drank." Dave made his presence known.

"I hope you're not going to let those Aussies get the best of us," laughed Al. "We've got our honor to think of. After all, they drank as much, if not more, than we did."

"While you guys keep talking about your honor, I'm going to set my alarm for 08:30 hours and hit the sack."

"There he goes again with all that military talk, but I'm going to do the same," said Jeff.

That was enough for Dave and Al, they too, set their alarm for eight-thirty and hit the sack.

The next morning all were up, and in spite of last night's activity, were raring to go. They met their friends from 'down under' for breakfast, after which they made plans to meet at the dock at 11 a.m. for a sail around the bay. There were some qualifiers though: the Aussies would have to rent life preservers from the resort's dive shop, and whatever other special gear they wanted.

It was a gorgeous day; the sun shone bright, and there was a slight off-shore breeze. The islets at the entrance to the bay acted as a natural barrier, resulting in calm waters the year round. The Dragon Lady left her port powered only by the main sail, with a total of twelve scattered all over the deck and in the cockpit. Al was at the helm. Richard Taylor was beside him. Dave Hollingsworth was seated on the back bench. Earl was positioned at the mainmast and Jeff at the bow. The rest of the Aussie were scattered on top of the cabin.

Everyone marveled at the sign of wealth that was evidenced by the many mansions that were along the shore, and the steep cliffs, covered with greenery that made a perfect backdrop to the bay. The boat dropped anchor at one of the islets, then it was in the water with snorkels and fins to gaze upon the submerged coral formations and all the sea life that darted to and fro among them. By the time the Dragon Lady returned to its berth there were a bunch of exhausted people. But not that wearied to prevent them from meeting again for dinner in the resort's dining room, and as an extra treat, the tab for the dinner and drinks, which there were many, was picked up by the Aussies.

It was a late morning breakfast after the reveling of the night before. The crew of the Dragon Lady was discussing plans for the next leg of their cruise.

"I was planning on a long day in the hopes of making Mindanao, but to do that we should have left three hours ago," Earl reported.

"Yeah, well we kinda missed that target so what's next?" Al asked.

"Funny you should ask," Earl answered. "I was studying the charts and I think the nearest jumping off place to Mindanao is the small town of Siaton. It has a

large bay called Tambobo Bay and the guide book
describes the water as calm and ideal for mooring.
There doesn't seem to be much of a pier as such. The
town itself is a few miles inland, so we probably
shouldn't count on much in the way of supplies.

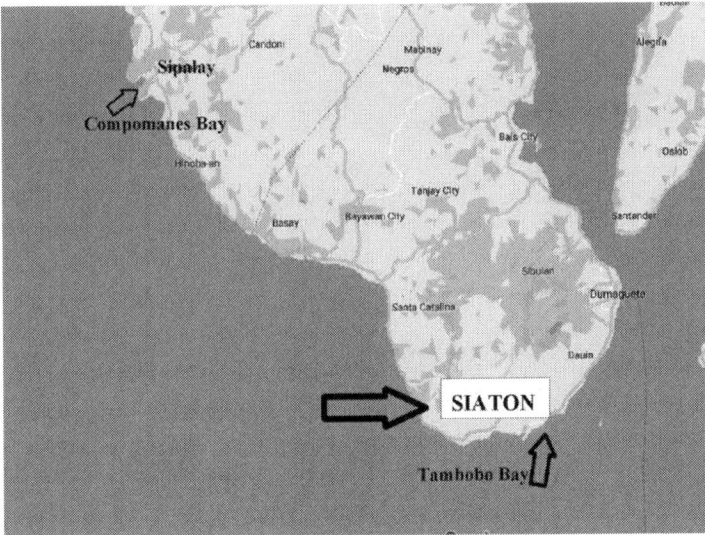

TOWN OF STATON AND TAMBOBO BAY

"That shouldn't be a problem," remarked Jeff. "We
can top off our fuel tanks here. We've got enough
provisions to last us a week."

"So, what do you think our ETA will be?" asked Dave.

"Assuming a decent wind, I'd say around five," replied Earl.

The fuel tanks were topped off and the sails set. Al set a tack that would take them southwest before coming about to a southeast course. The weather cooperated and they entered Tambobo Bay around five in the afternoon. Before entering, they had lowered their sails and motored into the bay where they had to round a tip of land that jutted out into the bay. It was there they dropped anchor. The bay was surrounded by mangroves, coconut palms, and jungle growth which backed to sheer cliffs. Fishing boats were berthed on a narrow strip of beach around a narrow wooden pier, giving evidence to the presence of a fishing village.

"What do you think?" asked Jeff.

"I don't know, it seems peaceful enough, no headhunters," laughed Earl.

"At least, not yet," added Al.

"I guess a couple of us could check out the village," suggested Dave.

"Or we could just spend the night on board, and depart at sunrise," Jeff remarked.

"Hey, what's the big deal?" asked Earl. "A village is a village. We've never been hesitant to mix with the natives before."

"Yeah, you're right, it's just that I have some uneasy feelings," said Jeff. "As near as I can tell, there isn't any kind of town. My guess it's just a collection of huts."

"I'll tell you what, Al and I'll go and get the lay of the land," suggested Dave once more. "We'll take the inflatable to the pier and see where it leads. We'll maintain communication with our walkie-talkies."

"Okay, but take some arms," Jeff suggested.

"Hey, you do have some misgivings, don't you?" observed Earl. "I don't remember your being so nervous before."

"I know, as I said, I have some bad vibes," remarked Jeff.

"Okay, I'll slip one of the Berettas in my pocket," said Dave. "But the last thing we want to do is give the impression that we're a landing party."

"Better yet, I'll go with Dave and Al, but stay with the inflatable "said Earl. "If they need to beat a hasty retreat, I'll be ready."

The plan was laid. After driving the inflatable to the pier, Earl secured it with an overhand knot so that if need be, he could release the boat instantly. He also had one of the walkie-talkies so that he was in constant communication with Jeff, as well as Al and Dave.

Al and Dave began a slow walk down the bamboo constructed bridge. It connected to a dirt path that led to a collection of bamboo huts raised around four to five feet off the ground. Their roofs were of coconut palm leaves. The walls looked to be pleated bamboo. Some had fishing nets drying outside. Farther down was a wooden structure with a peaked roof on which a cross was mounted.

Al and Dave spied a couple standing outside of one of the huts and walked toward them.

Dave greeted them in Tagalog, the official Filipino language. "Greetings, we are anchored in the bay for the night. What is the name of your village?"

"Greetings. Welcome to Tambobo. Are you Americans?" one of the men asked. He was small in stature and elderly in appearance.

"Yes, we are sailing around the Pacific," Dave answered. "Are you Tagalog?"

"No, not Tagalog, we are Ilonggo, friends of the Government," the other answered.

While the four were talking, other villagers came out from inside the church and joined them. Some of the men wore necklaces with crosses hanging from them. Others had what appeared to be amulets suspended from around their necks. The original two spoke to the rest of their tribe in Hiligaynon, their native language.

"You Americans? I speak some American," one in the group said to Dave and Al. His smile displayed a gold tooth. "Americans friends of the government, Americans our friends." Then he pulled from his shirt's top pocket a pack of Black Cat cigarettes, and offered one to both Al and Dave who politely refused.

"Is there a restaurant in the village?" Al asked the one who spoke broken English.

"A restaurant?" his face took on a puzzled expression.

"Yes, you know, where we can buy food?" Dave asked the question in Tagalog, and interpreted for Al. "He says that there is no restaurant as such. There is the local market where you can buy grilled fish and beer. They have a few tables where you can sit, eat and drink."

"What kind of fish?" Al asked.

"Snapper and mahi-mahi," the man speaking broken English blurted.

"What do you think?" Dave asked Al.

"Hey, it's gotta be fresh, let's call Earl and Jeff, and have them join us. Tell our friends here that we have two others who will be joining us."

Dave interpreted and the group seemed delighted. Al contacted Earl and asked him to pick up Jeff and join them. While they were waiting for Jeff and Earl, there were more questions.

"You Catholic?" another of the villagers asked. "We're Catholic, that's our church. Saint Joseph."

"I'm not, but Dave is," Al answered. "I'm a Baptist myself."

"Oh, like John," the villager replied.

"John? Oh, John the Baptist, yes, you're right," Al laughed.

"None of you are Moslems, are you?" the villager asked.

"No none of us are Moslems, why do you ask?" Dave replied.

"Because we hate Moslems," was the reply.

Al and Dave looked at each other as if to say, let's not pursue this.

Then another question was asked, "Are you a communist?"

"Communist? No, we're not communist, why, do you hate them too?" Dave replied.

"No, but they're not our friends, but the NPA is active in Siaton, just north of here. They are not our friends. The government is our friend," was the reply.

281

"NPA?" Al questioned.

"NPA, New Peoples' Army, the so called, military arm of the Communist Party of the Philippines," Dave explained. "They mostly intimidate and extort the local populace in the areas where they are active. I didn't realize that they were this far south."

Dave questioned the villagers in Tagalog to gain more information. He turned to Al and explained, "it appears that the NPA has a garrison just outside the city of Siaton. However, according to the villagers they are afraid to come here, because the locals here are not afraid of them. As one of them put it, 'they come here we chop off their heads and use them in our stew'. One of them referred to themselves as Ilaga or rats. They have been used by the government to put down the Moslem insurrection on Mindanao."

At this time Earl and Jeff joined the group, and the villagers greeted them like long lost friends. Expressions such as: we like Americans, our government likes Americans, that is good, we're Catholics and we hate Moslems, were heard all over again. Finally, after all was said Al, Dave, Jeff and Earl were led to the outdoor market, where they enjoyed grilled snapper and mahi-mahi and drank the local beer. It wasn't until they returned to their boat that Dave let them in on the so-called 'rats'.

"These guys are a bunch of Catholic fanatics, who are a vigilante group and are traditionally superstitious. Their targets are the Muslims in the region. It's even said that some of them are cannibalistic. I don't know if you noticed or not, some wore amulets with ears attached to them. They believe that these amulets will protect them from the Muslims and the NPA."

"See, I told you so, but nobody listens to me," Jeff ended the conversation, although he didn't sleep that well.

The Dragon Lady exited Tambobo Bay just as the sun was making its appearance. A southwest tack was set that would take the boat way out into the Sulu Sea, before coming about to a southeast tack, pointing the boat directly to the peninsula that comprises Western Mindanao and the town of Labason.

It was great sailing weather; skies clear, good stiff breeze and a fast-moving current propelled the 'Lady' toward her turning point, 8.60 degrees north latitude and 120.9 west longitude, where Al gave the command to come about, and the boat was turned about ninety degrees, heading southeast.

Earl was the first to see it. He was scanning the horizon from his watch position on the bow. "Land-ho off the port bow, about 10 o'clock" he yelled.

Jeff focused his binoculars on the 10 o'clock position and brought into view a light green object seeming to rise out of the water. Earl's shout brought Al and Dave from the cabin to topside.

"What is it?" Al asked.

"Earl has spotted land," answered Jeff. "Looking at the chart, I'd have to say it is Mount Malindang; some 7,000 feet in elevation. It's the highest point on the peninsula. Our course seems to be true. We need to come two degrees to our port, but other than that we're right on target."

LABSON, ZAMBOANGA PENINSULA. MINDANAO

It was a little over two hours when the seawall around the town of Labason was sighted. The tree covered islands and white sandy beaches of Murcielagos and Bayangan Islands, were on the boat's starboard as they entered Patauag Bay, Labason.

"What about those islands?" asked Jeff.

"They're a protective area; a nesting ground for turtles and some migratory birds, so our guide book says. There is a reef that surrounds the islands which provide protection and food for the turtles and birds.

The Dragon Lady was tied off at the wharf which protruded into the bay. The group stood on the concrete surface stretching their legs.

"It feels good just to be on terra firma again," commented Earl.

"Right you are, but what is the plan?" asked Jeff.

"Good question," replied Al. "I don't think there is much to see or do in this town."

"Yeah, you're right about that," echoed Dave. "Although it's a lot bigger than our last port of call."

"You mean Tambobo," Jeff laughed. "I don't consider that a port or anything like it."

"You got that right," laughed Earl. "Just a bunch of headhunters looking for a meal."

As they stood around, the ubiquitous motorized trike pulled alongside of them.

"Need a ride?" the young Filipino driver asked.

"Gosh, I don't know," answered Dave. "We haven't decided on what we're going to do yet."

"How about a restaurant?" asked Earl. "Are there any close by?"

"Depends on what you like," the driver smiled. "There is a small seafood restaurant at the end of the wharf. Or, there are some good restaurants and bars in town that have a limited menu, but have friendly bar girls."

"Yeah, that's what we really need, is some friendly bar girls," laughed Al.

"What about the seafood restaurant at the end of the wharf, is the fish fresh?" asked Al.

"Sí, the fish is supplied by the local fishermen daily."

"Well if you want my input, I say we go for the fresh fish," suggested Jeff.

"I agree with Jeff," Dave said. "We should make Isabela City tomorrow, and there will be plenty of things to see and do there."

"Well the decision is made," said Al. Then he turned to the Filipino driver. "Can we walk to the restaurant?" Then turning to the rest, commented, "I don't know about the rest of you, but I'd like to exercise my legs some."

"Sí, it's not too far. You see the warehouse; it is just past that. You walk there and I can bring you back."

"That sounds like a plan, I'm sure we all can do with a little exercise," commented Jeff.

The four walked to the restaurant. Its name, The Shack, was an apt description. Tables were both inside and out. Its meager menu was posted on a chalkboard and consisted of fried tilapia, mahi-mahi, strip steak, and chicken adobo, all served with rice, sweet potato or taro, and banana chips. The group opted to eat outside and enjoy the cool evening breeze while they downed their food with San Miguel beer. When they finished their meal, true to form, their ride was waiting for them and transported them to their boat. The four sat around the cockpit discussing the next day.

"Tomorrow's the big day," remarked Al to Dave.

"Right you are," replied Dave.

"What are the plans?" asked Jeff.

"My contact is a Catholic priest within the Our Lady of the Pillar Church. I guess, it will depend on what he has to say."

"What about us, what do we do while you're doing your thing?" asked Earl.

"Good question," answered Dave. "A lot of this we're going to have to play by ear."

"So again, what's the plan? Are you on your own?" asked Jeff.

"As far as my business with the MNLF, yes, I'm on my own," answered Dave. "But I was thinking how we still could maintain our cover as four Americans sailing around the Pacific. Four of us need to be seen in Isabela City. I thought we could hire a car and driver to do some sightseeing. One of the stops would be Our Lady of the Pillar Church. While visiting the church I'll try to make contact. Being Catholic I'd ask to make my confession. It's in the wording of this request that I communicate with my contact, and he'll give me my instructions within the protection of the confessional. It's after this happens, that we'll have to 'wing' it."

"I guess that's as good a plan as any," remarked Al.

"Earl, you're our navigator, how far is Isabella from here?" Jeff asked.

"Well, as the crows fly only seventeen miles, how-some-ever, we're not crows, and we'll probably encounter cross winds so obviously it's a lot farther for us mere mortals. The tack will be similar to today's; southwest into the Sulu Sea away from Western Mindanao, and then southeast to Basilan Island on which Isabela City is located.

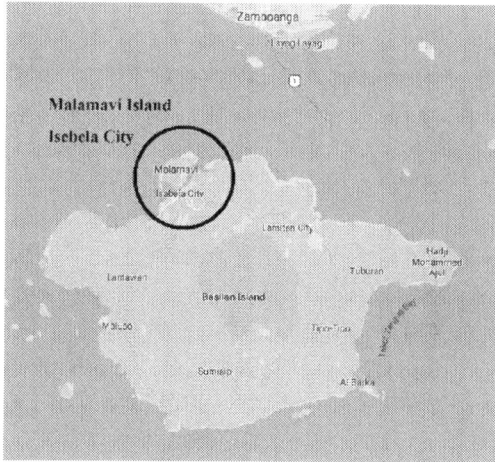

ISABEIA CITY, BASILAN ISLAND,MINDANAO

Chapter 12

Isabela City

The group departed the Labason pier just as dawn was breaking. A slight mist rose from the calm waters of Patauag Bay. Sails were raised as soon as the Dragon

Lady left the confines of the bay and the Murcielagos and Bayangan Islands.

Once in the Sulu Sea, a stiff wind and corresponding wave action was encountered that propelled the Dragon Lady swiftly toward its destination. It was after three in the afternoon when Al spotted land.

"I think I have Isabela City in view, where is the pier?" Al asked Earl, who was plotting their course.

"According to the navigational chart, the city is on Basilan Island. That's the big one just south of the smaller one. We have to enter a channel that separates the two. If we keep on our present heading it should take us to the channel," answered Earl.

"Okay, once we get closer, we'll lower our sails and go on motor," instructed Al.

Once the white sands of the northern shore of the small island of Malamavi came into view, the sails were lowered and the crew motored around the western side of the island, and entered the Isabela Channel. On their left, the white sandy beach and coconut palms of the northern side of the Malamavi Island, changed to mangrove swamps and forest foliage. As they approached the Isabela City pier, there were shacks on stilts on both sides of the channel.

"Look at all those houses that are literally built over the water," remarked Earl,

"Reminds me of some of the houses along the bayous of Louisiana," observed Al.

"Or what we've seen in Vietnam's Mekong River delta," added Jeff.

"And look at that mosque we're passing," remarked Dave, pointing to a while box-like structure, with the ubiquitous minaret and onion shaped dome; the characteristic of Muslim architecture the world over.

"It's not surprising since we're in Muslim country," remarked Earl.

"You say that, but Isabela is predominately Roman Catholic, although the rest of the island is Muslim," said Dave.

The group tied off at the Isabela City pier, next to the ferry landing, and down from the Malamavi Island shuttle. They decided to eat at the ferry terminal's café, and spend the night on board. At the café, they engaged the proprietor in conversation.

"What's with all these huts on stilts we saw as we entered the channel?" Al questioned.

"Ha, they are the Badjaos people. We called them sea gypsies, because they are a kind of nomads of the sea, moving from one place to another, to seek their living from the sea."

"Okay, next question, what's the name of the box-like, white building which we assume to be a mosque?"

"That is the Kaum Purnah Mosque, the oldest mosque on the island of Basilan."

"Are there any motels nearby, where we can stay for a couple of days?" Jeff asked.

"Motels?" questioned the proprietor.

"You know, hotels," Jeff answered.

"Well there's the Channel Hotel, just down from the ferry landing. It's not much to look at, but it is clean. Of course, you can get all sorts of information at the tourist office inside the terminal building. It's located next to Immigration and Customs, where you'll have to check in tomorrow and register your boat."

The group spent a restless night on board the Dragon Lady. In the morning, the four ate breakfast at the ferry terminal's cafe. After breakfast, they walked to the Customs and Immigration office located on the main floor of the ferry terminal building. After registering and paying the berthing fee, Al asked the custom official: "will our boat be safe at the pier?"

"No problem; there is twenty-four-hour surveillance at the pier. That's what a portion of the berthing fee pays for," the Inspector answered.

"How about personal safety?" Dave asked.

"Well that depends," the Inspector answered.

"Okay, I'll bite; depends on what?" Dave replied.

"Yes, well we do have the remnants of Abu Sayyaf; a Moro terrorist group. Most of their activity has been farther south, although there was some kidnapping in Isabela last year. As long as you stay in groups, and confine your visit to populated areas you shouldn't have any problem."

"I think the operative word is 'shouldn't'," Earl remarked.

"Just don't go on your own to isolated spots," the Inspector cautioned.

"How about the beaches?" Jeff asked.

"Most of our famous beaches have their own security, so there shouldn't be any problem," the Inspector answered.

"There goes that shouldn't again," remarked Earl.

"Well, no one can guarantee your personal safety. Manila and Luzon have had problems as well, but if you use common sense, and be a little more vigilant than you might be if you were in the United States, you won't have a problem. If you want to do some sightseeing, and there are a lot of beautiful and interesting places to see, we suggest you take a commercial tour, or hire a reputable guide."

"How does one find a reputable guide?" Dave asked.

"Check next door with the tourist agency. They carry a list of reputable guides as well as commercial tour companies."

"Thanks a lot. You've been most helpful," Al said.

"You're welcome, enjoy your visit. One last caution I need to add. We do have a lot of bars which offer nighttime entertainment. Some of the bargirls are willing to offer their own services. If you wish to partake, take them to your hotel; do not go to their home. You don't know who might be there to assist in relieving you of your money and maybe your life."

"Right, 'who knows what evil lurks in the heart of men'," added Jeff.

"What?" a puzzled Inspector asked.

"It's from an old, and I mean very old, radio program back in the States, named The Shadow," Jeff laughed.

"Roger that," exclaimed Earl, "A really old, old radio show."

On that note of attempted humor, the group exited the Customs and Immigration Office and made their way next door, to the Isabella City Tourist Agency, where they reviewed brochures on what to do and where to stay. They found the picking slim: The Farmland Resort outside of the port area, the Alano White Beach Resort on the northern side of Malamavi Island, and the Casa Rosario on Valderosa Street, in the port area. They opted for the Channel Hotel, since it was nearest to where their boat was berthed, and thus, they could keep the boat under some sort of observation. Next on their agenda was to get information on city tours, especially ones that included churches. The receptionist at the counter picked out a city tour brochure. It included a drive around the city, with stops at the Santa Isabel Cathedral, the Plaza and Kalun Park, Calvario Peak, Bulingan Falls and Calugusan Beach.

"What d'ya say guys," Al asked.

"I vote for the City Tour, and then if we see something that spikes our interest, we can return there via a taxi, tomorrow," suggested Jeff.

"I think Jeff makes a good point," added Dave. "After all, we're supposed to be tourists."

"Okay, I'll make it unanimous," Earl added.

Al turned to the clerk, "Can you make reservations for us for the City Tour, and find out where and when we can pick it up?"

"I'll be glad to make reservations; for how many, in whose name and when?"

"For four, and this morning if that's possible," Al answered. "And use my name." Al handed her his passport.

The clerk phoned the tour company where she engaged in conversation in the local language. Turning to Al she said, "they will pick you up in front of the terminal building at nine-thirty, if that is all right?"

Al looked at the large round clock over the travel counter. "Let's see, it's just a little past eight-thirty." Then turning to the others, he asked, "What do you say, can we be ready by nine-thirty?"

"I don't see why not, although I thought we wanted to see if we can get rooms at the Channel Hotel," Jeff said.

On overhearing the conversation, the clerk offered to make reservations for them at the hotel.

"That will be great," Al said.

Then a short conversation with the tour company pursued. "The tour bus will pick you up in front of the hotel if you'd prefer," she announced.

"How far is the hotel from here?" Al asked.

"Oh, it is a short walk, or you can take a tricycle," the clerk answered.

"Let's do it," said Jeff. "We won't have to get all our stuff from the boat; just what we'll need for the tour."

"That will be great," Al said to the clerk.

The clerk put the tour company on hold, and then called the hotel, then back to Al, "how many rooms?"

Al addressed the group, "how about two rooms with twin beds?"

All consented.

The clerk reported that to the hotel clerk, and then back to the group. "They have reserved two connecting, twin bed rooms for you."

"That's great!" Al exclaimed.

Then the clerk talked to the tour company and arranged for the group to be picked up in front of the Channel Hotel.

They were able to get a motorized trike in front of the ferry building, which returned them to their boat and waited while they collected what little gear they wanted on the tour, and then transported them to the Channel Hotel.

The four-storied Channel Hotel was faded-beige in color, and showing its age. The lobby was small, the dark carpet was worn but clean. Past the lobby was a small restaurant and bar. Two elevators separated by a potted palm, were located across from the reception desk. Placed between the reception desk and the elevators, was a small sitting area, consisting of a sofa and three easy chairs located around a rectangular coffee table.

The receptionist was a young, petite female whose straight black hair fell to her shoulders, and who wore a multicolored blouse and yellow skirt. She greeted them with a smile.

"Welcome to the Channel Hotel. You are the four Americans from the Tourist Agency, yes?"

"Yes, how could you tell?" Earl asked, a large grin lighting his face.

"Well there are four of you, and you are foreigners, so you must be the ones who the tourist agency just called about," she laughed.

"Elementary my dear Watson," Jeff remarked.

"Aw, I thought it was our good looks," remarked Earl.

"Well, yes, good looking foreigners," the receptionist laughed.

"Forget those two clowns," Al said to the receptionist. "Yes, we are the Americans and I believe you have reservations for us."

"Yes, we have two adjoining, rooms on the third floor overlooking the channel. But you first need to register," she said, giving each of them a registration card.

Once the registration formality was over, and everyone received a key to their rooms, the group proceeded to the elevator, and to the third floor for their assigned rooms.

"Well they're not the Taj Mahal, but they seem to be clean," Al said.

"And it does have a nice view of the channel, and whatever's the name of the island across the channel," added Dave.

"I like the idea of adjoining rooms," Jeff said, opening the door to the adjoining room, making a casual inspection.

"Right, we can alternate party rooms," added Earl.

"Well what say we go down to the lobby and wait for our tour bus," Al said.

"Good idea," agreed Jeff.

The wait wasn't long. A white passenger van with blue lettering denoting Basilian Tours, pulled up in front of the hotel. A Filipino, about five-feet in height, wearing a blue guayabera and white-slacks, entered the lobby and walked up to the group sitting around the lobby's coffee table.

"*Señor* Cooperman?" he asked.

"Yes, I'm Allen Cooperman," Al rose, and answered.

"*Bueno dias*, I'm Jorge Garcia with Basilian Tours," the Filipino answered. "I'll be your tour guide today. Are you ready to leave?"

"Yes, lead the way," Al answered.

"Is it just us taking the tour," Al asked, seeing a six-passenger van.

"*Si,* we don't have many requests for English speaking tours, so it is just you four," Jorge answered.

"That's great!" exclaimed Jeff. "We've got the van all to ourselves."

"Si, I am at your disposal," Jorge said, holding the passenger door open.

Earl and Jeff climbed in first and took the second row of seats, allowing Dave and Al the first row behind the driver.

"Our first stop will be downtown Isabella City via J.J. Alano Street. We will visit the city plaza, Rizal park and the Santa Isabel Cathedral."

"Okay, who was J.J. Alano on whose street we'll be driving?" asked Earl.

"Juan Alano was the Congressman who was responsible for raising the Island of Basilan to a provincial status," answered Jorge. "Before that we were part of Zamboanga Peninsula Region across the Basilan Straits."

"Okay, with that little piece of trivia let's be on our way," said Al.

Jorge pulled away from the Channel Hotel and drove through the crowded wharf area flanked by its fish markets and peddlers selling their wares from make-do stalls with protruding awnings, and onto the J.J. Alano street, to compete with the myriad of small trucks and motorized trikes.   The first stop was the capital building where Jorge began his narration.

"The Zamboanga Peninsula and the Island of Basilan were part of the same providence, but in 1948 they became separated thanks to Congressman Juan Alano. Because Isabela was predominately Roman Catholic a special plebiscite was held in which the people of Isabela voted to remain under the Zamboanga Peninsula Administrative Region while the rest of Basilan, which is mostly Muslim, chose to be under the Autonomous Region in Muslim Mindanao. When it comes to local politics Isabela and Basilan are one, but when it comes to Regional politics, they each go their separate ways. The capital building occupies the site of a fort which was destroyed by Japanese bombs during World War Two. Notice the building's arched windows, doorways and the two wings that converge on a central rotunda. They take on an Arabian flair. The building was designed to commemorate both our Roman Catholic and Muslim heritage." Jorge then drove to the City Plaza and Rizal Park and parked outside the plaza. Then he disembarked from the van and opened the double passenger doors. "We'll take about thirty minutes here to allow you to stretch your legs, and use the facilities and enjoy the parks," he announced.

The group alighted the van and gathered around Jorge to listen to his expounding on the two connecting parks. "You see the Plaza and the Rizal Park border on each other. We think of them as the same. The Plaza is the center of community life, but Razal Park with its tall obelisk, honors one of our greatest heroes, José Razal. He was a writer who advocated political reforms for the Filipinos when we were a Spanish Colony. He was executed by the Spanish because they believed his writings inspired rebellion."

After walking around the plaza and viewing the giant obelisk with its life-size statue of José Razal, the group walked across the street to tour the art deco styled Saint Isabel Cathedral. The entrance to the cathedral was under a tall modernist steeple. Next to it was the large statue of the patron saint of Isabela City, Saint Isabela of Portugal; a red cloak was draped around her shoulders, a crown upon her head, and the word 'peace' was placed above her.

Inside the cathedral, the ceiling was high, the vestibule and nave were flanked on each side by tall white columns and floor to ceiling, stained glass windows. In the middle of the asps stood a large altar. Raised high behind the altar, as if floating on a cloud, was a modernist depiction of a white-robed Christ with his arms extended, flanked by brown robed apostles, six on each side. On the sides of the chancel stood confessional booths.

A tall, slim priest met the group. "Welcome to the Cathedral of Saint Isabel of Portugal. I am Father Alfonso Gonzales and I will be your guide this morning. The Cathedral was established as the Territorial Prelature of Isabela from the Metropolitan Archdiocese of Zamboanga in 1963. We took the name of the patron saint of the City of Isabela, as our own. Saint Isabella was born in 1271 in Portugal. She married King Denis of Portugal. Isabella established orphanages, institutions for the sick, housing for the homeless and a convent for nuns. She is depicted with roses. Legend has it that one time she hid bread in her apron to feed the poor so that her husband, the King who was not supportive of her work with the destitute, would not know what she was doing. He confronted her about her apron's contents and when she opened her apron the bread had miraculously turned to roses. She died in 1336 and was canonized in 1625, almost 300 years later." With that brief introduction the Priest led the group through the church. At the end of the tour he asked if there were any questions.

"Yes, Father, I have one," Dave Hollingsworth spoke up. "I am a Roman Catholic and in need of confession. My companions and I have been sailing around the Philippines for the last couple of weeks and I have not had the opportunity to partake in the sacrament of contrition."

The Priest's eyes fell on Dave, scrutinizing him. Then he replied "the Sacrament of Reconciliation is offered every day from nine in the morning until six in the evening. I'll be glad to hear your confession today if you wish."

"How about tomorrow," Dave answered. "Right now, I'm in the middle of a tour, but I can return tomorrow if that is okay."

"Tomorrow will be fine, let's say at 10 a.m.," the Priest answered. "But do not put off the act. It is necessary to cleanse your soul and seek forgiveness."

"Yes Father, I'll be here tomorrow at ten," Dave answered.

Next stop was at the top of the 1300-foot Calvanio Peak, which provided a great panoramic view of Isabela City and its surrounding environs. Then on to Bulingan Falls in neighboring Lamitan City. Its water cascaded over, and between boulders feeding the river used by the locals as a favorite swimming hole. The last stop was Calugusan Beach, not far from the Bulingan Falls. This stretch of beach was strewn with broken shells and coral, and as Jorge explained, "this beach is used by locals. It is not as nice, or as scenic. or as pristine as White Beach on Malamawi Island, but it's free. To get to the beaches on Malamawi you need to first take a boat to the island and then a taxi trike to the opposite side. Public buses go to this beach, and Sumagdang Beach in Isabela."

Jorge dropped the four off at their hotel, and they all congregated in Al and Dave's room. What's this about confession?" Earl asked Dave.

"It seems that I scored on the first try," Dave answered. "Father Gonzales is my contact in Mindanao. My 'In need of confession and the sacrament of contrition', and his reply, 'the sacrament of reconciliation is necessary to cleanse your soul to seek forgiveness', and not today but tomorrow at ten o'clock, are all identification codes. I'll meet with him tomorrow and supposedly learn more while in the confessional booth."

"Man, the plot gets thicker and thicker," remarked Jeff.

"You got that right, old buddy," exclaimed Earl. "What's next?"

"What's next is dinner," replied Al. "Where are we going?"

"I don't know, maybe we could try one of the restaurants along the wharf," Dave suggested. "It seems to me that we passed two or three on our way here."

"I'm for that," Al replied. "At the same time, we can check our boat, and get what we need for our stay while we're at the hotel.

So, with the decision made, the four-strolled back along the waterfront toward the wharf. They passed bancas, some docked, with their owners peddling their goods dockside, while others vied for space to unload their wares. Opposite the water were stalls with all sorts of merchandise, from electronic equipment to clothes. The area took on a carnival-like atmosphere as bargain hunters crowded the pavement, hustling from stall to stall. The four ate at a cafe located on the ground floor in a warehouse which opened to the street across from the channel. After eating they continued their way to the wharf and the Dagon Lady. Upon showing their docking fee receipt to the blue-uniformed guard, they were allowed onto to their boat, where they packed a couple of duffle bags with changes of clothes, underwear and toilet kits, and caught a tricycle taxi to the Channel Hotel. After a couple of beers in the hotel's restaurant, they agreed to meet in the morning for breakfast. Then a restless night as each anticipated the morrow.

TIPP TIPO, BASILAN ISLAND, MINDANAO

Chapter 13

The Meeting

The three gathered around the motorized trike as Dave got into its sidecar.

"Still don't like it, but I know you are doing the right thing," remarked Al. "Just know we're here if you need us."

"Hey, don't be so glum, I'm not going to be thrown to the lions," laughed Dave.

"I'm not so sure about that," remarked Jeff.

Dave responded: "Well I hope not anyway. I don't know when I'll be back. I'll try to maintain some sort of communications with Fr. Mendoza."

"I assume he'll be our point man if we want to find out anything," said Earl.

"I'll mention it to the good Father," answered Dave. "In the meantime, tryout the nightlife."

"Nightlife? They probably roll up the sidewalks as soon as the sun goes down," laughed Earl.

"Actually, we should have tried it out yesterday while we were cooling our heels," laughed Dave. "Well so much for the small talk, I've got a date with the lions. Wish me well."

"That goes without saying," replied Al, slapping Dave on the back.

"I've got an uneasy feeling about this," remarked Jeff as the three watched the trike set out down the sandy path bearing their compatriot to his rendezvous.

"I hear you Jeff but I think we have to chalk it up to the unknown," said Al. "No different from when we were in Nam. I'm sure we all had that feeling before we embarked upon any type of mission; at least I know I had."

"Yeah, guess you're right," a subdued Jeff answered.

"I kinda liked Dave's suggestion," said Earl. "I think we should sample some of the night life."

"Well we do need to do something or this waiting will drive us nuts," said Al. "Let's call a taxi and go into town. We can grab a bite to eat and check out some of the bars and then decide what we want to do. We might even drop in on Father Mendoza just to let him know that we are still around."

"Good idea, said Jeff. "We can make sure he has the telephone number to the pier. Give him Senor Amparo's name as our contract. I assume he'll answer the phone."

"That will be fine except we don't speak Spanish and I don't think he speaks English," observed Earl.

"Probably not, but I'm sure that Farther Mendoza can give him a telephone number and he can write it down and give it to us. Numbers in Spanish and English are the same," observed Jeff.

"Good plan," said Al. "Let's call a taxi."

*   *   *   *   *

The motorized tricycle let Dave off in front of the Guardian Angel Ministries' chapel. Dave wasn't sure if he should enter the chapel or go to the mission building behind it. He elected the chapel but upon entering he didn't see anyone so he walked to the mission building and inquired about the whereabouts of Father Mendoza and was directed to his office. It was located in the rear of the building behind a large meeting room and storage area. The door to the office was open and Dave observed Fr. Mendoza engaged in conversation with a tall, slim, bearded man wearing a black skullcap with a zigzag design between white balls.

Dave knocked on the door frame causing both Fr. Mendoza and his guest to turn in his direction.

"Mister Hollingworth, come in. We were just talking about you," Fr. Mendoza greeted.

Dave entered and was introduced to Abdul Mutaal who greeted him with the customary 'As-salamu Alsikum (may peace be with you) to which Dave replied 'Wa alaikum assalaam (and peace be with you). Then Fr. Mendoza informed Dave that Abdul would be his escort. The formalities of greetings over, Abdul suggested that they be on their way,

The mode of transportation was the motorcycle with Dave ridding behind Abdul. They left the confines of the town and entered a coconut and palm tree forest. After a short ride into the interior Abdul stopped the motorcycle and tied a neckerchief over Dave's eyes. Then the travel continued with Abdul making a lot of turns to completely disorient a blinded Dave. It was obvious that they were on some sort of loosely packed dirt road because at times the motorcycle would slide and its driver would accelerate to straighten the vehicle, kicking up a lot of sand and dust at the same time.

Finally, the motorcycle came to a stop and both Dave and his escort dismounted and the neckerchief was removed. Dave looked around. There was a small house, actually more of a hut, in the middle of nowhere, surrounded by sand and palm trees. He couldn't see any sort of path leading to or from the house. Abdul opened the door and ushered Dave inside. The furnishing was meager, one room, a table and five or six folding chairs. They were the first. Abdul raised the screenless windows admitting a cool breeze.

"Have a seat, it shouldn't be too long before the rest get here," he remarked.

"How many are you expecting?" Dave asked.

"I don't know, I was just told to bring you here."

"Is it possible to go to the bathroom? The ride over took a toll on my bladder," Dave asked.

"I don't see why not. I'll show you the way."

Abdul opened the door and led Dave to an outhouse located behind the house. Dave, trying to get some fix on his location while remaining inconspicuous, glanced past the outhouse and through the rows of palm trees. He saw what he believed to be a body of water; maybe the bay? He also glanced to the sky and the sun to take note from which cardinal point the body of water was from the hut. At best he could tell the water was south which meant that the hut was north from the water. He also heard what he believed was the breaking of waves over rocks.

"I'll wait for you to finish," Abdul said.

"That's all right, I can find my way back."

"I'll wait," was the brief reply.

"Suit yourself," Dave replied, entering the outhouse.

Upon exiting the outhouse Dave thought he heard the sound of a motor coming from the direction he believed was the bay. Nothing was said as he and his escort retuned to the confines of the shelter. However, Dave took a seat near the window that opened to the rear of the hut so as to provide a view of that area in case it was an outboard motor he heard and the people he was to meet were on board. His assumption proved to be correct. He saw four men appear from behind the outhouse and make their way toward the front of the hut. Upon entering, Abdul and Dave rose and Abdul greeted the group. Then the group turned and one of the men greeted Dave with the customary Muslim greeting. Then he suggested that they all sit around the table which all but Abdul did. He sat in a chair next to the door.

"You wanted to meet?" the man who suggested the seating arrangement asked.

"Who do I have the honor of addressing?" Dave asked whom he assumed was the leader of the group.

"We are the leaders of the Moro National Liberation Front that is all you need to know," was the curt reply.

"I'm not sure I agree," Dave answered looking directly in the eyes of the leader. I have important matters which I am authorized to discuss but only with Mohamed ben Idom."

"And who are you? How do we know you are who you say you are?" the spokesman countered.

"My name is David Hollingsworth and I'm with the United States Embassy. I have my Identification in my wallet in my back pocket. Shall I show it to you?"

"By all means, we'd like to see it."

Dave produced his wallet from his back pocket and took out his identification card. It was examined by the spokesman and then by each of the other members of the group.

"I recognize one of the members of your group although I don't remember his name. He can vouch for me. My colleagues and I assisted him when his boat was disabled off Palawan Island." Dave pointed to one in the group.

"Yes, how kind of you to remember," the one who Dave recognized, said. Then addressing the rest of the group, he related how he was towed to Sipalay. "I am in their debt."

"Thank you for assisting our friend, Abdul Rahman ben Hasan. I am satisfied that you are who you say you are. I am Mohamed ben Idom," the spokesman of the group identified himself. "Now as to the important matter you wished to discuss. We have been informed through our sources that you are bringing a proposal from President Aquino."

"Yes. It is a short message but long in its significance. She is sympathetic to your desire for a separate country for the Moro people. She would also like to end the bloodshed which has endured all too long between the Filipino people. She believes that not just the Moro of Mindanao, but the predominate Muslim regions of Mindanao should have their own government but not an independent nation. She cannot relinquish her sovereignty over any part of her country but she can recognize the right of the Muslim people to form some sort of self-governance. She is willing to support creating an autonomous region for the Muslims on Mindanao. Obviously, she cannot do this on her own. She needs an act of the Philippine Congress. What she proposes is that an armistice be declared between the MNLF and the Philippine Government to end all this needless slaughter of the nation's people, and representatives of the government and the MNLF meet to work out the framework that can become the basis of a self-governing region."

"They're giving us nothing!" One in the group exclaimed with obvious rage. Do they take us for idiots? What have we been fighting for? Our own country, independent from the bastards in Manila, that's what."

"Allow me, if I may to address that issue," Dave spoke up. "President Aquino is limited to what she can do. She's going out on a limb in proposing a sort of self-rule. She'd probably be impeached if she agreed to complete independence. We Americans have a saying, a half a loaf is better than no loaf."

"Ha, you Americans fought a war for complete independence just as we have been doing. You didn't accept a half a loaf, as you so eloquently put it," the dissenter sarcastically replied.

"I apologize, I have no right to interject my thoughts into the discussion," Dave replied. "My role is strictly as a messenger. It just happened that I and my friends were in Baggio just two weeks ago and saw firsthand the slaughter of so many innocent men, women and children; and for what? What did it accomplish?"

"My friend Hashim Salamat has a point," Mohamed ben Idom scornfully interjected. "We abhor killing but it was such killing, as tragic as it seems, that brought Aquino to make the concession she is making. Do you think that if we approached her on our hands and knees and said 'pretty please grant our people freedom she would eagerly agree? Ha, she'd have us tossed in the dungeon as lunatics and continue to treat us as second-class citizens. No, don't lecture us on the use of force as a means to our ends. The Government has no qualms in turning their troops loose on our people to plunder, slaughter and rape."

"Again, I apologize. I didn't mean to judge you just to point out that she really is sincere but has no more room to negotiate. She's met with a lot of opposition already. Not just from the opposition party but from her own party as well. I don't think you're going to get a better deal. When I met with her, she emphasized that she can do no more and I believe her. She wants to put all the killing and maiming behind us and move forward."

"I think she is playing us for fools. She wants us to sit down with her government and do what? You already said she can't do anything without her congress approval. I see this is nothing more than a stalling tactic while her military regroups. We have them on the ropes now and she knows it!" Hashim Salamat exclaimed.

"We have no authority to make any decision either. We've heard the government's position, now we must sit down with our council and they will deliberate her proposal. It will not be easy. You can see that the feelings are very high. Abdul will take you back and you will be contacted when a decision is reached," Mohamed ben Idom said. Then he turned to Abdul and instructed him accordingly.

Once outside the meeting house Abdul motioned Dave to mount the motorcycle and then Abdul blindfolded him. Once again, the shifting and sliding until the motorcycle emerged from the sand and Dave felt the firmness of the tarmac beneath him. The blindfold was untied when they reached the outskirts of Tipo Tipo, and then he was taken to the Guardian Angel Ministries Chapel where he was unceremoniously left. Dave looked for Father Mendoza but was advised that he was away. Upon hearing that, Dave hailed a taxi and returned to the pier where he was excitedly greeted by his companions. Later, on board the Dragon Lady and eating sandwiches and drinking their favorite San Miguel Beer, the conversation took on a somber note.

"You don't know how glad we are to see you back, ole buddy!" exclaimed Al.

"Yeah and in one piece," added Earl.

"Everything turn out all right?" asked Jeff.

"First of all, you don't know how glad I am to be back, and as Earl so apply put it, in one piece. As to Jeff's question, I don't know. I delivered my message and it was not enthusiastically received. You might say, hostilely received. I know there was one person who'd be more than happy to shoot the messenger," Dave reported.

"What next?" asked Al.

"I was told that the leaders were in no position to speak for their followers. I gathered that there is some sort of governing body. Mohamed ben Idom, who I took to be the leader of the group told me that President Aquino's offer will have to be put before the council but he didn't elaborate. There was another, a Hashim Salamat, who I take, holds some sort of leadership position; I already know what his view is; hang the messenger and get back to what they do best: intimidate by killing and maiming until the government gives in to their demands for full independence. He actually compared their fight to our fight for independence, and he sees President Aquino's proposal as a sign of weakness."

"Is it?" asked Jeff.

"I don't think so. When I was briefed, and I was personally briefed by President Aquino herself, full independence is impossible. The Army wouldn't stand for it. They have a lot of deaths and injuries invested in their fight to put down the insurrection, as they call it. Also, the Congress wouldn't stand for it. As she told me, if she even proposed such an idea, the government would fall at a minimum and she'd probably be impeached and perhaps even tried as a traitor. I don't think she was over exaggerating. You can't imagine the intensity of the emotions. It's not an understatement to say, they run high."

"Okay, as I asked before, what next?" asked Al.

"I was told I'd be contacted; I assume through Father Mendoza. I tried to talk to him but he wasn't available. I think tomorrow I should give him a call and maybe meet with him and inform him of the outcome of my meeting with the MNLF," Dave answered.

"Okay, I think we should all go into town, maybe have lunch at the market place. Then depending on the outcome of your meeting with Fr. Mendoza, come back and plot our strategy," Al said.

"Plot our strategy?" quizzed Dave. "I don't want to get you more involved than you are already," replied Dave.

"Remember, one for all and all for one," quoted Earl.

"Yeah, the three musketeers," added Jeff.

317

"Well let's see what tomorrow brings. I must confess, I'd feel a little better with some backup," Dave said.

"Backup is what you'll get," added Jeff to the conversation.

*   *   *   *   *

Morning came early for the four. There was a light fog rising from the bay with no breeze to dissipate it. The four ate on top gazing at the palm and coconut trees; translucent images that faded into oblivion.

"It's going to be a hot one," observed Jeff.

"Sure, feels that way," added Earl.

"It's too early for the marina to open," observed Al.

"Do we need anything?" asked Dave.

"No, not really," replied Al. "I just thought that you might like to ask Senor Amparo to take the telephone number down if anyone should call."

"Good idea," replied Dave. "I thought I'd also call Fr. Mendoza to see what time he was available to hear my confession."

"That's good, but notwithstanding, I think we should still go into town; help us relieve some of the tension in waiting," Al replied.

The fog lifted, Dave talked to Senor Amparo, the telephone call was made to Fr. Mendoza who stated that confession was available all day, and now the four made their way to the Guardian Angel Chapel via the motorized taxi. They entered the chapel where they found Fr. Mendoza at the altar. He and Dave entered the confessional booth where Dave related his take on the meeting with the leaders of the Moro National Liberation Front.

"Thank you for your information," Fr. Mendoza stated. "We now must leave it in God's hands."

"Yes Father, I'm assuming that the MNLF will use your office to contact me. You have the telephone number where we can be reached and Senor Amparo, the proprietor of the Marina, has agreed to take any messages for us in our absence."

"Very well my son, I will pray for your success and your safety. Go with God."

With that blessing, the four left the chapel and walked to the market place where they once again occupied an outside table and chairs, ordered San Miguel beer and pork sandwiches.

"Now it's waiting time," commented Al. "Somehow, I feel we should be doing something."

"I was thinking of that," said Dave. "The safehouse was off the bay, at least I assume it was the bay. I got a glimpse of water and heard what I took to be an outboard motor. I also heard what I thought was surf breaking over rock which makes me think that there is some kind of reef action. Which means that there may be some sort of break in the reefs to allow access for a motorboat. The direction of the water was about south of the safehouse. I was thinking it might be a good idea to sail around this side of the island and see if we can find anything resembling reefs and a possible break through them. I'd like to find that safehouse before I meet there again, assuming that will be the place where we will be meeting."

"We can do that, it will beat just waiting," commented Al. "However, what if you get a call in the meantime. Will there be enough time?"

"Let's face it, there is no way they are going to meet and make a decision in a couple of days. My guess it will be at least a week. I mean there was some really vehement feelings coming out of that meeting. That's the reason I'd like to know the whereabouts of that safehouse, just in case," expressed Dave.

"We'll do it," replied Al.

"How about this afternoon?" asked Earl.

"I think tomorrow would be better," mentioned Jeff. "By the time we get back to the boat and make ready it will be late in the afternoon and we're going to need clear visibility and time to really reconnoiter."

"Yeah, I think Jeff makes a good point," agreed Dave. "We need lots of time to really do a good job. Who knows, maybe we have to spend a couple of days."

"Maybe we should buy a large-scale local map of Tipo Tipo and see if we can find any inlets around the coast," suggested Earl. "The scale of our charts is probably too small to help us."

"Good idea," replied Al. "Do you think Senor Amparo would have them?"

"He might, however, if he doesn't then we lose a lot of time. Let's see what we might find here in town," Earl replied.

"Dave, you're our language expert, why not go inside and ask the proprietor if he knows of a place where we can buy a large-scale map of the area," instructed Al.

"Will do," Dave answered. Then he rose from their table and went inside. It wasn't long before Dave joined his comrades at their table. "No sweat, there's a book and stationery shop two blocks from here. They sell all sorts of maps. The proprietor says we should have no problem in finding what we want. Of course, they'll be in Spanish."

"That shouldn't be a problem, you can read Spanish, can't you?" Jeff asked Dave.

"Sure, I assume the marking shouldn't be too technical. If I see something I'm not sure of I'll ask Senor Amparo. If fact, I bet he knows these waters with not having to resort to any chart."

321

The four left their table and walked the two or so blocks where they found the book and stationery store. They did have large-scale navigational charts of Basilan and other islands as well. Basilan had fringing reefs which were plainly marked, that encircled three quarters of the eastern and southern coast. After the chart was purchased the four hailed a taxi and returned to their boat. They huddled around the chart table with the navigational map of Basilan Island.

"Okay, here is Tipo Tipo, and here is José Razal Road. It runs pretty much east and west and the side streets intersect perpendicular to it," Earl said pointing at the main street of Tipo Tipo. "And here is the Guarding Angel Ministries' Chapel." Then turning to Dave, he continued, "you said you traveled down this road until you entered the palm trees, that is where you were blindfolded, right?"

"Yes, that's right, then my escort started traveling in circles. I don't know if he was missing palm trees or just trying to disorient me; maybe a little bit of both. But on the way back he didn't take that precaution. Although I was blindfolded and there was some slipping and sliding, it was more of a feeling of going against the sand. I didn't really get the feeling of riding in circles."

Earl reached for a straightedge and drew a line from the end of the street all the way to Tauket Tangug Bay. It ran through a copra plantation. Then he drew a wide circle around the point where his line intersected the bay. "I'd say, here is where we make our search."

"Damn Sherlock, that's pretty good!" exclaimed Jeff.

"Elementary, my dear Watson," Earl replied.

"That is pretty good," agreed Al. "But, look at those reefs," pointing to the fringing reefs that ran parallel to the shore." "How do we get inside those?"

"There must be a way," commented Dave. "The motorboat had no trouble. Let's take the chart and talk to Senor Amparo. Maybe he can give us a clue on how to get inside these reefs."

"Great idea!" exclaimed Earl.

The four entered the Marina and Dave showed Senor Amparo the large-scale navigational chart and pointing to the area where the copra plantation and the bay intersected, he asked "how do we get in here?"

"You mean with your sailboat? There is no way," Senor Amparo answered.

"Not with our sailboat, but say a motorboat," Dave explained. "We thought that inside the reef will be good fishing."

Senor Amparo face lit up. "Oh yes, there is good fishing. The snapper come for the little fish that feed off the algae on the reef. My sons and I have had a fine

feast off the catch around the reef. Now, as how to get there, see this island across from Al-Barka, it is Kauluan Island, and the narrow strait that separates it from the mainland, that strait flows between the reef and the coast. It's like the back door. The reef along this

323

part of the coast ends at the island." Senor Amparo said pointing to the chart. "You need to enter the strait from the west, here." He slid his finger from west to east along the strait. Great fishing. There is a public boat ramp and fishing pier here," Senor Amparo continued, pointing to an area across from the island."

"Is there room for our boat at the fishing pier?" Al asked Dave who relayed the question to Senor Amparo.

"Oh no, the strait is too narrow for your boat, explained Senor Amparo. "If you want to take your boat, you'd have to go around the island farther down the coast where there is a public pier just like this one. You could berth there and rent a motor boat."

"Could we anchor to the west of the island and enter the strait with an inflatable boat?" asked Dave.

"Oh yes, that you could do."

"Well thank you very much Senor Amparo, you've been very helpful," said Dave. "We won't take any more of your time."

"You are most welcome, good fishing," replied Senor Amparo.

The next morning the Dragon Lady powered by motor, set out from the Tipo Tipo pier in calm waters, staying as close to shore as was safe given the reef along this part of the Tauket Tangug Bay. Al was at the helm; Earl was with Dave at the bow who was scanning the coast with binoculars looking for anything that might be familiar. Jeff was in the cockpit comparing what was marked on the chart to what he could see along the coast. He turned to Al, and remarked "I don't see anything but dense foliage."

"But when we did a little reconnoitering the day before yesterday, we did make out some coconut palms and white sand although we were too far out to get a real look," commented Al. "That very well could be the spot we're looking for."

"Yeah, your right," replied Jeff. "It was so insignificant I didn't give it much thought."

It wasn't long after that conversation that Earl yelled back at the cockpit, pointing to a wide swath of white sand and coconut palms. "I think we found it."

Al turned to Jeff, "use those proportional dividers and see how far we're from the fishing pier at whatever is the name of that town."

"Will do," Jeff answered. "And the town is Al-Barka. The fishing pier isn't annotated on the chart but there is a larger pier at the southern side of the strait, which I assume is the public pier Senor Amparo mentioned. I'll use that and also make note of the time. We can use that to judge how long it will take us to get from the pier to here."

"Good idea," commented Al.

"It's about 5 kilometers, or a little over 3 miles," Jeff reported, laying the proportional dividers down on the chart table.

"We ought to see the island from here then. Why don't you go forward and take a look?" Al suggested.

Jeff grabbed a pair of binoculars and joined Earl and Dave at the bow.

"Howdy partner, what's up?" Earl greeted.

"We're about three miles from the island that's across from Al-Barka," Jeff replied. "I want to scan forward and see if I can make it out."

"Have at it, good buddy," Earl commented.

"Here, take my place," Dave said, stepping aside to make room for Jeff.

Jeff homed-in on the terrain in front of him, adjusting his focus at the same time.

"Yep, I can just make out the strait that separates the island from the mainland," he reported.

"Let me take a look," Dave said, lifting his binoculars to his eyes and looking in the same direction as Jeff, adjusting his focus at the same time.

"Your right," he said. "I see it too. I'll go back and tell Al."

As the boat continued toward Kauluan Island, the vegetation on the mainland changed once again to jungle foliage fronted by mangroves.

Once at the mouth of the strait, Al put the Dragon Lady's motor into idle. Dave, Earl and Jeff were at the bow examining the strait and the area on both sides.

"I can see the fishing pier," Dave announced. It's actually sticking out from a small inlet."

"Yeah, it's more than a fishing pier," observed Jeff. "There's a small community that's built around its end; probably a fishing village from the looks of it and the small boats that are berthed around it."

"What do you all think?" Al yelled from the cockpit.

Dave and Earl returned to the cockpit and informed him of what they saw. "It looks like Senor Amparo was right when he said it's too narrow for the Dragon Lady," Dave informed. "However, there appears to be s a small area between the island and the reefs that might allow our inflatable. It you look you can see the water cascading into the strait."

"I don't know," commented Al. "It wouldn't take much of rock to puncture its skin."

"I'm not sure we should take the risk," added Earl. "It won't take long to get around the island. We should have no problem anchoring there, or for that matter, the chart shows the larger pier that Senor Amparo mentioned. It's not that far from this pier. We could tie off there."

"I think that's the better course," commented Al. "Let's do that. One of you advise Jeff as to what we're going to do."

"I'll do that," said Dave. "I'll stay with him and keep watch."

Having made that decision, Al increased the throttle and started circumventing the island. It didn't take long. There was a small community on its southern side in the midst of what seemed to be a coconut plantation. At the end of this side of the island and across from it, were two piers parallel to each other extending from the mainland into the bay. Both had ample space to berth the Dragon Lady. The larger of the two seemed to extend way into the foliage where it disappeared from view. Built around the piers was a large community.

Al selected the smaller pier on which to berth the Dragon Lady. Jeff placed bumpers along the side of the boat facing the pier. Al put the motor into idle and let the boat drift alongside the pier. Earl jumped from the bow onto the pier with the bowline in his hand and pulled the bow into the pier. Then he tied it off to one of the pilings. Jeff stepped from the stern onto the pier and tied his end to one of the cleats that were strategically spaced along the pier.

Al and Dave joined Earl and Jeff, and spying two men working on one of the other boats berthed alongside the pier, walked to them and greeted them in Spanish.

"Good day, Señores, how are you?"

Both of them stopped what they were doing and looked toward the group. "Fine, thank you."

"We were told there is good fishing inside the reef," Dave said to them.

"Oh yes, snapper, mackerel and some grouper. They feed off the little fish, plankton, algae and seagrass that inhabit the reef. But your boat is too big," was the answer.

"We have an inflatable," Dave replied.

"That is good,"

"What is the best way to catch the fish?" Dave asked.

"Bottom fishing is the only way," one of the workmen answered. "I use shrimp for bait. All fish like shrimp."

"Is there a place that sells bait around here?" Dave asked.

"Oh yes, Al-Baka bait and tackle store at the end of the pier,"

"How about our boat, is it alright to leave it here?"

"Oh yes, no one will bother it."

"Thank you, you have been most helpful," replied Dave.

"You are welcome, good fishing,"

Dave relayed his information to the others.

"Fishing will be a good cover," said Al. "I'll bring a couple of our rod and reels out and Dave you're our linguist, why don't you buy us some bait. And Earl you and Jeff get the inflatable into the water."

Those chores tended to, the four climbed into the inflatable. Al and Jeff sat aft with Al manning the outboard motor, Dave and Earl sat forward. The rod and reels were placed lengthwise under the seats and a line to the bait bucket was attached to a cleat allowing the bucket to float aside the inflatable. They moved forward at a slow speed, keeping to the middle of the channel avoiding the sharp edges of the reef. Boys on the shore greeted them with shouts and waves displaying their catch. They passed the inlet and its pier as they reached the outskirts of the town and Kauluan Island. Then Al advanced the throttle a little more to increase its speed. The reef was on their left, and on their right mangroves were tucked in front of the four-foot high shoreline. After about twenty minutes more, the jungle vegetation gave way to coconut palms amid white sand that ended at the shoreline.

"I think we found our coconut plantation," remarked Earl.

"Yeah, your right," commented Dave. "However, there is no way you can get a boat onto the shore."

"I guess you can pull alongside the shore and tie off to one of the coconut trees and then climb up the embankment," remarked Jeff.

"Yeah, but first someone would have to jump four feet onto the embankment," pointed out Earl. "And that's not very likely."

"That may make it a lot easier to find the spot. Let's keep our eyes out for some break in the shoreline. That may be where the safehouse is," instructed Al.

Al put the throttle into neutral and let the inflatable drift. Jeff scanned the trees with binoculars while Al retrieved a rod and reel from where it was stowed under the seats. He laid it on his lap and releasing a little tension on the reel released the hook that was secured to it.

"Might as well see if the fishing is as good as they say it is," announced Al. Then he reached into the bait bucket and pulled out a shrimp and hooked it through its head.

"Good idea. I'll try fishing from this side," Earl said as he pulled a rod and reel forward from under his seat. "Hand me a shrimp," he said to Al.

"Will do," he answered. Once his line was in the water, he reached into the bait bucket and handed a shrimp to Earl who hooked it and then gently cast his line toward the shore.

Both lines were now in the water, weights keeping them near the bottom while a red and white bobber floated on top.

Jeff moved the throttle forward just a little to keep the inflatable moving forward albeit at a very small speed. Both fishermen were trolling while Jeff and Dave continued to look over the coconut palms for any sign of a break or the hut in which Dave had had his rendezvous. It was Dave who spotted it first; what appeared to be a breach in the shoreline.

"Jeff, steer in a little closer to the shore," Dave instructed. "Let's see what's on the other side of that break in the shore. It looks like a good spot in which to beach a boat."

That got everybody's attention and the rest joined Dave in examining a small cove in which the sand came down to the water. The fishing lines were reeled in as Jeff steered for the spot. He was able to propel the inflatable right onto the sandy beach. They all disembarked and walked up the short distance to the coconut palms. There it was just as Dave had described it; an outhouse with a small building in front of it.

"This has gotta be the place!" Dave exclaimed. They walked around the outhouse and in front of the building. The front door was as Dave remembered. It was unlocked and they all entered. The table and chairs were still in place.

"Well we now know where it is, what next?" Jeff asked.

"Good question," answered Dave. "I don't know."

"There's no place we can conceal ourselves; assuming the next meeting will take place here," remarked Al.

"Yeah, the bad guys knew what they were doing when they selected this place," added Earl.

"Actually, if we could get our inflatable up here and, say over by those palms," Jeff pointed to a cluster of palm trees not too far from the hut, "we could use it for a blind and keep watch from over there."

"Jeff makes a good point," Al said. "I was also thinking that if we could launch the inflatable from the mainland into the strait, we wouldn't have to go all the way down to the big island to make our entry. We need to talk to Senior Amparo some more. We were talking about the Dragon Lady and obviously we couldn't get her over the rocks, but we really never discussed the possibility of just using the inflatable."

"Good point, might as well return to the boat," said Dave. "Not anything more we can do here."

The inflatable was returned into the water; Earl holding a line while the rest climbed aboard. Then one final push and Earl joined the rest. Al engaged the motor and they were off. There wasn't any conversation as they made their way back to the Dragon Lady. Once aboard, the inflatable and fishing gear stowed, they motored into the bay before setting sail for the return to Tipo Tipo. They tied off at the Tipo Tipo pier and checked with Senor Amparo; no telephone messages, but they did discover that there were all sorts of places to access the straits from the mainland farther down. The question, how to get the inflatable to the access points? The answer was provided by Senior Amparo. His son owned a small Datsun pickup which was used to resupply the marina, and according to Senior Amparo, would readily agree to transport the inflatable to the nearest access point.

"Let's move out into the bay and enjoy the evening breeze," suggested Al.

That done, sandwiches were made and accompanied by San Miguel, consumed on deck.

The next week was sheer torture as the four waited for the telephone call. They busied themselves by retuning to Al Barka and exploring that town's sights which weren't many. As Earl so aptly put it, "you see one marketplace you've seen them all." While far off shore they checked all their weapons and fired-off rounds, just in case . . .They tried to think of ways they could offer Dave protection but just could not come up with anything. Each morning and night they checked in with Senor Amparo but no telephone messages. Just when Dave was ready to admit failure, the telephone message came. An appointment was made with Farther Mendoza for 11 AM the next day.

chapter 14

Second Meeting

Morning came early. Visibility was good. The plan
was made the evening before 14 implement Jeff's
suggestion of keeping the meeting hut under
surveillance while Dave met with the MNLF leaders.
They hoping of course, that their guess was right and the
meeting would be in the same place as the first meeting.
The mission was no longer Dave's alone but one shared
by all; all for one and one for all.

Using the inflatable, the four motored to the pier
where they met Senior Amparo's son, Luis. The day
before, Dave had arranged for him to transport the
inflatable with Al, Jeff, and Earl to the nearest access
point to the straits between the reef and the mainland, on
the pretext that they wanted to do some early morning
fishing. It was understood that when their fishing was
over, they would call a taxi from the nearby bait shop
and one of the three would return and alert Luis who,
when convenient, would transport everyone back to the
Tipo Tipo pier. At this point Dave left the group and
called for a taxi to take him into the city where he would
have breakfast at their favorite café across from the
market place. There he would wait until it was time for
his meeting with Fr. Mendoza.

The access point was a metal ramp that descended
from a height of about four feet to the water's edge. The
bait shop which Luis described was a dilapidated
wooden shack run by an elderly couple who sold shrimp

that they harvested from around the mangrove that hugged the shore. They used shrimp pots, a wire enclosed rectangular box that allowed shrimp to enter but not exit, which were lowered beneath the water at night and retrieved the next morning. In addition to the shrimp, soft drinks, beer and homemade sandwiches were sold. A payphone was attached to the outside of the store. Before Luis left the site, he purchased shrimp and sandwiches for the three and watched as they pulled their inflatable down the ramp and into the water. Once in the water and with the help of one of the two wooden paddles that were stowed under the seat, the boat was pushed away from the ramp and then the motor was engaged.

The copra plantation materialized from a break in the mangrove trees which lined the shore. It wasn't long after that that the cove and earthen ramp leading to the assumed meeting place was seen. The three were relieved to see that there was no boat berthed, indicating that there was no one there. The plan was for Al and Jeff to disembark and Jeff would confirm that the hut was empty. After making that observation, and assuming it was, Earl was to motor the inflatable back to the point where the mangrove began and the plantation ended. Al and Jeff would meet Earl and tie off the bow and stern of the inflatable to a mangrove tree. The thinking was that the members of the MNLF would be coming from the opposite direction and the inflatable would not be observed.

Jeff stealthily made his way to the hut where a quick inspection of the inside indicated no change to what they had seen the day before. He then walked back to Al where they signaled Earl that everything was fine and proceeded to meet Earl at the prearranged spot.

After the inflatable was secured Earl removed three M16A rifles each one to Al and Jeff. He had a **Beretta M9 holstered around his waist.** Then Al helped him from the inflatable onto the shore. There, he handed both Al and Jeff two clips of cartridges for their rifles and then relieved Al of one of the rifles, after which, they walked back to the hut.

"Okay, leader, what's the plan?" asked Earl to Al.

"I was thinking that we could take cover behind a couple of coconut trees that would give us a direct line of sight to the hut as well as to each other. You on one side. Jeff and I will find a spot on the other side. That way we've got both sides covered."

"Sounds like a plan," replied Earl. "We probably should stakeout our position now to make sure we have the hut covered and at the same time have each of us insight in case we need to signal the other.

"Good idea, let's do it," said Al.

So, the three separated; Al and Jeff to one side and Earl to the other. They found positions about forty yards from the hut which gave them a 45-degree line of sight to the hut and at the same time put them directly across from each other. They were able to conceal themselves by lying prone behind some fallen palm fronds. Then the tedious wait began.

Earl was sitting with his back against the palm tree musing on the events that led them here, of Mel in Taiwan, of Dave and his undertaking, when his thoughts were interrupted by the noise of an engine; the sound of an outboard motor? He rose to signal Al and Jeff. Jeff was standing looking at him and indicated that they had heard it too. Then they positioned themselves behind a palm tree and waited and watched. They heard the cutoff of the motor and soon thereafter they heard voices and then saw six men approach the hut. One was carrying what appeared to be a camcorder, another a machete.

Jeff turned to Al, "I don't think I like the looks of this. What would they be doing with a camcorder?" a puzzled Jeff asked.

"You got me there, maybe to record this historical event. I guess I'm assuming that they will sign some kind of peace accord."

"Maybe so, but why the machete. There's no dense or jungle foliage that they need to penetrate. In fact, I'm thinking of something quite different, like a beheading and if that is the case then whose head? You know these guys have done that before to make a point."

"Well if you're right, then we know whose head if will be. Motion for Earl to come over, let's talk about it."

"Right." Jeff stood up and saw Earl looking over to where they were. He waved to Earl to come to them. Earl acknowledged by moving from his position and making a wide sweep away from the hut, moving from palm tree to palm tree until he reached where Al and Jeff were concealed. They all moved farther back and keeping their voices low, almost to a whisper, they discussed Jeff's fear.

"I know at times my buddy Jeff tends to think that the sky is falling, but what if he is right? We know these clowns have no qualms in beheading. They proved that when they unceremoniously lopped off the heads of a couple of Filipino soldiers a while back."

"Okay, what do we do?" asked Al.

"Maybe we should try to stop Dave and alert him to our fears," suggested Jeff.

"What, and perhaps be responsible for ruining any chance for a ceasefire between the MNLF and the Filipino government," countered Al. "We don't know, there could be a logic and reasonable explanation. Afterall, the machete is used for other things beside beheadings, like, maybe opening a coconut to get to its milk or meat, and you have to admit that there are a lot of coconuts around here. And, as I suggested to Jeff, the camcorder could be for recording the beginning of negotiations leading to a peace agreement."

"Yeah, you're probably right, but what if you're wrong, then what?" question Jeff.

"It seems to me that we should try to get a little closer, say one of us get next to the hut and keep an ear to ground. Nobody knows we're out here," suggested Earl. "I could come from behind and get next to the window and overhear what's going on inside. You guys can watch the outside. I have a pistol in case I need to assist Dave. If you hear a gunshot you guys come running like the provable 'bat out of hell'."

"You know that just might work," said Al. "They haven't any sentries posted. They obviously feel they have nothing to fear. If it appears that all is on the up and up, Earl can beat a hasty retreat and inform us and we'll just fade into the woodwork."

"There's just one thing, none of us can understand Spanish or Arabic, or whatever is the language the Moslems speak," Jeff remarked.

"That's true, but I sure as hell can tell when things aren't going right," replied Earl. "If I hear a lot of commotion, or shouting or whatever, I'll take a peek in the window just to make sure they're not raising glasses in celebration."

"Well I guess that's the best we can do," remarked Jeff.

"Then it's a go," said Al. "Jeff, you take Earl's spot. Earl, I suggest that your first position should be somewhere across from the hut and when you see Dave enter then get as close as you can without exposing yourself."

"Roger that, I'm on my way," Earl said. Then he left Al and Jeff and cautiously made a wide circle away from Al and Jeff, before creeping to the far side of the hut, taking a position behind some palm trees that afforded him observation of the front of the hut and a side window. He noticed a curtain fluttering in the window indicating it was open.

. Jeff, taking the same precaution, left Al to maintain Earl's old position.

More waiting. Finally, the roar of an approaching motorcycle was heard navigating the blanket of soft and shifting sand interspersed with the palm trees. Then, from around a palm tree cluster materialized the motorcycle with a driver and passenger riding in tandem. The motorcycle stopped in front of the hut and the driver and passenger disembarked. The driver assisted the passenger who was blindfolded, through the door to the hut.

Inside the hut the blindfold was removed. Dave looked around and saw the six men looking at him. He recognized Hashim Salamat, the antagonist from his first meeting. Who he didn't see was Mohamed ben Idom whom Dave assumed was the leader at that meeting.

"*As-Salaam-Alaikum,*" Dave greeted using the standard Muslim greeting, Peace be upon you. However, there was not the customary return; just stares. "I was advised that you have a message for me," Dave added, after encountering no reply.

"Message for you," Hashim Salamat repeated with obvious scorn. "No, we have no message for the puppet of the infidels in Manila but, we do have a message for the blasphemous leaders of the government who would offer us crumbs and call it a feast thinking we are so ignorant that we don't know the difference. They would have us believe that they are magnanimous in their peace offering and that we should be grateful for whatever concession they make. Do they think that we're that naïve? We'll send them a message alright." Then he turned to his partners and issued a command.

Two men grabbed Dave while a third pinned his hands behind his back.

"What are you doing," Dave protested. "I came here in good faith and in answer to your request. Is your Muslim faith so lacking that you do not honor your guest as commanded by the Prophet?"

"Bah, what do you, an infidel, know of the Prophet?" Hashim Salamat sarcastically replied.

"I know that the Prophet said let the believer in God and the day of judgement, honor his guest," Dave answered defiantly.

"You, insolent pig, how dare you quote the Prophet to me," Hashim Salamat sneered and slapped Dave so hard that his head was thrown back. Then turning to those holding Dave commanded them to "take this dog outside."

Earl was frustrated. He knew things were not going well, but his view was blocked by all the bystanders. Then he saw Dave forced through the door. He immediately went to the edge of the building, at the same time, removing his M9 revolver from its holster.

"*I don't believe it!*" he thought. He saw Dave forced into a kneeling position. A man with a machete at his side, the man with the camcorder moving to the front of everybody. Then another man, apparently the one in charge started talking to the man with the camcorder who then proceeded to record what he was saying. Then he stepped aside and the man with the machete raised his weapon over Dave's head.

"*Damn, Jeff was right they are going to behead Dave! I don't have a clear shot, but I sure as hell can get their attention but will it be in time?*"

No more thoughts.

He stepped from the side of the building, firing his weapon in the air.

But it failed to get anyone's attention.

But the two simultaneous shots fired at the same time as Earl's shot, did!

Earl saw the executioner fall to the ground while the others stood there, dazed, Not knowing what was happening!

Then a burst, exploding the dirt in front of everyone and Earl running to Dave's side, his weapon pointing toward them broke their stupor and they all ran into the safety of the hut. All this happening in less than one minute.

Earl lifted an obviously shaken Dave to his feet. By this time Jeff and Al were at his side. Al untied Dave's hands, while Earl and Jeff kept their weapons pointed toward the hut,

"Okay, buddy let's get you out of here," Al said to Dave.

"Man, talk about the cavalry coming to the rescue, I thought I was a goner," uttered Dave.

"Naw, there ain't no way we'd let anything happen to our ole buddy," said Earl.

"Let's get our butts out of here," said Al.

"What about him," Jeff said, pointing to the executioner laying on the ground.

"Let his buddies inside the hut take care of him," Dave answered.

"You guys go on, I've got a couple of things I want to do," said Earl.

"Whatcha got in mind?" Jeff asked.

"I won't be long," he answered. Then he walked over to the motorcycle and put a couple of rounds into its gas tank. The explosion that resulted caused the motorcycle to jump two feet into the air.

"That's a good idea, I'll take care of their boat," said Jeff. Then he walked down toward the water's edge where he saw the boat lying on the earthen ramp. A burst from his M16 rifle put half a dozen, quarter-size holes in its bottom. Then another burst and gas from its gas tank spurted into the boat.

That done, Jeff joined the rest of the group as they made their way to their inflatable. It didn't take long before they were at the metal ramp leading to the bait shop. With Dave's fluency in Spanish, there was no need for a taxi. Dave called Senior Amparo and let him know that they were ready to return to the pier.

While they waited, Dave explained what the MNLF group had in their mind.

"They literally were going make a movie of my beheading and send it, with my head to the President's palace, along with a simple message, this is our answer to your offer."

"Ouch," remarked Earl.

"Yeah that's right," laughed Dave. "Thank God for you guys. I owe you big time."

"Hey, that's what friends are for," remarked Al.

"What now?" asked Jeff. "Does this mean no peace."

"That's a good question and one for which I don't have an answer," answered Dave. "I can't believe this Hashim Salamat is the spokesman for the MNLF. At our first meeting I got the distinct impression that Mohamed ben Idom was in charge. I need to get back to

Father Mendoza and let him know what just happened and get his opinion."

"Well you could call him from here and make an appointment," suggested Al.

"I'm sure you have a lot to confess," laughed Earl.

"That's a great idea. I'll do it now," Dave laughed. Then he made his telephone call and made an appointment for an urgent need of confession. "I've got an appointment for five this afternoon. I'd like you all to come with me."

Another hour passed before Luis arrived. The inflatable was loaded in the back of his pickup and they returned to Tipo Tipo. Then after explaining to Senior Amparo that fishing wasn't that good and what was caught was released, Dave called for a taxi. Forty minutes later they were speaking with Fr. Mendoza.

"Thank God and your friends, you are safe," Fr. Mendoza declared. Then he explained, "Although Hashim Salamat is in a leadership position he is not as high up the totem pole, as you Americans put it, as is Mohamed ben Idom. Although, Hashim Salamat does have a following, especially among the younger, more radical members. Return to your boat and call me sometime tomorrow morning; and the blessing of God the Father, Jesus his son, and the Holy Ghost be with you all."

"Amen," they all answered in chorus. Then it was back to the pier and the safety of their boat.

There wasn't much conversation back on the deck of the Dragon Lady where they were sipping beer and eating what little they had an appetite for. Some talk about Mel and wondering what he was doing. Even some talk about continuing their cruise once this small hiccup in their plan was over. And it would be over soon. Obviously, Dave or Mel would not be a part of it. It would only be Al, Jeff and Earl—like the Three Musketeers without D'Artaganan. After this afternoon's encounter, anything else would be anticlimactic. While not admitting it, some of the zeal was gone.

The next morning Dave took the inflatable to the pier and made his call to Fr. Mendoza. It was good news. Mohamed ben Idom would like to meet with Dave and in Fr. Mendoza's office; the sooner the better. Dave returned to the Dragon Lady and informed the rest.

"I'll be meeting with Mohamed ben Idom alone, but I'd still would like you all there. I've got some good vibes about this meeting. I can't help but think it will be a step forward and I want you all to be a part of it. I also got the impression that Mohamed ben Idom was with Fr. Mendoza when I talked to the good Father."

When the four returned to the pier to call for a taxi they found that Senior Amparo's son Luis was there with his pickup truck and offered to take the four into town. At the Guardian Angel Ministries, they went straight to Fr. Mendoza's office where they saw that Fr. Mendoza and Mohamed ben Idom were conversing. Dave knock on the door frame where he got both men's attention. Fr. Mendoza bid Dave enter and he exited to be with Al, Jeff and Earl, closing the door behind him.

After the usual Moslem greeting, Mohamed ben Idom got right to the point.

"First and foremost, I wish to apologize for the action of those who are no longer members of our movement. They acted on their own and without either the knowledge and approval of our Council. Which brings me to the second point. The Council has instructed me to advise you that we, somewhat hesitantly agree to meet with the government representative to discuss their offer for an armistice between the MNLF and the government with certain guarantees of course."

"That is good news," Dave answered. "I know that President Aquino will be pleased however, as to guarantees, I'm in no position to commit the government to anything other than the offer I bring to you but, based on my personal dealings with her, I know she will do whatever is in her power to convince you of the sincerity of her offer."

"I understand your position and will leave you to report to President Aquino our position and will await her reply which can be conveyed through the good offices of Fr. Mendoza."

"Thank you, as I mentioned earlier, I know that President Aquino will be pleased, but let me add my own personal pleasure at its outcome and will do whatever the President might want me to do to bring the results to positive fruition."

"Well we will leave it at that; *Assalamu Aleiykum* (Peace be upon you)."

"*Waleiykum assalam* (and peace be upon you)," Dave responded. The meeting was over.

When Dave, Al, Earl and Jeff were about to leave, Fr. Mendoza approached them.

"One word of caution; I am led to believe that Hashim Salamat is a very vindictive person and will seek some sort of revenge for yesterday's actions. Be careful. Go with God."

"Thank you, Father. We will take your warning seriously and thank you for your assistance in bringing about such positive results. Without your office and that of Father Gonzales's this would not have happened."

"You give us too much credit. The credit goes to God. We are just his messengers."

"Yes Father, as you say, we go with God."

The four left the confines of the Guardian Angel Ministry, elated by the news of Dave's success with the MNLF Leaders. They heard Fr. Mendoza's warning but they were so absorbed by the good news that they dismissed it out of hand.

They made a brief stop at the Philippine Long Distance Telephone Company next to the post office, where Dave called a number in Manila and left a message that the operation was a success and that his uncle was in the recovery room. He'd know more when he returned.

Then it was to their favorite café where they were sitting outside, across from the market enjoying pork sandwiches, black beans and rice and discussing their future plans.

"Now that your mission is over, will you be heading back to Manila?" Al asked Dave.

"Yes, I'll have to debrief the Ambassador and then I assume we'll brief the President and her Military Assistant," Dave answered.

"Where will you fly out of?" Jeff asked. "I don't think they have a commercial airport on the Island, probably due to the continuing fighting."

"Yes, I think you are right," answered Dave, but there is one in Zamboanga City, just across the straits on the Zamboanga Peninsula. I was hoping to impose on your good graces one more time and ask that we sail there tomorrow. Gosh, that sounds so final," a somber Dave remarked. "We've been together so long and I could never have succeeded without you all. It was literally one for all, and all for one."

"Hey, we're supposed to be celebrating, not holding a wake," remarked Jeff. "Your mission became our mission, your success our success! We can all celebrate."

"I'll drink to that," Earl chimed in, raising his bottle of San Miguel."

"Hear, hear, they all echoed Earl, raising their bottles at the same time.

"Okay," said Al. "Let get this show on the road. "We gotta prepare the Dragon for an early morning departure so our ole buddy Dave will get his kudos from the Ambassador."

The four paid their bill and was getting ready to leave when they heard the blaring of horns and the wailing of sirens. Looking from where the noise was coming from, they saw two police cars, their lights flashing red, a large firetruck, followed by an army jeep and two 2-ton trucks, all jungle camouflaged; the trucks carrying twelve soldiers each, all heading east on José Razal Road.

"Looks like they're going our way, maybe we could hitch a ride," laughed Earl.

They flagged down a motorized trike coming their way and all squeezed into its limited space; Dave riding behind the driver. They left the tarmac of José Razal Road and entered the sand-packed trail that led to the pier. When they approached the few hovels that comprised Banah Village they could sense something was amiss. The few residents that comprised the village were gathered around the roadway in animated discussions. The taxi driver stopped and conversed with the villagers. The three occupants of the sidecar saw the apprehension on Dave's face, engrossed in the discussion between the villagers and the driver.

"What is it?" Jeff asked.

"I'm not sure, but I've got a queasy feeling it's not good," Dave replied, addressing his three comrades.

"What do you mean?" Al asked.

"The villagers are talking about a large explosion that came from the direction of the waterfront. Then, they saw this line of police and military vehicles come zooming through their town. Their first thought was that it was some sort of terrorist attack."

"That's not good," Earl agreed.

The conversation between the driver and the villagers over, they resumed but it was obvious from the expression on the taxi drivers face, he wasn't too happy about continuing, not knowing what they were headed into. In fact, it took a lot of prodding on Dave's part to get him going. When they finally broke out from the palm and coconut trees, they found the road was blocked by one of the military trucks and two policemen were standing guard, not allowing them to proceed farther nor would he allow the taxi driver to leave. As Earl described later, "It didn't take a rocket scientist to know what was going on." The soldiers had fanned out into the copra plantation and policemen were going from house to house questioning the residents.

The four disembarked from the taxi, and Dave explained to the policemen who they were and what they were doing in this area. One of the policemen called his supervisor who came and Dave repeated what he had told his officers. Dave also suggested that if there were any questions, they could contact Senior Amparo who could vouch for them. After the police supervisor checked their identification cards, he then radioed to one of the military, and after a short wait, an Army Major approached them. The major could actually speak English so all could be included in the conversation. After checking their identification cards and was convinced of who they were, he dismissed the taxi driver and then gave them the bad news.

"I'm afraid your boat was the target of terrorists, at least it has all the hallmarks of one of their attacks. We have questioned most of the residents but they say they didn't see anything, which is not unusual. From the debris pattern we can tell the explosion was from devices that were placed on the outside of your boat, just above the waterline. Do you have any idea why they would target your boat or for that matter, maybe target you? We know that there are some anti-American feelings among the terrorist on the Island, but this is the first time we've had Americans, or their property targeted. For that matter, we have had very few Americans visiting the Island," he added smiling.

"Yes, I think I can provide the answer," Dave started the explanation. "As you saw from my identification card, I'm with the United States Embassy. We're here on an extremely important and sensitive mission on behalf of President Aquino. The boat was to take me to Zamboanga City to connect to a commercial flight to Manila to report to my Ambassador and your President. This action this afternoon tells me that all of us may be targets. It is imperative that I talk to the most senior military officer on the Island," Dave explained.

"Hmm, that would be Colonel Garcia. He is the commander of all military forces on Basilan. I can contact him and inform him of your request," the major offered.

"That would be great," Dave said. "Please emphasize that I'm the personal representative of President Aquino."

"Yes, of course."

Epilogue

Early in the morning a Philippine Air Force (PAF) C-130 landed at their abandoned Menzi Airstrip in Isabella City. An Army armored personnel carrier quickly met the aircraft and the four disembarked and immediately boarded the aircraft where they were flown to Manila's *Villamor* Air Base, the headquarters of the Philippine Air Force. A U.S. Embassy staff member met the aircraft where diplomatic documents were given to Al, Earl and Jeff and a check for $5,000 to each to compensate them for the personal items they had lost in the explosion of the Dragon Lady. In addition, they received tickets for a commercial flight to Kaohsiung, Taiwan. Then they were driven to *the Ninoy Aquino* International Airport.

Dave was whisked to the embassy where he reported to the Ambassador. After the meeting the Ambassador made a telephone call to President Aquino, then he and Dave rode in the Ambassador's official limousine to the Malacañan Palace, the principal workplace of the President of the Philippines. There, they were greeted at the steps of the entrance hall by an aide, who escorted them through the double doors and up the grand staircase to the President's study, where they met with President Aquino and the Chief of Staff of the Philippine Armed Forces. Dave briefed them on the results of his mission. President Aquino acknowledged the debt that her government owed Dave for his service to the Philippine government and to her personally. She recognized the risk he had taken and expressed relief that he and his colleagues had not been aboard their boat when it exploded. She then turned to the Ambassador and asked if Dave would be available to assist in the follow-on efforts to consummate the tentative agreement. And, of course, the Ambassador agreed.

Al, Jeff and Earl were met by Mel and Shao-mei when their flight landed in Kaohsiung, Taiwan. Then the hugs and kisses that normally follows with the reuniting of old friends. Mel questioned the lack of luggage and was informed of the explosion that had sunk the Dragon Lady.

The first order of business after checking into the Tainan Hotel, was to purchase enough clothing to see them through the short period of time they would be in Taiwan. Shao-mei's father hosted a banquet in their honor where he showed off his American friends to all his friends and business associates. Hung Li-chun and Sung Kuo-ying joined them at the head table. Their brief visit ended and the three boarded a United Airlines Flight to San Francisco, where each would go their separate way; Al to Washington D.C., Earl to Seattle where he would join his father's law firm, convincing his father that Boeings legal department was not for him, and Jeff to Long Beach, California and his brother's dive shop. At the San Francisco Airport they found a bar in which to have a farewell drink.

"Well, I guess its time to say goodbye," Al said.

"No, not goodbye," Jeff replied. "Until we meet again."

The end

Author's note: On, January 1987, the Moro National Liberation Front (MNLF) accepted the Philippine government's offer of semi-autonomy of the regions in dispute, subsequently leading to the establishment of the <u>Autonomous Region of Muslim Mindanao</u> on 6 November 1990. The signing of this agreement brought about a serious rift in the MNLF leadership, leading to the formation of a breakaway group known as "The New Leadership"; later, the Moro Islamic Liberation Front.

Made in the USA
Monee, IL
15 January 2020